SUPERSTAR

A ROOKIE REBELS NOVEL

KATE MEADER

Please see my website for content warnings pertinent to this book.

1

March

"AND I KNOW you all recognize this guy! It's everyone's favorite power forward—Bast Durand!"

"Jesus, what are we? Chopped liver?" Reid nudged his brother—everyone's favorite power forward—as the kids on the Lurie Children's oncology ward cheered on.

Bast grinned at Reid. "Jealousy is a good look on you, bro. That green tinge gives your skin an olive glow."

"Hilarious." Reid barely cracked a smile but then that was par for the course.

Never were brothers more different. Two years younger than Reid, twenty-six year old Bast was generally the optimistic, sunny Durand while Reid was the characteristic definition of a grump. He had reason to be, given how Bast's father, Hall of Famer Henri Durand—Bast's bio-dad and Reid's stepfather—had pitted them against each other as rivals from an early age. Bast liked to think they'd risen above that, and now that they lived in the same city at last, they were finally becoming friends.

Who would've believed it after the events this past December? The great cross-town rivalry between Chicago's hockey franchises was lately embodied by two Canadian brothers who notoriously did not get along—a narrative that was only twenty-three percent true. The press liked to create their own fairytales. Whatever it took to get clicks.

Reid had come on board the Chicago Rebels roster last year and what a year it had been. Rescued a dog, fell for a girl, nabbed a three-year contract after years of being the fucking new guy with several other teams. On the other side of town, Bast had been steady with the Hawks until last December when he broke his wrist during a clash with Reid on the ice.

The press had *loved* that.

Their dad, not so much.

Three months later, Bast's wrist was on the mend, and his appointment with the Hawks' PT this afternoon was going to tell him what he needed to hear: he would be well enough for the playoffs.

But first there was the PR stuff, a fun way to fill his time during his rehab. He was especially enjoying the mix of players from both Chicago teams. It never hurt to remind the Rebels that Bast Durand was still a star, even when injured.

"Hey, Bast, we'd love a pic of you and Cecy." Emily, the Hawks' PR lead, motioned for him to get closer to a little girl in a wooly hat playing with a cuddly toy, a gray rat-bird thing wearing a Rebels jersey. Not even his team! Still, he could be magnanimous.

No one was more magnanimous than Bast Durand.

"Hey, Cecy!" He took a seat beside her on the pink rubber mat and pointed at the toy. "I had no idea they made the jerseys that small. Who's this?"

"This is Rowdy."

Right, Rowdy Rebel, the Rebels' mascot. Whoever had come up with the design for this thing must have been having an off day. Maybe he'd had a fender bender on the way to work or spilled coffee on his laptop or someone stole his lunch from the staff breakroom fridge. Or maybe all three. Because as mascots went, this was probably the worst one in the league. At least the Hawks' mascot looked like a bird of prey. This thing seemed to have skipped several steps in the evolutionary chain. Was it a fox or a cat? Maybe a duck?

Cecy pushed the Rowdy toy into his face, close enough for him to see its beady eyes and ugly whiskers. "Want to kiss her?"

"Course I do!" He landed a smacker on Rowdy's rodent-like head. "So, Cecy, who's your favorite player?"

"Smooth, Durand, real smooth." That comment came from Theo Kershaw, D-Man with the Rebels.

Bast grinned. "Just makin' conversation, Kershaw."

"I like Hudson Grey," Cecy said because kids rarely kowtowed to the egos of big-shot hockey players. "But he's not here."

"Nah, but you know something? He's missing out big time."

She put her ear to Rowdy's mouth—beak?—and listened. With a diffident glance up at him, she said, "Rowdy thinks you're pretty good."

"You're one of her favorites," an older voice chimed in. An elderly grandma type had taken a seat beside Cecy.

"Who? Rowdy's or Cecy's?"

Grandma winked, the cheeky minx. "Cecy loves hockey and is crazy about the Hawks *and* the Rebels."

"Oh, yeah? That's pretty rare, Cecy. Most people stick to the one team."

He took a closer look. She couldn't have been more than ten—though the way cancer ravaged these kids' little bodies had the unnerving effect of making them look both younger and older. "That's a cool hat. Where I come from we call that a toque."

The hat was in the Hawks' red and purple and was probably the worst example of a knitted cap he'd ever seen, all crooked with uneven chevrons. But it looked warm on top of Cecy's hairless head and was probably made by her grandmother.

Confirming his suspicion, Gran had a big smile on her face as she held another toque in her outstretched hands. "I made one for you."

"Love. It." And he did, despite the dodgy design. The heart that had gone into this made him smile. "Are you Cecy's mom? Or maybe her sister?"

The woman giggled. "You are a cheeky one, aren't you? I'm this one's grammie and probably your biggest fan, Bast Durand."

"Only probably?"

"Okay, absolutely." Another girlish giggle as he pulled the hat on. "I'm Gwen by the way." She blinked as PR Emily snapped a photo.

"Great to meet you, Gwen. Hey, Ems, get one of me and Cecy wearing our hats, created by Gwen the Knitmeister." He leaned in close and placed an arm around her frail body. Pulling on the little one's toque bobble, he earned a shy grin.

Gwen placed her hand on Bast's arm and gently squeezed. "You're such a nice guy, Bast. I just knew you would be in person."

That's what people said about him, and he enjoyed living up to their expectations. He was the peacekeeper, the bon vivant, everyone's friend and no-one's enemy, not even his so-called rivals here. He caught Reid's smirk, but he didn't care.

The last three months had been rough—though he was careful to keep that to himself. Reid didn't need to feel any more guilty than he already did. Sure Bast had missed the regular season *and* the Olympics, but he'd managed to smile his way through. No point in complaining, not when he was this close to wiping the slate clean.

He was on his way back.

Playoffs, here I come.

2

This Diamond's Got It Rough!

Kent Gallagher's trajectory continues to descend at an alarming rate with the latest news from the Denver Diamonds org about the left winger's demotion to the AHL affiliate. Of course you'll recall that Gallagher was scratched from several Diamonds games in January, and that was before the three-game suspension following his arrest at Blistering Moe's in downtown Denver. These days, it seems the Minnesota native is better at getting trashed and punching teammates than dressing for games. Sources say Gallagher is still heartsore over his broken engagement to Pepper Calhoun, but those same sources remain cagey as to whether Dustin Marsh was punched because of his rumored dalliance with Gallagher's ex or for another reason entirely. Pepper has yet to make a statement supporting or denying the allegations or explaining her part in Gallagher's downward spiral. But you know that if and when she does, you'll hear it first on the Dish.

— BENTON KOVAX, *THE DENVER DISH*

TABLOID-FAMOUS PEPPER CALHOUN inhaled a calming breath, decided that didn't quite cut it, and tossed her phone on the sofa. How was the madness only becoming more, well, mad? That people were still parsing her days with Kent and looking for reasons to blame her for his mistakes was crazy. Yet here they were.

Explaining her part in Gallagher's downward spiral?

She shouldn't have to explain a thing. People broke up every day. Fact. Sometimes one person was more to blame, sometimes it took two to tango. Fact. The things she could say ... but wouldn't because she was classier than that.

Pepper had never considered herself classy, but she did consider herself loyal. Blabbing about her breakup with Kent would only make things worse, and sure enough, he was apologetic whenever the press put her name in their ridiculous, trash-filled mouths.

On cue, a message from the man himself came in, though she had to admit the follow-up texts to each tabloid accusation against Pepper seemed to be taking longer and longer as time went on. In the early post-breakup days, she could rely on receiving that apology before she even had a chance to read the thing for which he was sorry. Now, almost two months after she'd broken up with him—or broken his spirit, depending on which rag you read—Kent's check-ins were rolling in later and later. Case in point: this "article" was published three whole days ago.

KENT

Hey Pep, I'm guessing you saw the
Denver Dish piece. Or maybe not! It
might be better for your sanity if you
ignored it.

PEPPER

Sure did. Hard to miss when Connor insists
on sending it on. That's my brother, stirrer-
in-chief!

KENT

Damn, I've told him to ignore it. As should
you. They're just looking for a reaction,
which I won't be giving them. I'm sorry
you're still caught up in this. I've told the
Diamonds' PR to be more definitive about
your part in all this.

Had he? Because she saw little to no evidence that she
was under his protection. Still, she knew this was a tough
couple of weeks for him, so she was prepared to cut him
some slack.

PEPPER

Don't worry about it. I'll survive! How are
things with your new team?

KENT

It sucks, Pep. I know it's my fault I'm in this
position. I should have listened to you.

KENT

...

KENT

I really appreciate you having my back.

Even if it meant *her* back was oozing from all the knife
wounds she'd sustained, with the entire hockey world
blaming her for Kent's misfortune. She dug her nails into

her palms, fighting for inner serenity. Stay classy. When they go low and all that.

PEPPER

Have you made up with Dustin?

KENT

Yeah, we're buddies again. Just alcohol and bad decisions. Listen, I gotta go—practice. Let me know if you hear any more trash talk. I'll set the PR dogs on them!

PEPPER

Sure. Have a good practice!

Off he went, secure in the knowledge he'd done his duty by checking in on the woman who knew all his dirty little secrets and had somehow convinced herself that keeping them at the expense of her reputation was justified.

He hadn't even asked about her latest interview. Not that there was much to tell.

Pepper Calhoun? That's an unusual name ... ah, right. That *Pepper Calhoun.*

End scene.

Invariably, that was the script for her last three interviews, and she assumed it would be the same for the next three. Of course, the one for the Growing Minds Daycare Center had lasted a little longer. She actually got a tour of the facilities with their bright pastels and cute drawings of families and pets and purple trees while the interviewer pumped her for information about her personal life. A lot of, "Oh you're back in Chicago with your dad. We're all such huge fans of the Chicago Rebels, and we love Coach Calhoun! He must adore having you around."

Well, you'd have to ask him, but he would probably only sigh deeply and say, "Family's a blessing."

Another text came in, this time from her friend Bridget.

> Heading to Bridgeport for dinner with the
> fam this evening. You want in?

If there was anything worse than suffering the questions of potential employers, it was suffering the questions of Bridget's big Irish family over corned beef and cabbage, the usual Sunday meal at the Shaughnessys'. They were a lovely, rambunctious lot but awfully nosy.

PEPPER

> Said I'd eat dinner with Dad. Could meet
> you after?

BRIDGET

> Perfect! I could use you as my excuse to
> bail before Grandma Eileen force-feeds me
> a fifth cup of tea and a slice of fruitcake.
> That shit's dense enough to stop a door!
> Jimmy's Tap at 7?

Ugh, a sports bar. She didn't even need to text that reaction because Bridget was already weighing in with a counter-argument.

BRIDGET

> Time to get over yourself, girl! No one will
> recognize you, not when you look like a
> completely different person these days.
> Stop being a hermit!

PEPPER

> Okay, but this is just us, right? No making
> eyes at some South Side jabroni who only
> knows how to talk in hockey stats.

BRIDGET

> I promise.

But she added a wink emoji, so all bets were probably off.

Pepper would have gone anyway. She needed cheering, and even if it was in the middle of a crowd of hockey bros, at least she would feel like she was part of something again.

3

THE ONLY THING worse than watching a hockey game where your team was losing was watching a hockey game in which you should be playing when your team was losing.

Bast eyed the screen above the bar at Jimmy's Tap on Chicago's South Side and tried his best to conceal his disgust at the Hawks' performance. One thing he appreciated about Jimmy's, apart from the three-dollar Pabsts for weekday happy hours, was the gloom. Dark enough that you didn't notice how sticky the surfaces were unless you fingertipped them—inadvisable—but more important, dark enough that a usually recognizable star hockey player might travel incognito.

Hey ho, the beard and toque were also doing a top-notch job.

Per his latest text, Reid was running late, which was code for "I'm banging my gorgeous girl." Bast tried not to be put out. After all, his brother was happy now whereas before Kennedy and their cute little mutt Bucky arrived on the scene, he'd been one miserable fucker.

A bit like how Bast felt right now. The news he'd received yesterday was not good.

He was going to need surgery on his wrist.

The Hawks' ortho had told him it wasn't healing as well as it should be. *Maybe*, in his eagerness to get back out on the ice, he'd gone overboard with his training. Surely an extra thirty minutes with a few wrist flexions and extensions shouldn't have been so catastrophic. Yet here he was, with the possibility he might not be back at all.

The org had been previously supportive but were waiting for the injury update before they entered into contract negotiations. Now? He was damn sure his current overlords were going to dump him. After all he'd done for them, the team was willing to give him up with the flick of a wrist—or wrist fracture.

The numbers for wrist injuries aren't good, Bast. Statistically it makes more sense to give you up and get the better draft pick.

Asshole management, always looking for the new and shiny.

He re-focused on the screen again. Right now his boys were on the wrong end of two and zip, and they still thought they could do without him. Sure, he might be useless this minute, but it wouldn't always be this way. He'd be back to form soon.

If he said it enough times, it might come true.

A few minutes into his visit, he was still riding under the radar. He rarely went this long without a fan coming up to ask him about the Hawks' Cup win four years ago or his goal-scoring streak from a couple of seasons back. Lately those queries had gone by the wayside, only to be replaced by more bothersome ones like: *How's the wrist, man?*

Well, I thought it was better, but maybe I was trying to convince myself that I'm not a washed-up loser after all.

His phone buzzed with a text from Reid.

> Twenty minutes out.

He shot back a quick response.

BAST

> If you need extra time to kiss your girl goodbye …

REID

> She's trying to kick me out the door. Won't be long.

Before he could react to that, another text came in, this time from his agent, Kit Mallinson.

> Got a second?

He'd been waiting for this. Dialing Kit, he headed outside to get some privacy. "Hey, what's up?"

"Just had a chat with Fitz over at the Rebels. He'd like to talk to you, sooner than later."

Fitz, as in Hale Fitzpatrick, the Rebels' newer GM. He'd been sniffing around for a while but Bast had been putting him off, not ready to make a move. Now all that had changed.

"But my contract isn't up until July."

"And you know in your heart they won't renew. You're essentially a free agent in all but name, and if you want to stay in Chicago—which I know is important to you—then having the Rebels in your back pocket would be the way to go."

Kit had said Bast might have other offers, but he hadn't sounded all that hopeful. *Wrist injuries, man. So tricky.*

"Does he know about the likelihood of surgery?"

"Yeah. Didn't faze him, but the Rebels are gamblers. Always have been. This would be either the most forward-thinking move of the modern hockey era or a huge mistake they'll never recover from."

Let it be the former because his agent was right about one thing: Bast loved Chicago and wanted to stay here. The on-ice clash with his brother might have broken his wrist, but it started them on the road to fixing their relationship. It had been a childhood dream to play with Reid instead of against him. If his damn wrist would only cooperate, this season they could create magic together on the same team.

"Set up the meet. Can't hurt to hear what they have to say."

"Will do."

Bast hung up and took a moment to let the March chill awaken his senses after the bar's heat, but really he needed the time to assure himself all was not lost. That he still had something to offer. This was good. Moving forward with his career and not letting the bastards beat him down.

Only this wasn't how it was supposed to go. He should be getting the full support of his current org, not having to make nice with the top brass of a different one. He flexed his wrist, like that could convince him he was in good enough shape for this fight. It felt good, but apparently not good enough for the Hawks. And then because he was feeling unusually masochistic, he checked Marina's Insta.

A bikini pic, of course, Marina by a pool with Brian Costa, a linebacker with the Packers, her mouth in that sexy pout he knew so well. The hashtags were typical of her usual posts. #PostSeasonRelaxation #Poollife #Balilife #Islandlife #fuckthis

Okay, not the last one. Marina would never. She was

incredibly conscious of what it took to be the perfect WAG. The designer duds, the toned body, the carefully curated images. They had dated for a few months off and on last year, took a break and were back together just before his injury. He had hoped she'd see him through that, but by January—only a month after he was decked—she had given up. He was too sad-faced in her pictures, too "real," completely harshing the vibe she was trying to create. By the time the Superbowl rolled around, she had found another guy who better suited her image.

A winner.

(Okay, not completely, but Costa had graduated to the most popular sporting event in the country, and while the Packers didn't win, he had remained injury-free. Much more in tune with Marina's narrative.)

Annoyed with himself, Bast closed the app and snatched another cold influx of air. He was almost tempted not to return to the bar, to tell Reid he'd decided to head home to wallow. Watching a game he couldn't play, surrounded by the fans who would normally adore him when at his peak, chatting with the man who had caused the injury in the first place, seemed like a special kind of purgatory. A punishment for how easy he'd had it until now. The press liked to compare his road to Reid's, always pointing out that he hadn't had to fight to get to his position. Not like the elder Durand who had struggled every step of the way. These days that kind of underdog backstory held more appeal.

Just thinking that put a stopper in Bast's self-pity outpour. If he went home now because he was #sadface about his ex and not being ready for primetime on the ice, then what did that say about him? Besides Reid deserved every piece of good fortune coming his way. He had worked his ass off to get there and Bast's injury was an accident. Shit happened.

His thoughts strayed to Cecy, the little girl with cancer. How fair was it that this beautiful soul had to suffer like that? Not fair at all. Yet here he was whining about a delay getting back to the sport he loved more than anything. Because that was all it was: a temporary setback. Life went the fuck on, and Bast needed to remember he was in a blessed position.

Another team wanted to talk to him—how lucky was he to still be in the conversation?

He headed back inside and retook his seat, just in time to see Smithy, the Hawks' left winger, send a wicked drive that whizzed past the wrong side of the pipes. A collective groan went up in the bar, the crowd operating as one roiling beast in pain.

Except for the woman beside him.

She hadn't been there before he left to call Kit. He would have noticed this raven-haired beauty, but in his five-minute absence, she had settled in and ordered a Rolling Rock. Not only that, but an empty shot glass sat sentry beside the green bottle.

With sleek, dark hair pulled back in a ponytail, a stubborn tilt to her chin, and rosy cheeks, she looked like Snow White on a bender.

A touch presumptive? Perhaps. That shot glass could have been left over from a previous customer, only that conclusion was laid to waste when she raised it in the direction of the bartender and immediately got it refilled with Patron. This woman meant business.

The TV screen didn't interest her. Bast Durand didn't interest her, which was interesting in itself. Usually you'd take, at least, a cursory glance at whoever sat down beside you. Guess the beard n' beanie disguise was working just fine.

Something that was confirmed when she turned to him with a blank, slightly unfocused stare and said, "That seat's taken."

There was a challenging set to her chin, like she expected trouble but a shot of tequila would see her right. Because she'd spoken to him, he took that as permission to look his fill. Even sitting, he could tell she was possessed of amazing curves, shapely hips, and a nice rack, though it was covered by a University of Denver hoodie. He couldn't see her ass, but he suspected it was as hot as the rest of her.

"Sure is," he said in response to her comment about the seat's current ownership.

"No, I mean by my friend."

"Where is she?"

"Who?"

Oh boy. "Your friend?"

"Why do you assume it's a female friend?"

"Fifty-fifty guess."

She corkscrewed a finger in the air. "Typical."

"What is?"

"Your assumption that there are only two genders. *Fifty-fifty guess.*" Her voice went deeper on that last phrase, an impression of him, he supposed.

"One in three odds, then."

She twitched her nose. Damn cute, even if it signified disapproval of his hasty take on gender identity.

"It's a woman." She picked up her Rolling Rock, readied to take a draft, then changed her mind. "My friend is a woman and that's her seat."

He nodded slowly and took an eye at the screen. Another miss, another crowd-swollen groan.

"But she's not here."

She sighed. "Not yet. But you have to leave when she arrives. That's the deal."

He smiled, figuring there was no need to argue the fact he'd been sitting here first. They had a deal.

"Fair enough."

She fixed him with an inscrutable look through eyes an unusual shade of golden-hazel, and big, like a children's book illustration. Did she recognize him or—his pulse rate picked up—*did she not*? Which would be better. Much better.

"Why so sad?"

That surprised him. "You think I'm sad?"

She pointed at his mouth. "Looks like one of those paper-over-the-cracks smiles." Followed by a lazy wave at the TV screen. "Is it because of these losers?"

These losers, his teammates. That, and so much more.

"No one likes to see their team on the wrong end of that kind of score line."

She snorted. Clearly, she wasn't on board with that sentiment.

"Did you ever think that it might be because of your hat?"

"My hat?"

"No one else here is wearing one, which makes you the odd one out. Or maybe you're having a bad hair day. I get it. Truly." She gave a general motion of her hand at her own, to his mind, perfect, hair.

He wanted to laugh, but she seemed so serious about his funny hat, his bad hair, or both. "I'm always cold. Hence the headwear."

"Tough to be you."

"The stories I could tell."

She chuckled, a raspy sound that went straight to his dick. It had been a while, so he was extra-susceptible to sexy chuckles with just the right amount of gravel.

But there was something else about that chuckle. Something strangely familiar. Her eyes, too ...

"It's a good-looking hat," she said before he had a chance to examine this weird sensation of déjà vu. "Your grandma knit it?"

An insult, perhaps, but he had her there.

"Someone's grandma did. A sick little girl gave it to me as a gift."

She studied him again, checking his story out with a lie-detecting cast to her expression. He must have passed the test because she nodded. "Cool. You're a saint."

True enough, it wasn't the best crafted of hats, but Granny Gwen had given it to him and that meant something. Especially when he wasn't feeling a lot of love.

The crowd let out a loud groan. Winnipeg had scored again, so now the home team was down by three. He shook his head.

"Sucks to be a Hawks fan right now," she said just as the bartender slid another Rolling Rock across the bar. Her second to add to the shots.

She offered a twenty, but he held up his hand to the bartender.

"Add that to my tab."

"You don't have to do that."

"Why not?"

She blew out a breath, which caught a stray dark curl near her forehead and gave it a half-hearted lift. "Because ..." The moment was held suspended. "I'm not here to be picked up by some jabroni."

That would normally be enough to deflate his dick, but

instead it pulsed, inspired by the challenge she presented. "Is that the only reason I'd buy you a beer?"

She waved her hands, taking in the entire bar. "Trying to think of any other."

"You must be an incredibly suspicious type or severely lacking in imagination because I can think of at least three."

For his efforts, he was rewarded with an inordinately cute kick to the corner of her lips. The charm was finally penetrating and the success sent an endorphin rush barreling through him.

"Oh yeah? Hit me."

Reason #1: I'd like to talk to the one person in this bar who seems to have no clue who I am.

Instead he went with, "First, you put me in my place about my gender assumptions. Much appreciated."

"True, true," she murmured, with what sounded like a tipsy pride.

"Two, you said nice things about my hat"—though she hadn't really—"which me and my hat really appreciate. And three ..."

He tried to think of something else, wishing he didn't have to. He was Bast Fucking Durand after all. Never in his life had a woman considered *not* accepting his offer to buy her a drink in a bar. He would've liked to say this need to convince her was refreshing, but after his recent funk, he was eager for a win.

Maybe he should introduce himself. Take the easy way out. She might not care who he was, but letting her know could be the boost he needed. Yet something in him longed for the stretch to his charm muscles, one he hadn't had to confront since he'd made his name as a star athlete at U Mass seven years ago.

While he searched for a third reason, she spoke. "I

suppose you could be trying to make sure Rolling Rock stays in business? It's not the most popular of beers. Kind of past its heyday."

"Exactly!" He flourished his hand to make his—or her—point, then let loose a grin.

She returned one of her own, and wow, little firecrackers went off in his chest. The gravity of before was replaced with a sunshine that warmed him through.

"Thanks for helping me out there," he said, inclining his head slightly. Something floral tickled his senses, and the closer he got the more that feeling of familiarity came back to him. But he would remember if he'd met her. A woman like this would stay lodged in his consciousness for sure.

"Looked like you could do with the assist." She took a sip of her beer, eyeing him over the neck of the bottle.

He leaned on the bar, his laundry list of troubles no longer on his mind.

They had been replaced by the perfect distraction.

4

PEPPER HAD NOTICED him the moment he sat down beside her. Sooner than that. He'd been outside the bar on the phone in hushed tones, tall, bearded, and broad-shouldered. Impossible to miss.

Once she found an empty duo of seats, she should have placed her purse on the stool beside her, but she'd been anxious to get her order in while she had the bartender's attention. Anxious to smooth out her jagged insides after her exchange with Kent earlier and the ultimatum from her father.

You can't get a job? Then take the one I give you.

By the time her drinking buddy had sat down, she was a shot to the good, the warmth in her body making her brave. She would usually never tell someone that an empty seat was taken, not if she hadn't employed proactive steps to secure it. That was the unwritten code—claim it with property, not expect that people would be mind-readers.

The moment it came out of her mouth—"that seat's taken"—she wondered if it sounded rude. She was a polite person, as a rule. It was one of the tenets she taught her kids, that and kindness.

Or had taught them in distant months past. Before her association with Kent blackballed her from doing anything meaningful with her life. Now her father wanted her to take a job that was, frankly, a joke.

When this stranger sat beside her, something in her reared up. Maybe it was the tequila. Maybe she wanted to be rude. Maybe she needed to assert herself after so long of doing the opposite.

That was before she realized who he was.

Because there was no doubt that this was Bastian Durand—and right now, in this bar, he appeared to be hiding that fact from the world.

Little wisps of dark hair, pushed flat by his headwear, curled along his high cheekbones. He had a perfectly-square jaw—or she imagined so as it was covered by a rather lustrous beard. The bluest eyes she had ever seen stared back at her, tropical beach blue, forging a connection that was likely all in her imagination.

Removing all doubt that her tequila goggles were playing tricks on her, a wrist brace peeked out from the cuff of his jacket, a reminder of the season-ending injury he'd sustained in a game back in December.

He didn't seem to recognize her. Not that she was all that famous, but she'd had a short spurt of painful attention that had left her damaged. She'd worn her hair differently then. Blond because Kent liked it that way, and now she was back to her natural brunette. So in a way, she was also incognito, a bit like Bastian who hadn't been assaulted by a single fan in the time she'd been here.

She should leave, tell Bridget that she'd meet her some-where else because this situation had trouble written all over it. Yet she felt a pull here, something drawing her closer to him, even if the sensible part of her preferred to label it as stubbornly sticking to the spot.

A few minutes enjoying that charming mouth wouldn't hurt. After the last few months, didn't she deserve a little fun? She was twenty-two years old, a college dropout, sleeping in her old childhood bedroom. She hated that version of herself, so tonight she would be someone else. Flirty and carefree, at least until Bridget showed her face.

Still, it would be easier to pull off if she played dumb about *his* identity. Time to establish some ground rules.

"I hate hockey, by the way."

He narrowed his eyes, like she had told an off-color joke. "You hate ... hockey?"

"Yeah, I just thought I should put that out there in case you wanted to use it as—" She waved, searching for words the tequila made unreachable.

"Conversation fodder?"

"Uh huh. Gotta find different fuel for this, Mister."

"Okay." He nodded, looking a touch whiplashed by the prospect of a hockey-free chat.

Oh, she enjoyed how that felt, the silly victory in it. She bit back her smile, eager to see where he went next.

"Well, I'm sort of a fan," he said, with one eye on the screen above the bar. Several competing emotions danced over his face as he puzzled out how to make progress without the inherent advantages of the Bastian Durand mythos. "But we don't have to talk about that. Let's talk about you."

No, thanks. "You first. What do you do?"

"What do I do?" As if it was the strangest question in the world. She'd caught him on the back foot, so now she waited for him to give up and spill the beans.

I'm Bast Durand, power forward with the Hawks, the team that's playing on that screen right now. Winner of the Stanley Cup, twice-winner of the Hart Memorial Trophy. Hey, I could go on.

"Yeah, how do you earn a crust? Pay for food and shelter?"

"It's, uh, kind of boring."

Interesting. "Can't be that boring."

"Super boring. I give advice on retirement funds."

"Oh, right, that is boring." She couldn't help her giggle, though it was tempered slightly by a flicked glance at his braced wrist. Maybe he'd weighed the benefits of being Bast Durand against the annoyance of being asked about the one thing keeping him from what he loved, and decided, *today I give advice on retirement funds.*

Maybe, like her, he was trying on a different mask. She wasn't planning on being all that truthful either.

"But important work," she affirmed with a hand on his arm. She wasn't sure why, but she had an irresistible urge to touch him. Make sure he was real.

Or okay.

"Everyone needs that kind of advice."

"Yeah, super important." He smiled, evidently relieved that they'd overcome that hump. There was also a touch of, *did I really get away with that?* So cute. "Let me guess what you do. You don't like hockey, so I'm going to say nothing to do with sports."

"That leaves quite a lot."

"Something in the beauty industry. Or law enforcement. Or maybe you cook."

She laughed, though it was tinged with sadness for the career she'd had to abandon. "We could be here all night."

"I wouldn't mind," he said, which was either a glib line or shockingly honest.

Rather than overthink it, she offered up the first thing that came into her head. "Right now, I tend bar."

"And you hang out in bars on your night off."

"Always looking for inspiration. How are other tenders cutting up limes these days? Quarters? Eighths? Against-the-grain thirds?" She held up her hands, hoping the gesture could somehow convey the meaning of fractions. The tequila was lighting up her veins.

He chuckled. "Right, I can see how you'd want to keep your finger on the pulse. So why the hockey hate?"

"Most hockey players and fans are jerks, I find."

"Kind of harsh."

About ten feet away, a couple of guys reached for each other across a table, wrestled for long enough to spill a drink before they were separated and forced to hug it out. One of them started crying. Fifteen seconds of idiocy in three acts.

"Did you plan that?" he asked in amazement.

"Didn't need to." An ex-fiancé, a hockey-mad brother, and a father who lived and breathed it had informed her world-view. "But I don't follow hockey all that closely." An image of Kent tried to ruin the vibe, and she desperately pushed it deep.

"You okay?" He moved in closer. "You looked like you had a flurry there."

"A flurry?"

"Yeah, like a bad memory manifesting."

We've got a sharp one here. "Something like that."

He held her gaze and after an age, said, "Flurry be gone." Like he was an old-timey magician.

"Flurry be gone," she repeated, as if the mantra could

help. Silly, but strangely it did. Like together they could wish away all the bad things.

Instead of making her happy, it touched her with sadness. *If he wasn't who he was and she wasn't who she was ...* No point even thinking it. Which meant she needed to exit this situation immediately.

Before she could come up with a departing line, he spoke again. "So, in about three minutes, my brother's going to arrive."

That settled it. "Okay."

"And it's going to be different. I can't say why right now, but it will be. So I wondered if you'd give me your number now so we can remember how good it was before it all changed."

He had no idea just how much. Would Reid recognize her? The elder Durand brother had played with the Denver Diamonds for almost a year. But when she had moved in those circles, he hadn't been very social. She couldn't recall a single instance of Reid at a Diamonds' team party or an after-game meet-up.

She couldn't risk it.

Number exchange was out. Flirt time was over. There was no future here, she'd had her fun, and it was time to wrap this up.

"I hardly know you," she hedged, pulling herself to a half-stand. It brought her closer to him, so much so her breasts brushed against his chest.

He leaned in, maintaining the bodily contact. Her nipples popped hard against her hoodie. "You don't know me at all, but admit it, you want to."

She laughed to cover up the yearning. She did. A little too much, which was the sign that she had to call time on this moment of madness.

Her phone vibrated on the bar.

"I really should be going."

"I thought you were meeting someone."

"I-I was. But that's all changed."

He held her gaze for a charged beat, then took out his phone. "Maybe we could meet up later."

"So you can talk about hockey?"

He smirked. "There won't be much talking, sweetheart, hockey or otherwise."

That should have signaled him as a Grade-A dick, but she admired his confidence and his irrepressible charm. Being the subject of his attention, his effort to woo her, was exhilarating. Only she remembered how quickly that feeling could fade, how the darkness could easily swallow up the light.

She needed to let him down gently. He'd made a valiant play and couldn't be faulted for failing.

But first, or last, she allowed herself one more moment of indulgence. That clean, male scent; those charm-stoked blues; the facial hair she wanted to run her fingers through. Those lips she imagined pressed against hers and other more intimate parts of her body.

In return, his gaze catalogued her features. He might be questioning where he'd seen her before.

"I have to leave." She moved past him, all too conscious of his hard body, teasing mouth, and curiosity about why she was playing so hard to get.

"But I don't know your name, Cinderella."

"And I don't know yours, Prince Charming."

Challenge issued. He could lie, like he had about his job, or he could fess up.

She watched as his mind churned with the weight of indecision. He was wondering if telling her who he was would make a difference.

But she had the advantage. Knowing it would make all the difference in the world, she held a finger to his lips. "Let's not. You'll thank me later."

His eyes went dark. "Not sure I will."

He didn't realize the favor she was doing him. "Bye, it was nice to meet you."

But as she tried to leave, someone pushed her from behind, back into his orbit. A universe bitch move, telling them this moment was far from over. Bast's hand landed on her hip, steadying her, and that heated touch was the best thing to happen to her in months.

Yes, so pathetic.

"Hi," he said, his eyes twinkling, as if he'd planned the whole thing.

"Hi," she murmured back. She felt sluggish, dazed by his sensual aura.

People weren't this overwhelming in real life, surely. "So, about that number," he said. "Because it seems you're still here and that's got to mean something."

"Only that it's crowded with all these hockey idiots."

Another challenge. If he could accept her blatant contempt of his profession, maybe ...

Maybe what? Maybe nothing. So far, no harm had been done. Just a drink purchased, some light-hearted banter exchanged, pulse rate spiked. Neither of them would remember it in the morning.

"Well, this hockey idiot would like to learn more about

the error of his ways. You seem like the kind of girl who could teach me where I've been going wrong all this time."

"Let's start with you calling me a girl."

His brow crimped. "Have I screwed up on the gender identity business again?"

"No, I mean that I'm a woman."

A thoroughly disarming head tilt was his answer. "That you are. Tell me what else I need to know."

That I'm the last person you need in your life right now, just as you're the last person I need in mine.

Yet she wanted to bathe in his brightness a little longer. It came out of nowhere, a blinding flash of inspiration and daring.

"Could I ask a favor?"

"Anything," he whispered.

"Could I ... touch your beard?"

He didn't even look surprised. He merely nodded, like her request had taken away his power to speak, so she reached up and allowed herself this one little luxury before he came to his senses. A feel-up of his jaw, her fingers shaping that strong curve, her thumb close to his lips.

The longer she indulged this, the harder it would be to break away.

One more second. Five. At twenty, she dropped her hand, marveling at how, for the briefest moment, this one connection felt like truth.

He was breathing heavily. "Tell me that's not worth pursuing."

"I can't." *Tell you that.* Neither could she stay another second longer. This was his career she was trying to protect.

"Pepper!"

Damn. Bridget waved like she was directing an airplane on a runway and began making her way slowly through the crowd. The last thing Pepper needed was to have her friend, who was a bit of a star-fucker, recognize Bast.

"Sorry, that's my friend." One step back.

"Wait." He frowned, recalibrated. The dreamy expression had fallen right off his face. "Is that your name? Pepper?"

"I really should go."

He mouthed her name, her somewhat unusual name, and snapped his gaze to her.

Here it comes.

"I thought I was imagining things, but you *are* familiar. I just couldn't place you. Pepper Calhoun? Connor Calhoun's sister?"

His expression yielded to darkness, likely recalling the last fifteen minutes and—*there it is*—the tabloid craziness of the last three months. Confusion reigned, veering on annoyance and probably two clicks away from anger.

"We had a no-hockey-talk rule, and now I'm thinking we shouldn't have agreed to that." His hand was still on her hip, superglued, as if determined to keep her on the spot until they sorted this out. Her heart rate was going bananas.

Before she could defend herself, he barked out a question. "Did you recognize me? Who am I kidding? Of course you did."

"No. I mean, not at first, but when you spoke ..." She added in a small, insignificant voice, "Yes." Her tequila inspired bravery was fading fast.

"And you decided to keep that to yourself." Fact, not query.

"You didn't announce it, so I assumed you had your reasons." They both had.

Oh, he did *not* enjoy that. No one likes to be reminded of their own lies, even ones of omission, and a cocky big shot like Bast Durand would always assume he could do no wrong. He took another long look at her, his mouth harsh, so unlike the man from moments ago and the amiable guy she recognized from press interviews.

A need to defend herself after months as the universe's punchbag reared up, the last buzz of the tequila giving her a boost. "I never thought this was going anywhere."

Ice-blue eyes cut through her, a skate blade eviscerating her organs. "Instead you thought you'd yank my chain and pretend you were someone you weren't."

"Hey, that's not what happened. I'm not the only one who was enjoying the anonymity."

His snort of disagreement put her back up. He had most definitely been enjoying it. One last surge of screw-you had her driving the point home. "How's the retirement investments business going these days?"

He flinched before another emotion took hold. Disgust. "Heard you have a thing for pro-hockey players. Well, I'm not another guy whose career you can destroy."

It wasn't the first time she'd heard that accusation. But hearing Bast Durand, one of the nicest guys in the hockey biz, spew the party line struck a blow lower than she expected. Her shady past was going to follow her around forever.

"I thought we were having fun, but it's best that it's out in the open and we go our separate ways."

"Exactly." But for some reason, he remained still. His fingers hadn't unfurled their possessive grip on her hip. Neither had his eyes averted from her face, as if locked in place by some supernatural force. "Is that what you want?"

That he was giving her a choice after his tantrum from a moment ago was baffling, to say the least. But there was this magnetic pull between them. It had scrambled her brain sufficiently enough for her to stick around longer than was safe, and apparently it was confusing the hell out of him, too.

He hated that he wanted her.

She wasn't a fan either, but she sure as hell wouldn't give him the satisfaction of knowing he'd snuck under her skin.

"Yeah, it is."

His stare drilled into her, stripping her to the bone and removing all hope of salvaging this. After an age, he stood back, giving her room to leave.

Room she had no choice but to take.

5

———————

July

News just in: Bastian Durand has signed with the Chicago Rebels after several months of rumors he would be headed to the city's less successful hockey franchise. After his wrist surgery, Durand's days with the Hawks were numbered, though his acquisition by the Rebels wasn't always a sure thing. Most people are of the opinion that even an underdog outfit like the Rebels has its limits (or should have). But here they are throwing their chips in on a player who might never attain the dizzying heights of yore. Quite the gamble, but owner Harper Chase and GM Hale Fitzpatrick have never been ones to play the odds.

— CURTIS DEACON, *CHICAGO SUN-TIMES*

"WHERE SHOULD I put the inlagd sill?"

Erik Jorgenson held up a Tupperware container of something gray and slimy. Everyone in Theo Kershaw's kitchen recoiled in unison.

"If you've brought fucking herring to my July 4 cookout, J-Dog, I'm going to kindly inform you of two things: the exit's behind you and you can leave your lovely lady here." Theo grinned at Casey, Erik's girlfriend. "Hey, Higgins, can I get you a drink?"

"I'd love one of those lime and mint spritzer things Elle was raving about."

"Coming up."

"It's best on rye toast," Erik said, oblivious to his host's distaste—or maybe this was the vibe. Indulge the weird Swede with the funny taste in potluck foods.

Curious, Bast took the container from the Rebels' goalie and squinted through the plastic. It looked almost alive. "I'll give this a shot later, but maybe let's refrigerate it for now?"

Reid looked on indulgently. "Only a Rebel for three days and already the peacemaker."

"Seriously, I want to try it. But I'll start with a beer first."

For the last few months as Bast's path toward the Rebels had firmed up and his wrist healed (again), he had spent time playing poker and hanging with his brother's teammates. All good guys, who were cool enough to welcome him into the fold. So while he might technically be a Rebel on paper for just three days, the roots stretched deeper than that.

Confirming this, Theo passed him a Blind Pig IPA, Bast's favorite brand.

"Thanks, man."

"No problem, Baby D. It's good to have you on board. I can't fucking wait for the season to start." He turned to Reid. "Hey, Duracell, I've got La Croix for you, but if that's too out there flavor-wise, we can also stretch to regular filtered H2O."

Reid was well-known for his restrictive diet. "It's the off-season. Even *I* take a break in the summer." He grabbed an IPA instead.

"Heard you're headed to Thailand in a couple of weeks after Foreman's nuptials." Gunnar Bond, one of the Rebels' centers, weighed in. "That food's kind of spicy. Sure you can handle it?"

"I'm always up for trying new things," Reid said, completely straight-faced.

Bast wouldn't have believed those words out of his brother's mouth a year ago, but since Kennedy and Bucky entered his life, Reid was a changed man. Open, engaged, happier than he'd ever been.

"Trying new things?" Kennedy walked into the kitchen with Tara Becker, who was dating Fitz, the Rebels' general manager. She placed an arm around Reid's waist, her pink-streaked blond tresses barely rising above his brother's pecs. "I can't wait to see that."

"Reid burning his mouth off with some Tom Yum Kung ..." Erik offered.

"Sleeping in until, oh, 7 in the am," Foreman said.

Kershaw finished with, "Wearing a banana hammock in Rebels colors," which inspired plenty of guffaws.

Kennedy's eyes sparkled with mischief. "I would totally be up for that. Baby, you gonna model that for me later?"

Reid shook his head, trying to look annoyed but failing. The team had embraced him, and he was finally in a good place, both professionally and personally. Sure, the Rebels hadn't made it out of the second round of the playoffs this past season, but they'd done better this year than they had in a while. A lot of that was down to Reid's play, which had strengthened with each week of the last six months.

Bast was thrilled for him, truly, even if it was accompanied by the slightly nagging sensation of being left behind.

He didn't want to feel this way, but their fraternal competitiveness was ever present, and Bast wasn't used to being the underdog in the Durand family unit.

"Alright, time to get out there and grill these babies." Theo held up a platter of burger patties and trotted out to the yard. Usually this annual cookout was held at Chase Manor, lorded over by Rebels' owner Harper Chase and her husband, former player Remy DuPre, but they'd just had a baby, their fourth girl, and were keeping it quiet this year.

As Kershaw didn't know the meaning of quiet, he'd offered to host at his place. Most of the Rebels had brought their wives, girlfriends, and kids. Bast wondered if he should have brought a date, though he was out of practice since Marina. And while his ex would think she was the reason he was keeping his dick in his pants, Bast knew better.

It was because of *her*. Pepper.

She was still on his mind, sneaking into his fantasies late at night and wrapping her hand around his cock. Rather absurd, considering they'd barely spoken and it had ended the way it did. Lusting after a woman who was trouble for a whole myriad of reasons wasn't usually his vibe. Bast usually preferred the easy road: the puck bunny in a bar, the adoring fan at a coffee shop, not a woman who hated hockey and lied about her identity.

He'd even entertained the idea that she might be here, given she was Coach Calhoun's daughter, which meant he had it bad. For fuck's sake, what would he even say to her?

He was musing on this when he caught the eye of Hudson Grey, a newer player to the Rebels roster. And still on the topic of tabloid junk, there'd been some minor scandal about his boyfriend, Jude, a firefighter who was currently chatting animatedly to Tara.

"What's up?" Bast asked Hudson, feeling weirdly bashful. Like he was the newbie, and in a way he was.

Evidently waiting for that invitation, Hudson closed the gap between them quickly and held out his hand to shake it, all while blushing to the roots of his reddish-blond hair. "Hey, it's great to meet you. I mean, we've met before on the ice, but we haven't really talked much. I just wanted to welcome you to the team, officially."

"Thanks so much." That was nice of him—maybe even tough because he seemed shy. "You had a great season, man. Absolute barnburner."

"Well, I got lucky," he said diffidently. "Things just slotted into place." He threw a quick glance at his boyfriend, who might have been talking with Tara but had complete spatial awareness when it came to Hudson. A couples' thing, Bast supposed.

"I don't believe in that," Bast said. "You've worked hard to be so lucky."

Hudson smiled, like he wanted to disagree about the importance of luck in the game, but wasn't ready to challenge a veteran player. "Can't wait to play with you. The team's going to really benefit from your experience."

"I hope so." Bast couldn't believe he had to wait the entire summer before he could put that to the test. "Just want to get out there."

"If you need someone to train with—of course, you have Reid so, forget I said that. Kind of stupid."

"Not at all," Bast assured him. "I haven't got the all-clear yet, but as soon as I do, I'll be looking to re-start my regimen, even if it's just gym work or running. I'll definitely hit you up."

Hudson looked like that was the best news ever. Bast often forgot how much some of the younger players looked up to him, and being on the receiving end of that kind of adulation sure helped to ease his doubts.

"I think your guy wants your attention."

Looking over his shoulder, Hudson smiled at the handsome, tattooed firefighter and colored again. "That reminds me. Alex at Engine 6 says hi. Jude works with her."

"Oh yeah? Alex and I go way back." One of Chicago's few female firefighters, Alex Dempsey was an old friend, now married to the former mayor of Chicago and popping out babies right, left, and center. "Small world. I'll have to give Jude all the gossip."

"Sounds good. Talk later?"

"Sure. And thanks for the welcome. I appreciate it."

People were now heading out to the yard, and Bast would have been right there with them—he was starving—but someone placed a hand on his arm.

Tara Becker gave him a light squeeze. "Hey, Bast, have you got a sec?"

"Sure."

Normally, he would be suspicious of a beautiful woman like Tara wanting a little alone time with him. Only a few months back, she'd been in a relationship with Dex O'Malley, one of the Rebels' forwards, and had even accepted an on-ice proposal from the guy while she wore the Rebels mascot costume. Crazy stuff. But within days, the engagement was off and Tara had hooked up with Fitz, the GM.

Bast had met her once before when Fitz was courting him for a spot on the Rebels roster, and something about the way she was looking at him now said he was about to be reminded of that night back in March.

"So, could I ask about Pepper?"

Yep, that was exactly what he thought this was about.

"What about her?" It came out as defensive as he felt.

"I recall you two crazy kids running into each other a few months ago at the Empty Net, and there was a weird vibe. Want to tell me what that was about?"

"Why do you want to know?"

She touched a finger to her chin. "Question with a question, eh? I see this is going to be trickier than I anticipated. Well, that night I was talking to Pepper and she was in a marvelous mood until *you* arrived, and then she wasn't. Now I'm not the sharpest knife in the drawer, but even I could tell that there was history there. So help a gal out and spill the tea, handsome."

He didn't owe her an explanation, but something in him wanted to talk about this woman who still haunted his dreams. Maybe Tara might have some information he could use.

"I'd met her before and that was the first time I'd seen her in a while. That's all."

"Just a reunion of old acquaintances?" Tara gave off a distinct does-not-pass-the-smell-test vibe. "Because one look at you and Pepper scooted faster than you do on skates. In fact, she looked kind of annoyed with you. What did you do?"

"Why do you assume I did anything? And not sure it's any of your business."

That yielded a smirk. "It's my business because one, Pepper is a friend of mine and I'd hate to see any awkwardness now that you're on the team that her father coaches. And two, Hale—that's Fitz to you, also your boss—doesn't like complications."

He scoffed. "Kind of rich."

Tara grinned, that beautiful smile that had guys falling at her feet. "Yeah, I know, he's one to talk. I am the *ultimate* complication, more than enough for him to deal with.

Really, I just want to be sure that whatever you and Pepper have going on doesn't affect the team's close dynamic. By the way, I'm loving this longer hair, but I think you could do with a little trim." She touched her fingers to the hair over his ear. "Come see me at the compound. First cut's free! And you can tell me all about you and Pepper."

Tara was the team's hair stylist and had apparently assumed some sort of priest-confessor role in the org.

"I met her once"—*and we connected, but she's a liar and a troublemaker and have you heard about what happened with her and Kent Gallagher?*—"and we went our separate ways. There's nothing to see here."

In truth, he was a little embarrassed about his behavior. After that meet at Jimmy's Tap, he'd run into her in the Rebels watering hole, The Empty Net, a couple of weeks later, the night Tara was referencing. He'd tried to apologize, but Pepper had run off without letting him get a word in.

So he *might* have overreacted. He'd been so uptight about his surgery news and possibly signing with the Rebels that he'd let that overshadow the fun flirtation he'd been having with this mystery girl. So she had her reasons for keeping her identity under wraps. He'd had his own, so why had he been such a dick because she was playing the same game?

Maybe he should have been more understanding of her desire to keep her name to herself. Her engagement to Kent Gallagher had gone tits up a few months before he ran into her at that bar, and not long after, Gallagher's career had taken a nosedive with a bar fight, suspension from his team, and an unceremonious dump into the AHL.

The press hadn't been nice to him, but they'd been especially nasty to Pepper, like she was to blame for Gallagher fucking up. Made it sound like she was bad news, and the fleeting memory of that had tainted his parting words to her.

Heard you have a thing for pro-hockey players. Well, I'm not another guy whose career you can destroy.

As if he knew a thing about it. The tabloids and the truth were rarely on speaking terms, and it wasn't as if he could ask her brother Connor, who he happened to know from their college days.

He could, however, pump Tara for information, though it would set the gossip tongues wagging. Luckily he didn't get a chance to decide because his phone buzzed with a text from his best girl. Or his best girl's grandma.

GWEN

Someone wants to say hi!

Grandma Gwen had sent a photo of Cecy with a giant teddy bear in Rebels gear. She was hugging it hard, and the joy on her face made him so damn happy that for a second, he forgot about the rest: his worries about his career, his trepidation at having to start over, his regret over a missed opportunity with a hazel-eyed girl and her crooked smile.

He looked up at Tara. "Sorry, I've got to answer this."

"Sure. Talk later—and don't forget to hit me up for that cut." She headed out to join the party.

BAST

Looks like she's forgiven me for switching teams.

GWEN

She's a Bast Durand fan, honey. We'll be following you wherever you go.

Good to know he had some support in his defection to the enemy.

PEPPER WAS the ghost at the feast.

If any of the partygoers were to turn around, they'd see her spectral image at the window and wonder if the Kershaws' Winnetka mansion on the lake was haunted.

Bast was in the yard, chatting with his new teammates, laughing at something Cal Foreman had said. Not unlike that night in March, which was vividly imprinted on her brain: the ease of their conversation, his charm in the face of her dissing his profession, his shallow breaths when they stood a little too close. So she might have been a couple of tequila shots past sense, but she hadn't imagined the connection, the way her heart rate sped up when he touched her hip to steady her.

And then it all went to shit.

"Hey, Pep, come join the party."

Pepper turned to Elle Kershaw, who had just breezed in. About a month ago, Elle had asked her if she'd be available as a part-time babysitter for their ten-month-old Hatch, and Pepper had jumped at the chance to be useful. The Kershaws didn't seem to care that she had a reputation as a career-wrecker; all they appreciated was that she was six credits short of her early childhood education degree and liked hanging with little kids. Simple as that.

But working for a Rebels hockey player meant she risked crossing paths with other Rebels hockey players—which wouldn't have been a problem except for the news Bast Durand had signed on with the team a few days ago. Her fervent wish was that she never had to run into this guy again.

Because she rarely got what she wished for, here he was ruining her day by being a handsome idiot.

"I kind of like hanging with my guy here. He's being a little fussy."

"He is?" Elle bent over his crib and rubbed his tummy. "You being a little diva like your dad?"

Hatch gurgled and snatched at the air, making a tiny fist of fury.

Elle came over to the window where Pepper was standing and looked out. "Not in the mood to hang with a bunch of players and WAGs, I suppose." Her tone was kind.

"I'm sure they're all lovely people."

"But you were sure of that the last time. I could tell you they're the coolest bunch in the world, but you had a rough go of it in Denver, I'm guessing. Or maybe there's another reason you don't want to take the baby monitor downstairs and sample one of Theo's sliders." She shook her head. "Sorry, that came out kind of dirty."

Pepper laughed. "I'll grab something later."

That should have been Elle's cue to leave, but she still hovered. "Actually, I overheard a conversation about you just now and—"

"What are people saying?"

Elle placed a hand on her arm. "Oh, nothing about what happened with Kent Gallagher. Tara was asking Bast Durand about some run-in between you two at the Empty Net a couple of months ago."

Tara Becker was a one-time wannabe WAG who'd been friendly toward Pepper, though Pepper was suspicious of Tara's motives. After her experience with Kent, she questioned anyone who wanted to get to know her.

"You mean she was looking to stir things."

Elle frowned. "I wouldn't say that. In fact, she was concerned that Bast had offended you in some way, and she wanted to know what had happened."

Looking out for her or looking out for gossip? So hard to tell.

"Nothing. We met once, but he didn't know who I was, and when he found out, he wasn't pleased."

"Oh, I see." Elle's gaze turned sharp.

"It was nothing, really. We barely talked, and when we ran into each other again at the Empty Net, I wasn't in the mood to hear him out. That's what Tara saw. He didn't do anything wrong."

Elle snorted. "Nice of you to defend him, but let's be clear. You should not be the one hiding away in here, using my kid as cover, all because you want to avoid Bast Durand. Or anyone else for that matter." She held Pepper's gaze, her own filled with compassion. "I kind of know what it's like to want to go dark. Stay under the radar." At Pepper's querying look, she added, "My family is pretty toxic."

This sharing was unexpected—and unexpectedly comforting. "How did you deal with it?"

"Badly. I tried to hide my pregnancy from them—from everyone—because they tend to make everything worse. Which was especially tough on Theo, who wanted to shout the news from the rooftops. You know how he is."

Theo was one of the nicest guys in the NHL, a little like Bast—though how true was that? He hadn't been so nice to her when he heard who she was. Everyone had a darker side, she supposed.

"Now you're with Theo, so that's not possible anymore, is it? Hiding, I mean."

Elle smiled. "Theo craves the spotlight, but he's careful about splashing our private lives all over the Internet. But I get where you're coming from. Sometimes it's easier to put your head down, ignore the haters."

Which is why Pepper was here, holed up like a criminal

on the lam. The last time she'd tried to let loose and forget about the past, she'd ended up on the receiving end of Bast Durand's disdain.

Outside the Kershaws' window, the world was blooming, filled with noise and laughter, and there was Bast Durand, superstar hockey player at the center of it.

She wanted no part of it, not anymore.

"Just looking for a quiet life." Even if it meant a stunted one.

Right now, it seemed the safest option all around.

6

———

November

Hockey season is in full swing, and with it an old face in a young—and bruised—body. Bastian Durand, Cup winner, once the league's highest season goal scorer (sure it was three years ago, but the record still stands), and former Hawks super-star has made the jump across the city to appear on the roster of the better team's rival, the Chicago Rebels. Of course, there's the drama surrounding his brother, Reid. Can the two patch up their differences long enough to put in the performances a team like the Rebels sorely needs this upcoming season? Only time will tell if the younger Durand's wrist—and mind—are strong enough to handle the pressure.

— CURTIS DEACON, *CHICAGO SUN-TIMES*

A HOCKEY LOCKER room was probably the worst place in the world to try and center yourself ahead of a game, but never had Bast been so glad to have the opportunity.

Two months of healing for his fractured wrist, three plus

months of physio, wrist surgery to make it stronger, more healing, more PT, practice every day for the last four months in the off-season. Ten months since he'd set foot on competitive ice.

He flexed his wrist. It felt good. He felt good.

Even if he was the new guy on the team.

Even if it was on his old team's crosstown rival.

Even if it might be awkward being teammates with his brother, the guy who caused his wrist injury in the first place. (The press *still* loved that shit.)

No, Bast didn't mind any of that. He loved hockey too much.

"How do you feel?" Reid asked as he sat beside him.

Nervous. "Good. Really good. This year, we're going to win a Cup together."

"You think so?"

"I do." He flexed his wrist again. "Now I'm on this loser team, we're going straight to the Big Time."

"Cocky fucker."

Yeah, he was, even if it was partly a front. There'd been moments over the last ten months when he worried he might not make it back. Every athlete harbors a latent fear that he's one fall away from permanent retirement, but Bast's ego was outsized enough to help him overcome any serious doubts. He was meant to play, ergo nothing would stand in the way of that. A man possessed of such natural gifts on the ice wasn't meant to sit around feeling sorry for himself. He'd take that "cocky fucker" label and raise it to a run for the Cup every time.

A text came in on his phone from Gwen.

These seats are amazing, Bast! Thanks so much.

She'd also sent a pic of her and Cecy, who was looking so much better now, her eyes bright, her skin no longer that gray pallor. That fucker, the big C, was in remission, and just seeing her smiling face lifted his heart.

Reid smiled. "Is that the little girl from Lurie Children's?"

"Yeah, with her gran. If you can have a bunch of cougars in your corner, so can I." Kennedy's grandmother Evie had formed a superfan group for Reid from her old folks' home. They regularly attended Rebels games to cheer him on, often getting into granny-offs with Kershaw's fan club.

Another buzz on his phone and he checked, expecting more from Gwen, but no. It was from his old college friend, Connor Calhoun, a forward with the Denver Diamonds, who was also the son of John Calhoun, the Chicago Rebels' coach.

And Pepper's brother, information he would've liked to have in his possession sooner that night in Jimmy's Tap eight months ago.

CONNOR

Break a wrist, buddy!

Typical Connor, zero to asshole in 0.1 seconds.

BAST

Aw thanks, dickhead. Sorry about your three-game losing streak. Sucks to be a Diamond right now.

A month into the season, and the Rebels were 5 and 4, a damn sight better than a losing 2 and 7, Denver's record to date. Bast had hated every second on the sidelines for the last three weeks, but this was the first regular season game the Rebels' medics had approved him for play.

Another text from Connor zinged. Jesus, he had a game to get ready for, but of course this dick in Mountain zone thought Bast had all the time in the world.

CONNOR

Say hi to my sister for me.

Something in Bast's chest lurched. He'd never told Connor that he knew Pepper—if fifteen minutes of conversation counted as knowing someone.

BAST

Your sister's here? At the game?

Did that sound casual enough?

CONNOR

LOL. Yeah, "at the game".

LOL? What was so funny? And why was "at the game" in quotes? So Pepper wasn't a big hockey fan—she'd made that clear. It probably was kind of strange that she'd show up to a game, but her dad was the team's coach, so maybe she was here for him?

Or maybe she knew it was Bast's first game back, and she'd shown to give him some moral support. He liked that idea a little too much, but he didn't have time to interrogate Connor about it because they were called for the walk to the tunnel.

"You ready?"

Reid held up his stick for tapping, something they used to do all the time when they were younger before heading out to practice and looking for any excuse to beat the shit out of each other on the ice. Now they were on the same team, and Bast couldn't wait to show the world how well they worked together.

He winked at Reid, rolled his shoulders back in preparation for battle, and touched his stick to his brother's.

"Eh bien, mon frère, allons-y."

THE FIRST PERIOD FLEW BY. Bast spent about four minutes total on the ice, and while he didn't do anything major, it was awesome to be out there playing the sport he loved. Not on the same line as Reid, but that would happen soon. He couldn't wait.

Coach Calhoun tapped him affectionately on his lid as the first period ended with the Rebels already two goals up. "Not bad, Durand. Not bad at all."

"Thanks, Coach. Glad to be back."

As they skated off for the break, he looked up into the stands and waved to Cecy and Gwen, who looked so happy to be here. Cecy had something gray and furry in her arms. Man, she sure loved that Rowdy Rebel toy.

Vadim Petrov, the Rebels' captain, came alongside him. "Good work, Junior."

"Junior?" Hell, Petrov might be an elder statesman in the game, but it wasn't as if Bast was a complete noob.

"With two Durands on the team, we must come up with a way to distinguish you."

"Yeah, but Junior? That's ridiculous."

"Is it though?" Petrov grinned that smirk that lit up catwalks during his modeling side-gig. "You can't fight a nickname if it's bestowed by the team. But do not worry. Kershaw is working on something special." Kershaw was, by all accounts, the team's nickname generator.

"Guess I'll have to see what he comes up with."

"Yes. Stay on the tenterhooks. Or the blades. For now,

bask in the worship." He waved a gloved hand toward the crowd. "Looks like you have fans on this side of the city already."

Sure enough someone was holding a sign against the plexi: *We love you, Bast!*

Aw, that was nice and definitely made him feel like he'd made the right call. And when the sign was lowered, he was damn sure he had.

The woman with the sign was gorgeous. Blonde, apple-cheeked, full red lips—a real stunner. A little like Marina, in truth, which soured the moment a touch. But then Marina Two waved and he forgot all about his ex. He usually had no shortage of female attention, but it felt different when he was getting it for doing his job instead of being hit on in a bar.

That had him thinking of Pepper. Was she in the crowd somewhere cheering him on? Hell, that would be some-thing. Where would she be sitting? Most of the Rebels' comps were in the same area, where Gwen and Cecy were, so maybe Pepper was up there, too?

As he moved closer to the tunnel, the blonde leaned over, giving him a prime view of a great rack with what looked like a tattoo of ...

He squinted ...

This woman had his name tattooed on her tits.

Christ, it was good to be back.

With one last flash of a mouthguard-covered grin at his superfan—one that let her know he might be looking her up later because hell yeah, he needed to get back on that horse—he headed for the tunnel, realizing absently that the other players were already inside. All but him, but then he was moving a little more slowly these days. Hot blondes will do that.

The next few seconds happened fast.

Someone checked him—not hard, but enough to make him lose his balance. Usually that wouldn't be an issue, especially as he was about a foot from the tunnel's entrance and one of the team assistants holding skate guards, but for some reason he didn't react like a professional hockey player.

No. He reacted like he suddenly had no idea how to stay upright on his knife-shoes and, with a Looney Tunes Roadrunner-style foot move, went down like a sack of pucks.

And because he had the self-preservation instincts of an ant, he put his hand out to break his fall.

His wrist—fuck!

Praying that his instinct about what happened was wrong, he made a move to push himself off the ground.

Pain ripped a fiery path up his arm. *No, no, not again.*

He looked sideways ... into the eyes of a huge feathered being.

The mascot, Rowdy Rebel. That weird Frankenstein of a bird and a dinosaur, with the grace of neither. Was this what he collided with on his way into the tunnel?

He hadn't even seen it. But then he rarely noticed anyone around him except the other players. He barely even registered the fans, except that cutie he'd just been making eyes with.

If he'd been paying more attention ... no, this wasn't his fault.

It was this person—this thing's—job to stay out of *his* way!

Okay, don't call the mascot a thing. There was a guy inside that costume, though God only knew how he saw anything, never mind stayed upright.

The mascot was talking to him, its voice oddly pitched, like a woman's. Was he making fun of him?

"Are you alright?"

The stupid mascot reached for his elbow, and there it was again: excruciating pain. And then the medics were on him, cannoning him with questions about where it hurt and hauling him into the tunnel and an exam room.

After he stripped off his jersey—no picnic—the team doc, Dr. Nasir, took a closer look. "It doesn't appear to be broken, but maybe a ligament tear? We'll know better after an X-ray."

This could not be happening.

He had just come back. New team, new season, new wrist.

Same bad luck.

Waiting for the image results, he iced and elevated it. The door opened and Reid put his head in.

"Are you fucking kidding me?"

Bast could barely get the words out. "One minute I was skating toward the tunnel, the next I was in a heap and —this!"

Reid stared at Bast's wrist, his expression a mix of guilt and disbelief. "Does it feel broken?"

"I don't think so? It doesn't feel as bad as the last time, but it's not good, bro. The fucking mascot! I can't believe they let this lunatic on the ice. Don't they get training of any kind?"

Reid looked as clueless as Bast felt. Neither of them was up on the training regimen for NHL mascots, but bitching and moaning were the only tools in their arsenal.

Twenty minutes later, the result wasn't quite as bad as he feared but gloomy enough.

"Wrist sprain." The doc grimaced. "Unfortunately, you

know what it takes to heal. At least another couple of months before you can hold a stick again."

All because he bumped into the fucking mascot?

No, the mascot had bumped into him, and there was going to be hell to pay.

7

———

Twenty minutes earlier ...

Pepper liked to think of her side hustle as performance art.

After all, not everyone got a chance to wear a fun costume and dance in front of thousands of people apart from a Broadway show or a strip club. Though dance might be a stretch. And fun was possibly not so accurate.

The art part? So she was making lemonade here.

Most people failed to realize that, just like the emergency backup goalie crew for the NHL, the teams also had one for mascots. A list of people to call when the regular mascot was unavailable.

And tonight, Pepper was the one to save the day.

"Has anyone figured out what this thing is yet?" Pepper held up the mascot's head. She'd always considered it as a cross between a cat and a fox, but now that she looked at it more closely, it had a weird birdlike appearance with those feathers coming out of its forehead.

"Something prehistoric," Danny, one of the equipment managers, said as he helped her into her skates. With the body of the cat-fox-bird, she couldn't reach them herself. "Thanks for doing this. I know it's not your favorite thing."

Yeah, well, she'd promised her dad that she'd help out whenever she could. Saying no to John Calhoun, head coach of the Rebels, was generally impossible. About nine months ago, she'd stepped in for a couple of circuits when the previous mascot had been fired, as a favor to her dad. They had since hired someone else, but the new mascot's wife had gone into labor this afternoon and the usual backup was out of town, so Pepper was the next best thing. A one-night only performance.

"I'm surprised there isn't someone here who could do it." All the support staff could skate and basically, that was the only requirement. That, and to be at least five feet ten so the costume would fit right.

Danny wouldn't look her straight in the eye.

"Danny?" It dawned on her. "My father insisted I should be called, didn't he?"

"I offered, but he said you should be the one. Sorry."

Damn it. But lately her father didn't approve of anything she put her mind to. *You need to snap out of it, Pepper! No more of this aimless lack of application.*

Of course, he didn't think team mascot was a valid career, but he thought it might shock her into doing something real with her life.

Joke's on you, Dad. I don't mind this gig.

Few people in the Rebels org knew it was her, and she was determined it should stay that way. The press would find it hilarious that the former fiancée of a pro hockey player, daughter of a revered coach, and sister to a hot shot NHL winger, was reduced to this. Better to stay on the downlow. A figure of fun, high-fived by fans, punched by children —and sometimes their dads.

At least, it paid well and was the perfect cover for the invisibility-seeking gal about town.

"Okay, we're just nearing the end of the first period." Danny glanced at the screen over her head. "The crowd's going nuts for Bast. Big night for him."

She swallowed at the mention of his name. After their run-in at Jimmy's Tap and her dedicated efforts to avoiding him ever since, she'd done her best to put him out of her mind. After all, she had an ex-fiancé renting space in her head; she certainly didn't need another pro-athlete subletting.

However, living in a sports-mad town like Chicago meant it was difficult to avoid the news. Players and teams were always trending on Twitter, or showing up in her Facebook feed, or mysteriously appearing in search results. (So maybe not so mysterious. She'd been more than a little curious about the star Canadian with the God-given sporting prowess and the killer smile.)

This comeback game was all anyone could talk about. She'd tried to ignore it, which was hard to do when her brother insisted on reminding her with multiple texts over the last hour, telling her to say hello to his college buddy when she got the chance. (Apparently, her brother knew every other player in the NHL *and* had a heads-up on her performance this evening. *Thanks, Dad.*)

"Ready?"

"Lay it on me, Danno."

Grinning, he helped her with the head. The first period timer was ticking down, which was her cue to skate onto the ice and do a few circuits dancing to Pink's *Get the Party Started*. The song was over twenty years old but still yanked the crowd to their feet like no other.

Danny added blade guards to her skates and helped her

upright. As he took her arm, he looked up at Rowdy's eyes, about a foot north of Pepper's actual eyes which were lined up with the mouth. Peripheral vision was not a thing in this costume, but that was generally okay. She was a good skater, and even with the top-heavy costume, she knew how to balance all 160 pounds of woman.

"Let's do this," she said, the sound muffled, but Danny understood well enough. He guided her down the tunnel, past the players coming off, who paid her little heed. Too busy hyped up over the first period, which had them two goals to the good.

"Great start, guys," Danny called out, high-fiving a couple of the players as they passed. None of them looked at her, which was fine.

Invisible. Just how she liked it.

"Okay, when the last player comes off, that's when you go on."

Like she didn't know how it worked!

All the players had filed by her, heading toward the locker room. One of them must have been Bast, though she hadn't seen him, her efforts to ignore amazingly successful. At the entrance to the rink, Danny knelt and removed her blade guards.

"You ready?"

"Yep. See you in a few!"

"Go, Rowdy!" He called out just as she stepped onto the ice, her right foot taking a long stride to give her the momentum she needed to make an entrance.

That momentum took a hit as her skate collided with something.

Another skate.

Another *skater*.

They both went crashing to the ice.

The top-heavy Rowdy head weighed a ton, so all Pepper could do was look up at the arena ceiling through the costume's mouth-hole, trapped on her back like a giant bug. She managed to move the head enough to turn to whatever she had plowed into, a prayer on a loop.

Please let it be an official. Please let it be an official.

No such luck—the blue of a Rebels jersey confirmed her worst fear. She'd hit a player.

Okay, this didn't have to be a disaster. She moved down her list of wants.

Someone on the fourth line. Someone ... disposable.

Through Rowdy's mouth, she strained her eyes, trying to get some sense of her victim's identity through the howl of pain echoing above the crowd noise.

A sweater emblazoned with the letters D-U-R ...

No, no, no. If it had to be one of them, let it be Reid. Reid was an asshole, but he'd eventually forgive her. Please let it not be ...

Him.

It was Bast. And he was cradling his wrist, the one he'd broken last year.

No one was bothering with her, assuming the mascot costume had cushioned her from any real injury.

Though really it was because the Rebels' most recent acquisition, the man, the legend, Bastian Durand, was flat out on his back in front of twenty thousand people. In this moment, no one cared about the stupid mascot.

Invisible, just like she'd wished.

8

———

THE DOOR to the office where Pepper had been stashed, for want of a better word, flew open. She hoped it was Danny, but alas, no.

Her father, John Calhoun—or Coach Calhoun as he was known in these parts—slammed the door behind him.

"What the hell, Pepper?"

"I thought the ice was clear. All the players were behind me in the tunnel, and Danny said I—"

"This isn't Danny's fault. You exploded onto that ice like a bull in a china shop, blind to everything around you!"

"That-that's how the costume works, Dad. I have no peripheral vision." She was relying on people to tell her it was clear. She had the go-ahead, or thought she had. "How is he?"

"Doc's with him now. It might be a bruise or a sprain, but whatever it is, he'll be out for weeks at minimum."

"Oh. That's awful."

He looked exasperated, and absurdly, she understood. She had done nothing but disappoint him lately, not to mention herself. She just couldn't seem to get her life out of first gear.

"Jesus, Pepper, I got you this job so you could make something of yourself. Get back some pride."

"Not really much upward mobility in the mascot business, Dad."

Too flippant. The disgusted downturn of his mouth agreed. "There's only so long I can support you."

"I don't need your support, Dad." At least not financially. "I have savings"—ever dwindling—"and I have my nannying gig."

"You barely make enough to pay for your car. Pepper ..." He paused, seemed to course-correct. "I just want you to be happy."

She inhaled, a supreme effort to hold off the tears. It was almost easier when he was pissed at her. "Can we not talk about this now? You probably should check in on your player."

What the hell was Bast Durand doing on the ice after everyone else had left it? No way would she have skated on if she thought a player was still present.

Her father was still standing there, hands on hips, mouth like a hyphen. "Pepper, you need to start figuring things out. Establish some real goals."

Easier said than done. One quick Google search told everyone all they needed to know about Pepper Calhoun.

"Dad, I'm sorry. Could you tell Bastian that it was an accident? If I can do anything, let me know."

"You've done enough. You and I are going to have a chat about your future later." With that ominous pronouncement, he left the room in a chill and Pepper in a dejected heap.

She changed into her regular clothes, an unassuming

Henley with rolled-up jeans and ballet flats. Despite what happened, she felt exposed without the Rowdy Rebel costume. Sure, no one could see her face when she wore it, were barely aware that she was the human inside it, but there was comfort in that. Now that she had set it aside, she was determined to get out of here as quickly as possible. She would go home and wait for her father to ream her out properly.

She snuck a peek outside the door. All clear.

One step toward the exit, then another.

"Hey, Pepper."

She turned at the sound of a familiar voice. Elle was walking toward her, holding the hand of Hatch, who at fourteen months, was an absolute delight. She still helped out as a part-time babysitter for the Kershaws a couple of days a week, which was about the only thing that kept her sane.

Just behind her was Sadie Yates, who was married to center Gunnar Bond, with a Babygro containing their three-month-old, Matti, wrapped around her body.

Pepper pinned on a smile for Hatch. "How's it going, little guy?"

"Peppa!" He reached out and grabbed her leg.

Elle tried to hold him back. "He's running me ragged. He was getting a bit over excited in the box, so I thought I'd bring him down here for a walk. We saw what happened."

Pepper felt incredibly foolish in the presence of these uber-successful, have-it-all women. Elle was taking classes online toward a business degree, and Sadie was a famous fashion designer. And here was Pepper the mascot—a *failed* mascot, at that—wishing she could find an Internet-free desert island and hole up there for the rest of her life.

"I'm so embarrassed. You wouldn't think I'd taken

skating lessons until I was fifteen. I'm usually better than that."

Hunkering down beside Hatch, she inhaled as a wave of nostalgia for her previous life washed over her. As much as she loved watching this little tyke, she missed the kids she used to work with, all those developing minds she wanted to influence. How uncomplicated things were before she met Kent. Just as she took tentative steps to get back on an even keel, a cartoon sledgehammer was on hand to knock her off course again.

"Hey, buddy, you excited to see Daddy at work?"

He was too young to understand her question, but he seemed to sense her distress. He touched her face, a gentle gesture that almost broke her. If she wasn't ready to cry after tonight's events, that would do it.

Blinking back the emotion, she stood and leaned in to take a gander at baby Matti and inhale a lungful of his soothing baby scent. "He looks so peaceful."

"Yeah, he sleeps like a champ through the games," Sadie said. "Not so much at nighttime."

"Already bored by hockey." She stroked the feathery wisps of hair on his head. "Keep up the good work."

That drew laughs from the two women, and while Pepper would have liked to join in, it wouldn't come.

"About tonight," Sadie started. "It was just bad luck. Could've happened to anyone."

But it hadn't. "I should get going." The exit beckoned, and she wanted to be anywhere but here. She turned back to Elle. "See you tomorrow?"

"If you'd rather take some time ..."

"I'd like to keep busy. But if you'd prefer I didn't ..."

Elle shook her head vehemently. "Of course we want to see you! Let me know if anything changes."

"You know, if you need to talk about anything, feel free to reach out to either of us," Sadie said. "You know Elle a bit better, but I'm here too if you need a friendly ear."

"Thanks!" She infused as much cheer into it as possible, then watched as Elle, Sadie, and their little ones headed back toward the exit that would lead them to the executive suites.

Pepper let out a breath. That might have been her life if it hadn't all fallen apart so spectacularly a year ago. These women seemed nice enough, but then Pepper had thought that about the Denver Diamonds WAGs as well.

She turned the other way, anxious to put this night behind her.

Ten more steps and she'd be clear, at least until her father was ready to yell at her again.

"Pepper!"

The roar made her jump and almost tempted her to slam through the exit and remove herself from the threat as fast as her legs could carry her.

But she wasn't going to run. Not from him.

WHEN COACH TOLD Bast who had bumped into him on the ice, he couldn't believe it.

"Pepper? As in your daughter?" That's why that prick, Connor, had been so cryptic. *Say hi to my sister. She's "at the game."* Very funny.

Bast had never heard of a female skater taking on mascot duties. Not that it needed any special skill other than the ability to stay upright.

And oh yeah—avoid the fucking players.

Coach had been furious, then apologetic.

It should never have happened, there'll be hell to pay, and so on.

Well, of course. There should be, maybe a full-scale investigation into how something so catastrophic could have occurred. After a good ten minutes of oscillating between fury and sorrow, in which Bast didn't get a word in, Coach had gone off to shout at someone. Pepper, probably. Though that should really be Bast's right.

Tonight she'd screwed with his career, and here she was, scrambling for the exit. Old habits with this girl.

"Running away? Again?"

Turning, she faced him, those hazel eyes blown wide as they dipped to his arm in a sling. "How are you?"

The twin blades of anger and embarrassment were nicking at his organs. Bad enough he'd fallen over on the ice in what was sure to be the most meme-able gif doing the rounds this year, but why in the name of all that was fucking fucked did it have to be her?

Coach's daughter.

Connor's sister.

The woman he'd spent far too many nights fantasizing about.

While a cavalcade of curses did the rounds in his foggy brain, she approached him, her expression full of sympathy he neither wanted nor needed. "How bad is it?"

"Out for the season. Again." An exaggeration, but he wanted her to feel as terrible as he did.

Her face fell, and he cheered the reaction. Maturity was on sabbatical.

"I'm sorry. I thought I had the all-clear. Usually I need someone to—"

Impatiently, he cut off her excuses. "Why are you even here?"

"I'm just filling in."

"Durand, how are you feeling?" Coach Calhoun appeared in the corridor, looking as fierce as a Grizzly. He didn't even glance at his daughter, and oddly that made Bast feel … awful.

"Could be worse," Bast muttered, because he suspected that if he complained, it wouldn't reflect well on Pepper. Why the hell he felt a need to protect her after the stunt she'd pulled was beyond him.

"No need to be brave. I know this is a blow." He squeezed Bast's shoulder. "Pepper will drive you home."

"Nah, I can—" Bast said at the same time Pepper blurted, "Dad, I can't—"

They both stopped talking, any agreement here feeling criminal.

She turned to her father. "Wouldn't it be better if one of the official drivers took care of it?"

"You will drive Bastian home and make sure he gets inside his place without any more hassle, okay?"

She exhaled, utterly defeated, and there it was again: that pang of sympathy. But then she spoke with an abrupt "You ready to leave now?" and the feeling passed.

The third period had just started. He could probably view it from the press box, but he wasn't in the mood for the inevitable questions. Neither was he in the mood to argue with Coach, so he'd take the ride.

"Sure."

She walked toward the exit and he followed, trying his damnedest not to admire those curves he'd hit on months ago. What freaky kind of universe shit was happening that reunited them in these awful circumstances?

"We can take my car," he said as they exited.

"Better to take mine. I need to drive home after."

True. And it might be best if she wasn't behind the wheel of his SUV. She wasn't the most coordinated as tonight's incident demonstrated. Someone from the org could drive it home for him tomorrow.

Her car was a Honda Civic, an older model. Not that he was a car snob or anything, but his SUV was nicer.

"Embarrassed to be seen in my crappy car?"

When he didn't rise to the bait, she made a face of *whatever*. What was he supposed to say? It was gorgeous, the most beautiful mid-size economy car in the world? He clambered in, careful to favor his arm.

He couldn't believe he was in this position again.

Because of her.

"Not sure why you're pissed at me," he said. "I'm the injured party here."

"I'm—I'm not pissed at you. Honestly, it was an accident. You weren't supposed to be there."

"On the ice? Doing my job?"

"Everyone else was off." She added quietly, "Except you."

He didn't like the implication that he might be in the wrong here, not dissimilar to how he felt about the first night they met.

"I was connecting with my fans. I've been out of the game for a while, in case you hadn't heard."

"I know. We all know."

She sounded annoyed again. Fine, he didn't have to talk to her.

Instead he snuck glances her way, furious that she was still beautiful with those dark, inky lashes framing hazel eyes that would happily cut him dead if he looked directly at her. As if this was somehow his fault. He couldn't believe he'd spent every night since he'd last seen her wishing they could get horizontal.

Well, dreams do come true!

"What?" When he didn't answer, she said, "You made a weird noise."

"Just thinking about how—never mind."

How she'd smiled at him that night. How he would have happily dumped his brother for a chance with her. How a fifteen-minute conversation with her was the boost he'd needed after the worst months of his life.

He could admit that now. He'd kept on smiling through his rehab so no one would question his mental state. So Reid wouldn't feel bad when everything was going so good for him for the first time. So Bast wouldn't have to think about a life outside hockey.

Yeah, that fifteen minutes in Jimmy's Tap had done a lot of heavy lifting.

But then he remembered the rest: she'd known who he was. And there was all that business about hating hockey. Was that something to do with her ex, Kent Gallagher?

Maybe that was her game: mow through life, screwing up the lives of pro-athletes. He was trying to reconcile the woman with this tabloid-drenched past with the girl he'd talked to in that bar and the person who'd crashed into him tonight. Something was off here, but he was too tired and emotional to figure it out.

His phone buzzed with a text from Kennedy, his brother's wife.

You okay?

BAST

Sprain. Going home to rest up.

KENNEDY

Damn, that sucks. Let us know what we can do. We'll check in tomorrow.

We. A little spark of envy ignited inside him. Reid and Kennedy had married this past summer in a private ceremony in Thailand, then had a bigger one when they returned to Chicago. It must be nice to be part of a team like that, someone to unload your troubles on when you needed it.

The sourness he felt turned him unusually hostile. "I thought you were a bartender—was that another lie?"

"I have a couple of jobs. Lots of people take on multiple gigs. We're not all possessed of one singular talent."

"Some people aren't possessed of any."

She turned the car sharply onto his block and pulled up outside his building. On a shaky inhale, she said, "I wasn't trying to make a fool of you that night we met. I thought you preferred anonymity, and so did I, and as I had no intention of going anywhere with it, it felt harmless."

No intention of going anywhere? Well, that was about as clear a statement on the topic as could be made. He'd obviously misjudged the whole situation.

"Got it," he muttered. He gripped the door handle with the one good hand he had left and clambered out of the passenger seat, careful to shield his wrist. He'd had plenty of practice.

Pepper was already waiting by the passenger door, probably estimating how much more damage she could do. Wisely, she stood back to give him space, and he made sure to be careful getting out so he wouldn't need her special kind of help.

"My bag is—"

"Let me." She opened the back door and pulled it out, then headed for the door to his building.

He followed, not even having it in him to appreciate her ass. That's how bad of a mood he was in. Besides, what would be the point? He might have thought about her far too much than was sane over the last few months, but now he knew this was more than a non-starter.

It was an erase-from-existence.

They got to the front door of his building, and thankfully Pete, his doorman, was on hand, his face crumpled in sympathy as he spotted the sling.

"Hey, Mr. Durand, tough game tonight." He gave Pepper an appreciative look. Bast was tempted to tell him not to bother because he was in the presence of Rowdy Rebel, Dream Destroyer. "Can I get that bag, Miss?"

"Oh, right." She passed it over and turned to Bast. "Can I help you in?"

"You've done enough, don't you think?"

Ignoring the look of hurt on her face, he walked into the lobby and didn't look back.

9

___

"HI, DAD."

Pepper jumped clear across the kitchen to grab a mug for her father's coffee.

"You cooking?"

"Sure am. Making eggs just the way you like them with herbs. Thyme and rosemary." She placed his coffee down before him. "Have a seat."

With a noisy sigh, he did as he was told and added half and half to his coffee. Pepper returned to stirring the eggs to make them fluffy. "How did you sleep?"

"Terribly. One of my players is out for weeks, possibly months. News like that is going to keep me up, y'know."

"Right. I get that. Have you heard anything else? More definitive news?" If he was out for that long, it would be disastrous. She knew her father was banking on Bastian's participation to put the Rebels back in contention.

"It's a sprain so not a break, but he's just come back from surgery and rehabbing that wrist. Over ten months out. And now another few months at least."

She bit her lip. "I'm sorry, Dad. I screwed up big time. If there's anything I can do to make it right."

"You've done enough."

"Right, I get that, but—"

"Enough, Pepper."

She swallowed back her hurt. So she had no right to feel this way because she was in the wrong, but a part of her felt she shouldn't even be in this position. She was only on that ice because her father thought she needed to be jolted into getting her act together. According to him, she was wallowing over her life collapse—a collapse she'd brought on herself by breaking off her engagement to Kent.

She wished she could speak to her mom, but she was currently on a round-the-world tour with her new girl crew. Since her parents' divorce last year, Claire Calhoun had been doing all the things her ex-husband had promised would happen when he retired. When he re-upped for another three years as Rebels coach, her mother called time on their marriage and broke for the hills.

Her father's phone rang, and he answered it with a gruff bark, which was quickly followed by a string of very salty swearwords. Whoever was on the other end was trying to explain something, but her father was having none of it.

"I'll talk to him. Jesus Christ, these kids don't know their asses from their elbows."

Her father stormed out of the room, which gave her a chance to check the pings she'd been ignoring on her phone all morning. The text thread was twenty messages plus in, so she had to scroll back.

The first message had come in last night from Tommy Toga, the mascot with the New York Spartans.

> Did you really just take out Bast Durand?
> Wicked move!

Trigger with the Nashville Country had responded with:

> Give her a break, TT. She can't have meant
> that to happen. Uh, did you?

ROWDY REBEL

> No, I didn't. It was a complete accident!

Soon the rest of the gang were weighing in. After she first filled in as Rowdy Rebel nine months ago, she received an invite to a text group called Mascot Mania. When she questioned how they knew to invite her—her identity was supposedly private—she'd been told that all mascots *and* backups were included in this super secret group where they could ensure the "mascot profession" was respected. Or something.

She'd expected discussions about unionizing, better protections for the mascots, and how to monetize a mascot gig. Instead she got an extreme bitchfest about which players were the biggest assholes. The thread had been quiet for a while, given the off-season, but Pepper's crash into Bastian Durand had exploded a bomb under it.

THE THREE BRANCHES (DC)

> Did they fire you?

ROWDY REBEL

> Not yet, but I can't see them asking me
> back.

She almost said this was just a temp gig, but that might be considered insulting to the lofty profession of mascotting.

HOWIE HOLLYWOOD (LA QUAKE)

It was clearly an accident. Whoever sent
you on should be hauled across the coals.

Danny was crushed about what had happened. Last night he'd told the team org that he was at fault, but no one cared. The buck stopped with the awkward rat-bird on the ice, apparently.

BIG CAT (BOSTON COUGARS)

They'd rather blame the person in the
costume.

So far, no one knew it was her except the mascots on this thread and a select few in the Rebels org. If people found out that the Coach's daughter had screwed up in such a monumental way *and* that same woman was once engaged to Kent Gallagher, she would never hear the end of it. She may as well dig a hole in the backyard, crawl into it, and go to sleep until it was over.

Which would probably be Rip Van Winkle lengths of bedrest because it would never be over. She would live on in the annals of sports scandal, a notch below poor Steve Bartman.

While Sammy the Shark from Vancouver debated with Charlie the Bear from Edmonton (those guys had an avid rivalry going on) about which players *deserved* to be tripped on the ice, her phone rang with a call from Tara Becker.

"Hi, Tara."

"Hey, girl, what's up?"

"Other than wishing I could fall asleep for a hundred years, not much. You?"

"Oh, honey! That was not your fault. Have you seen the replay?"

"I'm trying to avoid it."

Tara chuckled. "That boy was making eyes at some chick in the crowd. That's what really happened!"

It shouldn't have surprised her, yet she failed to see how it improved her situation. "No one's going to care about that. They'll just remember that the mascot took him down."

"Maybe, but he needs to take *some* responsibility. I told Hale that very thing ..."

She continued talking while Pepper listened to rumbling from the other room, maybe the sound of something smashing?

"Listen, I've got to go." She'd promised Elle she'd look after Hatch this morning while the busy mom ran errands. "You'll let me know if you hear anything?"

"Sure, hon. But just know that this is not on you. Flirty eyes are the culprit."

Like that would get her off the hook.

"Dad?" She ventured tentatively into the living room. Her father was seated on the sofa, and it looked like a lamp hadn't survived the phone call. "Was that about Bastian?"

"There's a press conference scheduled so we can explain how the damn mascot set a key player's recovery back by months and possibly ruined this team's chances for a good season."

Pepper wasn't sure that could be explained in a press conference. Or at all.

"Should I be there?"

Her father narrowed his eyes. "No. What I want is for you to figure out your life. Ten months ago, you came back here after the stuff with Gallagher. I know relationships don't always work out, but I'm still not sure why it had to turn so nasty."

Because the Denver Diamonds would rather protect

their asset than worry about the woman who tried to help him. But she couldn't tell her father the real story, not without betraying Kent's trust.

"It's complicated. Like all relationships." She was speaking to a man who was recently divorced. Surely he got it.

"What's next, Pepper?"

"I'm figuring out some things."

"Such as finishing your degree? Better that than child-minding."

She blinked. "I'm working on it. I needed to take the time away after what happened and rethink the future. I'll be out of your hair soon, I promise."

The look he gave her was a mix of pity and love. She hated that look, how easy it was to recognize, and that dark pit in her stomach whenever he brought it to the table.

"Breakfast's ready," she said.

"I'll get something at the arena." With a heavy sigh, he headed for the door.

"Peppa!"

Hatch ran into her arms, and Pepper let herself absorb his soft breathing and little boy smell, possibly for a little too long because soon he was squirming, trying to escape the clutches of the needy lady.

He touched her face with sticky hands.

"Hey, buddy. Whatcha been working on?" She unfurled his chubby fist. "Peanut butter *and* glitter? Wow, that's quite the combination."

Elle had let her in three minutes ago, pointed at her artistic child, and hurried upstairs. Now she was back, donning a super-cute burgundy leather jacket. "I'm sorry, I turned my back for a second! He got into the play bucket under the stairs after eating his PB on toast."

"Mama!" Hatch held up his hand and giggled, then moved toward the harried woman who had borne him.

"Oh, no, baby. I just put on a clean shirt."

Pepper scooped him up. "I'll take care of it. I know you have an appointment, so don't worry about a thing."

Elle eyed her critically. "I kind of expected you to take a mental health day. I would've understood completely."

When this was her only source of income? Not likely. Besides, she hated to let anyone down, even though it seemed that lately, that was her brand.

"I know you had something important to do." She turned to Hatch. "We're going to be just fine, the two of us. Right, buddy?"

"Peppa!" Another grab at her hair, mixing the butter and glitter in good. Wonderful.

Elle picked up her purse and looked around. Pepper handed her a set of keys that were hiding under a SpongeBob toy on the hallway entry table.

"Thanks. Now, when I come home, we should talk about what happened at the arena. I'm hanging with Mia and Jordan later, so maybe you could join us? Theo's on daddy duty tonight."

As much as Pepper recognized how sweet Elle was, she wasn't quite ready to confide in the Rebel WAGs, or even hang with them. Mia *was* lovely, though, a super talented player who had married Cal Foreman over the summer. Pepper had yet to meet Jordan, a well-known hockey reporter, hitched to another Rebels player, Levi Hunt. The idea of chatting with all these high-flyers, including a member of the press, brought her out in hives.

"Sorry, but I have something going on."

Elle looked a little hurt at what sounded like an obvious excuse.

"Okay, just throwing it out there." Elle popped a kiss on Hatch's head. "See you later, Dino-baby!" Then to Pepper, "Text me if you need anything."

"Will do."

First thing was to wash this little monster's hands, then see if she could get peanut butter and glitter out of her hair. She felt awful about turning Elle's offer to talk down, but she'd been there before. Confiding in a clique of women only to have them turn on her. Not that she thought Elle would ever do that—she was such a nice person, and not the usual type for a WAG. In fact, none of the Rebels WAGs would be considered typical of the genus, except for Tara. And technically she wasn't one because she was dating Fitz, the general manager.

Tara had gone out of her way to be kind to Pepper, though Heavens knew why. She guessed that maybe Tara, with her somewhat outsider status, saw something similar in Pepper.

She lifted Hatch off the stool he used to reach the bathroom sink and stowed it away. "Okay, hands all clean."

"All kee!" Hatch yelled then devolved into giggles while pointing at Pepper.

She caught sight of herself in the mirror. Yep, a clump of blue glitter mashed into her hair with a gob of peanut butter. Lovely.

"I bet you're pretty proud, H-Man."

More giggles and pointing. The story of her life.

"Stay there while I work on this."

Of course, expecting a very active fourteen-month-old toddler to stay still was a little like expecting people to refrain from making jokes about being pounded *Pepper-style!* The meme game was strong on Twitter this morning. She had tried to ignore it, but her brother had already sent her several gifs showcasing her failure on the ice.

CONNOR

Nice job, Pepperoni! Eliminating the competition. Very kool!

Sure, that's exactly why she did it. To help her brother's career.

But Connor didn't really think it was cool (or kool!). He thought this was just one more example of Pepper's ability to court disaster at every turn.

Like the time she lost her pet hamster in the backyard (*Beauregard, I hope you're enjoying your retirement.*)

Or the time her hair turned carrot-orange after a spectacularly unfortunate home-dying accident.

Or the time she got food poisoning the night before her first-year college exams—and then again the night before she was supposed to repeat them.

Pepper wasn't a particularly lucky person, but until now, her hexed life had never impacted someone else, even if people thought she was the reason for Kent's career failings. This time, she was *undoubtedly* the reason for someone else's career stall. Poor Bast. He must be so miserable.

But she had no time to dwell on that because Hatch was trying his best to reach the bathroom doorknob so he could get into something else sticky. She gave a quick swipe of water through her matted hair, lamented the glitter that remained, and grasped her charge by the collar.

"Hold up there, champ. Where ya going?"

"Puddle!"

That meant "puzzle" or at least, Pepper hoped it did

because she didn't relish the thought of taking him out to play in the rain, which had a distinctly frozen look to it. The forecast was for snow, an unusually late Fall storm to brighten everyone's day.

"Okay, let's get out the dino-puzzles." The wooden dinosaur puzzle blocks were one of Hatch's favorites, so they spent the next ten minutes playing with them on the living room floor. Pepper loved watching how his little cheeks puffed up while he tried to figure out the placement of the puzzle piece, then his jubilant smile when he got there.

"You are so good at those, H-man. How about this one?" She gave him the pieces for the T-rex. Someone had written "HEO" after with a silver Sharpie, so it spelled "Theo-Rex." Weird. As smart as Hatch was, that was a little beyond him right now.

While she puzzled that out, her phone rang with a call from Bridget. She put her on speaker, so she could keep her hands free for potential toddler-wrangling.

"Hey, Bridge."

"Hey, you! So, still coming over this afternoon?"

A moment of panic reared inside her. "Are you telling me I can't stay?"

"No, not at all! You're more than welcome. I can't wait to hear all the gory details. Like just how mad at you is Bast Durand? Do his eyes flash that delicious blue or go dark when he's angry?"

"No, they turn green like the Hulk." Pepper sighed. "I just need to get away from my dad's place for a bit. He's furious with me, and it's making things really tense."

She had her luggage in the car and planned to stop by Rebels HQ on her way to Bridget's to let him know she was getting out of his hair for the foreseeable future. Just seeing her face reminded him of how awful she was, so she'd fix that the best way she could. Exit, stage left.

Hatch pounded his little fist, trying to get a puzzle piece to fit where it shouldn't.

"Hey, buddy, don't try to force it." She took the cardboard out while musing on how she was the wrong puzzle piece in her family. The one who didn't fit.

"You watching Theo Kershaw's kid again?"

"Yep." Pepper smiled as Hatch turned the piece around. "So smart, H-man!"

"So what's their marriage like? Do you think he plays away?"

Pepper rolled her eyes. Bridget was the worst gossip, always trying to get juicy nuggets out of Pepper because of her proximity to pro-athletes. "I don't know a thing about their marriage, but from what I can tell, it's perfect."

"Aww! I love hearing that. I would not throw Theo Kershaw out of bed for eating cookies, ya know?"

"I do know. You never stop talking about it."

Bridget plowed on. "Well, he's so hot, but Bast Durand is in another league entirely. I wonder if he'll get back with Marina Morgan. I heard she broke up with Brian Costa."

To her shame, Pepper had done a little research on Bast and come across several pics of him with Marina from before his wrist injury last year. They'd looked positively golden together, a true supercouple. People like that just fit so well, and Pepper should really have known better than to think she could flirt with a guy like Bast Durand in a bar and not suffer some consequences.

By the end of that meet-disaster, the guy had not liked her. But somehow she'd called that and raised the stakes to true hatred with this latest effort. Nice job, Rowdy.

"Hey, I need to go. Hatch is getting into all sorts here."

Sorry, little guy! He was completely involved in his puzzle and behaving like an angel, so it was unfair of her to make him the fall guy. "See you later this afternoon?"

"Of course. Text me when you're on your way. And Pep, don't worry about it. It'll all blow over."

She wished she could believe that. But as bad as she felt now, she suspected that Bast had to be feeling a whole lot worse.

His head hurt. So fucking much.

Which, given the amount of bourbon he'd downed last night, really shouldn't be a surprise. But his wrist was only throbbing today instead of shooting shards of pain down his arm, so he counted that as a win.

Sitting up in bed, he waited for the dizziness to subside, then stumbled zombie-like out to the living room. His sweats lay on the floor where he'd kicked them off about halfway through the bottle. A T-shirt lay in shorn rags, meat scissors beside it. Because he couldn't find real scissors and he had thought cutting the tee off was better than trying to peel it over his head.

That decision courtesy of three-fourths of the bottle.

His phone was on the sofa, its screen riddled with notifications. Missed calls, left voicemails, a parade of sympathetic text messages.

To hell with them.

Uncharitable, perhaps. People were being kind, but he'd been through this before. He'd used that experience the best way he could—as a means to re-connect with Reid and put his father on blast. *Quit being an asshole, Dad, and I might let you talk to me.*

And it had worked. He and Reid were closer than ever, and he and Henri had recognizable boundaries. He wondered how this latest injury would change the dynamic.

Coffee was probably the best solution, but he wasn't sure a sober Bastian Durand was the better option right now. In the kitchen, he pulled open the cupboard and grabbed a bottle of Jack Daniels. He'd already drunk the good stuff, but he wasn't looking to appreciate a single sip. The goal was to stay smashed so he wouldn't think about anything else.

Pouring a couple of fingers, he recoiled slightly as the fumes reached his nostrils. Maybe this wasn't such a good idea. While he considered that, his phone vibrated with a text.

HUDSON

Hey, Bast, I'm guessing you're not up for visitors. Let me know if you want to talk.

He and Grey had trained together during the summer while Reid was traveling with Kennedy, and had become close. The kid was pretty sensitive so Bast really should text him back and let him know all was good. Before he could do that, a text came in from Dex O'Malley, another of his new teammates. Nice guy, O'Malley, a devil for the ladies.

O'MALLEY

Fuck, man, hope you're okay. This might cheer you up.

He'd attached a photo of himself with ... was that the blonde from the game? The one with the Bast tattoo on her tits?

Through his bleary, hungover gaze, he squinted to confirm that yes, indeed, that was her. With O'Malley. How was this cheering him up again?

O'MALLEY

I might have given her your number.

Your fucking welcome.

It's spelled "you're," dickhead. That was all he needed. Sure, he'd noticed her before the clash … there it was again, that slither of discomfort down his spine, the feeling he'd fucked up. That his focus might have been elsewhere as he skated off for the break.

But that didn't mean the mascot was supposed to charge into him like a rampaging elephant.

BAST

Stop giving out my number.

O'MALLEY

wink emoji

He pushed the glass of JD aside and reached for the Keurig cups, only to be interrupted by the intercom. He'd instructed Pete that he would not be accepting visitors until further notice, so that noise was enough to rile him up all over again.

The buzz repeated. He picked up the phone. "Pete, what did I say about—"

"It's me."

Reid. "Managing the door today, bro?" His voice sounded like a frog was spawning tadpoles in there.

"You haven't been answering your phone. I need to come up."

"I'm not home."

Reid sighed. "C'mon. Talk to me."

Bast shut his eyes, but all he could see was her. Pepper Calhoun and her hazel eyes and gorgeous lips, close to tears because he'd hurt her feelings.

He was the victim here!

And just thinking that word—victim—was enough to shock him out of his haze. "Tell Pete I said it was okay." He hung up the phone.

Thirty seconds later Reid waltzed in, but not alone. Kennedy was with him, along with their cute dog Bucky, who immediately jumped on his uncle Bast.

"Hey, boy, how are ya?"

Reid pulled Bucky back, then undid his leash. "Okay if he has free run of the place?"

"Sure. As you can see the maid hasn't been in."

Reid took a long look. "You okay?"

"I've been better."

"Brother, this sucks."

"I know." Of course Reid was going to feel bad. At this rate, it would be almost a year since the last time Bast played a full game. He'd missed most of last season, the Olympics—Reid was alternate and came home with the gold—and now he would probably be out of action until the New Year at the minimum.

"Not your fault," he muttered to soothe Reid's guilt. Again. They'd been playing this game all year, and now a sizzle of irritation zipped through his chest.

"Well—"

"Seriously, bro. We're good."

Reid winced, fronting that look he got on the regular, the one that replayed the dynamics of their childhood. The weird protective streak.

Back then Reid had stood up for him when other kids were dicks but reserved the right to be a bully of his own. Bast had adored Reid, even when he was cruel to him. He had let his older brother push him around because one, he was smaller, and two, he knew on some instinctual level that Reid was treated unfairly by Henri. The more of a prick Henri was to his stepson, the more Reid took it out on Bast.

But eventually Bast was the same size as his brother and Reid stopped shoving Bast around, which coincided with them going their own ways. Different colleges. Different cities. Different routes to the NHL. Henri continued to grind on Reid, criticizing his diet, his regimen, his play. Picking at every part of him, all with the goal of making him stronger and getting him from the AHL to the big leagues. And Reid made it, then finally found his place on the Rebels.

Bast's journey had been different, a top-ten draft pick straight to the Hawks, his trajectory assured. There'd been no surprise when the team won the Cup a couple of years later. It was the kind of success expected in their family.

Reid had been there, cheering him on, never hinting he was jealous, though he had to be. While Reid liked to pretend he didn't feel like other people, he was the most emotional guy Bast knew. Bast saw that favoritism shown by Henri extend into their adulthood. Saw how it cut Reid to the quick, made him turn inward. He tried to make it up to him by being kind, and when they were both in Chicago, by extending the hand of friendship. But some part of him enjoyed being Henri's favorite, felt he deserved it because Reid had been such an asshole when they were younger.

When things came to a head and Reid lashed out at Bast during the game that resulted in Bast's wrist injury, Bast realized how much damage Henri had done to his older brother. But also, how much damage Bast had done by never standing up to his father on Reid's behalf. Maybe that wasn't his job, but ... he'd felt guilty anytime he heard Henri telling Reid he needed to work harder or spend more time in the gym or eat the right foods. Things he rarely told Bast.

Bystander revenge, Bast had labeled it.

But things were better between them. Reid had apologized, and they were tighter than ever. Now this re-injury felt like all the work they'd put in on this relationship, the closeness they'd forged over the last year, was destroyed.

She was to blame. Pepper Cal-*fucking*-houn.

Kennedy put her arms around him. She was short and barely reached his collarbones.

"Hi," she murmured into his pecs.

"Hi," he said to the top of her head.

The most important member of the tight-knit triumvirate trotted over and nuzzled his leg, which was Bast's cue to hunker down and give him a good rub. "Hey Buck, you okay, boy?"

Bucky gave him a lick in return, then seemed to recoil. "What, don't like bourbon?"

The dog sniffed and wandered over to Reid, who had taken a seat on the sofa.

"I'd offer you a drink, but I need it all to stay paralytic."

Kennedy handed his sweats to him from the floor. "I'm loving the view, but it's cold in here. Suit up, Bast baby."

While he pulled them on, he took the armchair so Kennedy could cozy up to Reid.

"You guys don't need to be here. I'm just having a day, okay?"

Kennedy looked at him seriously. "We're here because we're family. Whatever you need."

"A new wrist would be nice. But failing that, I'm thinking

of getting away for a bit. Could I stay at your place in Belhaven Harbor?"

Reid frowned. "How would you get there? The Upper Peninsula is over five hours away from Chicago."

"I can drive." He shouldn't, but if he took breaks, he'd be fine.

"Yeah, but why not stay here?" Reid looked at Kennedy then back at his brother. "With people you know."

This was rather rich coming from a hater like Reid, but Bast understood his intent. Family meant more to him now that Kennedy and Bucky had opened his heart. There it was again, a spark of annoyance, one he couldn't attribute accurately. If he was sober, he might think he was jealous.

The skate was on the other foot, apparently.

"There's been such a build-up to the season, all this expectation, and now I have to wait again. Not sure I want to be in a sports-mad city with sports-mad opinions. Some fucker online said I deserved what I got because I left the Hawks."

"Asshole," Reid said. "But why the fuck are you online?"

Because he'd been running an intel op on one Pepper Calhoun while he got progressively more and more drunk and became distracted by a few choice morsels about himself.

Reid was still talking. "You're seriously going to head to a lonely cabin like some serial killer. Are you trying to get away from us?"

"You're not that annoying. Even if you and Ken and Bucky are the picture-perfect happy family that's just sugary-sweet enough to make my teeth ache—"

"So you *are* trying to get away from us. Hey, have you talked to Dad?"

"He's left several messages." Mostly about the potential

for a lawsuit with Pepper and the team org in his crosshairs. "I can't deal with him right now."

Reid nodded in sympathy. Henri Durand's input would not be helpful here.

Kennedy patted Reid's knee and leaned forward. "Bast, are you sure it's okay to be so far away from the team docs and physios?"

"I've been through this before. It just needs rest for a while."

"And you need some peace."

"Yeah, I do."

Kennedy got it, but then his sister-in-law was very intuitive. At least he'd always thought so until she made her next statement.

"I feel really bad for Pepper."

He perked up. "Why? This is her fault."

Kennedy's nose twitched. "Technically, I suppose."

"Uh, not technically. Actually. Full-bodied, mascot-suited blame can be laid at her clod-hopping feet."

"That's kind of harsh. You know she didn't do it on purpose, and you *were* taking your time coming off the ice. Flirting with that fan."

"I was not—"

But Kennedy had already moved on. "So you're friends with her brother?"

"Yeah. Connor and I knew each other in college. But I'd never met Pepper until ..." He paused. "A few months ago."

"Really?" Kennedy said, perking up herself. How could she tell that was even perk-worthy?

"Yeah, in a bar on the South Side." Annoyed that he had to recount this, Bast filled them in on his original meet with Pepper, and while any number of her sins could get top billing, he focused on the true offense.

"And she kept her identity to herself."

"Wonder why," Kennedy mused.

"To make me look like an idiot."

"Really?"

Reid sniffed. "She has a rep with athletes."

Bast squirmed, not liking Reid's response. But it was true, wasn't it? Or at least, one athlete.

Kennedy looked confused, so her husband picked up the slack. "Last year, she was engaged to this guy called Kent Gallagher. Plays hockey with the Denver Diamonds."

"Didn't you play with them?"

"Yeah, for less than a year. Anyway, apparently she broke his heart, and not long after, he got into some legal trouble, fighting in a bar, and his career took a nosedive."

"These days, he's floundering in the AHL," Bast said.

Kennedy's mouth scrunched up as she addressed her husband. "But wasn't that where you started? What's so wrong with that?"

"It's okay to start there," Reid said. "It's *not* okay to get dumped there after a semi-successful career in the NHL. People blamed Pepper."

"Kind of absurd, though." Kennedy looked supremely skeptical. "A guy gets into fights and tanks his career, and we blame the last woman he dated?"

Last night Bast had dug a little deeper into the gossip about Pepper's time with Gallagher. He rarely placed much credence in that kind of thing—if the rags were to be believed, he was baby daddy to more women than Nick Cannon—but he was curious about the broad brush strokes.

He hadn't seen Connor much over the last couple of years, but Bast recalled skimming the stories about Gallagher's love life, his interest piqued because it was

Calhoun's sister. She'd looked different back then. Blonde, sleek, sophisticated. Such a change-up from the curvy, hoodie-wearing brunette he'd met at Jimmy's Tap.

Back in her Gallagher days, the press had focused on her job, a preschool aide or something like that. There were even a few pics of her in a classroom, surrounded by kids, who clearly adored her. She'd looked happy, and he'd wondered what it would take to make her smile like that again.

Not your problem.

The breakup had apparently come out of nowhere, but there were rumors of cheating. Not Gallagher but Pepper, which had surprised Bast, though it shouldn't have. After all, women were capable of affairs. The Denver Diamonds' PR machine went into overdrive to protect the star athlete while Pepper was hung out to dry. She was the one at fault, her roving eye the problem.

A month post-breakup, Gallagher was arrested after getting drunk at a bar and punching a teammate, apparently the start of a downward spiral for his career.

The press had a field day.

Want some Pepper with that, Kent?

You got Peppered!

Revenge is a dish best served with Pepper!

Scraping the headline barrel, to be sure.

There was obviously more to the story, but he wasn't prepared to cut Pepper any slack just yet.

"That night she told me she hated hockey players. To my face."

"But can you blame her after this business with the ex?" Kennedy's brain was ticking over as she thought it through with the benefit of objectivity. "If I'd ended up dragged through the tabloid mud because of some crybaby hockey player, I wouldn't be automatically making nice with the next one I met. And *yet* she flirted with you? Even though you're part of this hated subgroup?"

"Probably can't help herself," Bast said morosely. "Any athlete in her sightline is fair game." But his heart wasn't in it. He wanted to hate her because at one time he'd liked her, and now everything was so fucking complicated.

"Yeah, but that doesn't really make any sense, does it?" Said gently, like she was talking to a child. Or a pathetic man with a hangover and a possibly career-ending injury.

"Are you trying to break my brain, Ken? Besides, this is all moot—"

"Moot?" Reid offered.

"Yeah, moot. As in hypothetical. Pepper Calhoun's the reason why I am currently back on IR, or hadn't you heard?"

"I get it," Kennedy said. "You want to escape right now. It's understandable."

The way she said it implied his escape was related to Pepper. That was all wrong, so maybe Kennedy wasn't the read-between-the-lines savant he'd assumed.

A moment of silence to acknowledge Bast's ass-hurt feelings was broken when Kennedy said, "She's getting trashed in the press. Again."

"Good." And then because that didn't sit well, he asked, "How?"

Reid looked up from petting Bucky. "Journ-holes are talking shit, the usual. Saying she's a menace."

"Well, that's the press for you," Kennedy said. "Always with the opinions."

"But they're probably right about this," Reid continued. "She kind of *is* a menace."

"That's fucked up," Bast said, not sure why that was his first response.

Silence followed, then Kennedy chuckled. "Okay, then." Code for, "Very interesting response there, Bast."

Maybe it was. He was perfectly within his rights to blame her, but he refused to hear shit talk about her from anyone else.

Jesus, he was tired. All he wanted to do was curl up and sleep, but he'd rather do it away from here.

"I need to pack."

Kennedy shot to a stand. "Let me help," and when Reid frowned, she leaned in to kiss him. "Baby, he needs to do this. Don't be mad because I agree."

Ken dragged his duffle from last night into the bedroom while Bast did his best to one-handedly retrieve spare sweats and tees from his dresser. Kennedy folded them and started inserting them into his bag.

"Do you really agree with me on this?" he asked her.

Kennedy smiled. "I totally get it. And Reid does, too. He just doesn't want to admit that he can't help here. Things between you two had been going well."

He took a deep breath. "If I stay, there's a good chance I might not want to play nice. With anyone."

She patted his arm. "Take the time for yourself. But please keep in touch so we don't worry about you. We love you, okay?"

He kissed the top of her head. "I love you both, too. I'll be back in a few days once I've had time to process the disappointment."

It took him a good ten minutes to get them to leave. He knew they meant well, but right now, he was the worst company. On his way out, Reid handed him a key.

"I'll text you the alarm code. But I really think you'd be better off here."

"I know, but I'd like to have the option."

Reid looked like he wanted to say something else and had to be dragged out by Kennedy, leaving Bast to breathe a sigh of relief.

He'd prefer to ignore social media right now, given how he didn't want to read shit posts about himself, but after Kennedy said Pepper was being dragged by the press, he needed to know the details.

Nothing good, most of it in the vein of, *How many stupid bitches does it take to ruin two athlete careers?*

Bast scanned the rest, the bad jokes and tasteless jibes, all at Pepper's expense. He was getting out of it largely Scot-free. No one was talking about his inability to stay upright—one of the requirements of his job. Instead it was all about the "lump" who had collided with him. There were even insults about her weight.

He checked back on his messages, noting he had one from Connor. Of all the people, it seemed Calhoun might be the one who could answer some of Bast's niggling questions. He dialed the guy's number.

"Durand, I can't believe my sister took you out!"

"It was an accident."

"Yeah, sure, but it looked rough, man. I had no idea Pepperoni had such wicked checking skills."

Bast's stomach curdled. "Give her a break, okay?"

"Why? Should have known this would end in tears. She's kind of a jinx. Ask Gallagher."

"Or I could ask you."

Connor snorted. "Look, I love my sister, but she has the worst luck. When we were kids, she was always breaking shit—bones, glasses, you name it. Usually other people's stuff." He chuckled in memory, then got serious. "And she broke poor Gally's heart. The guy was a mess after she was done with him."

"So she made him get into fights with teammates and lose his mojo so badly he was sent down to the AHL?" Kennedy was onto something there. "Assigning an awful lot of credit to your sister, Calhoun."

"Listen, I would never introduce anyone to my sister if I didn't think he was a good guy. Hell, I've warned off enough jerks to last a lifetime. But Gally was crazy about her, and when she broke it off, he went a bit nuts." He scoffed. "I'd never let a chick get to me like that, but some guys are obsessed, y'know."

Bast had seen that, mostly with his brother. But for a woman to have that kind of impact on a guy's play outside of physically knocking him over ... "You really think your sister is to blame for Gallagher's downward spiral?"

"Hey, I know it takes two and all that, but the guy was doing great one day, not so great the next, and my sister is in the middle of it. I'm just sorry you had to get caught up in her orbit."

Sure, some chicks were magnets for drama, but Bast didn't think one person could have that much influence. She wasn't Lady Macbeth, for Christ's sake.

"Maybe it's your fault."

Connor sniffed. "What?"

"Maybe you're the common denominator. You're friends with Gallagher and me, so maybe you're the reason for all this fuckery."

"That makes no sense, man."

Exactly. "Just like one person isn't to blame for the demise of several careers."

And Bast's career was doing just fine! This was a temporary setback.

"Still sticking with the 'this is an accident' line?" Connor asked, sounding amused. Fucker. Why they were friends was beyond him.

"Yep."

"You know there's one good thing about all this," Connor went on.

"Enlighten me."

"With your wrist injured this past year, you've already gotten plenty of jerk-off practice with your other hand."

"Bye, dickhead." He hung up on Calhoun's laughter and headed to his room to finish packing.

11

SEVERAL ESTEEMED MEMBERS of the press were hovering near the entrance to the player lot, eager to get a jump on whatever sound bites Bast would be spoon-feeding them during the presser.

"Bast, how's the wrist?"

"Any word on your expected return?"

"Do you think you're a victim of the Pepper curse?"

The Pepper curse? He turned to the speaker of that one, some idiot he didn't recognize. Even his fellow journos were giving the questioner the side eye because that was absurd. So her own brother had mentioned her being a jinx, but really? A curse?

Fucking sports people.

He dialed up his good humor, though it was in short supply lately. "I'm going to keep the good stuff for in there."

When Sophie had called to tell him about the presser, his hungover ass had responded with a surly, "Why the hell do I need to talk to the press?"

Sophie had sighed, well-used to the whining of diva hockey players. "Because you're still a member of the team and have required press duties. And people are going to want to hear about your injury straight from the horse's mouth, so to speak. This way we can assure everyone that you're on the mend and there's nothing to see here."

Whatever. He usually enjoyed press stuff. He had a good relationship with the reporters, and he recognized the give and take necessary so people liked you and said nice things about you.

You're such a people pleaser, Reid would say.

As his brother spoke mostly in scowl to his wife and teammates, Bast would not be taking criticism from him, even if today he was feeling more like the Reid of old: grumpy, taciturn, unwilling to bend.

"Surely Coach can give the usual spiel," he'd said to Sophie, a last-ditch effort to escape.

"Nope! I'll send a car in an hour."

He just wanted to stay home and wallow, or better yet head to an isolated cottage by the lake to lick his wounds. Again, not his wheelhouse at all. Was he becoming more like his brother? Was there only so much happiness allotted to the Durand brothers and now Reid was using it all up?

"I can drive myself."

"The team's medics won't sign off on that."

"I'll see you at eleven. Don't bother with the car." He'd hung up then hit the shower, a thirty-minute effort to wash away his hangover and show the world he was absolutely fine. He had plenty of experience over the last year putting on a smiling front. He'd also dumped his overnight bag into the trunk so he could head straight to Reid's lake house afterward.

Walking into Rebels HQ, the first person he met was Fitz, the Rebels' general manager, who must have been hovering near the entrance.

The guy did his best, but there was no missing his surprise at seeing Bast looking so rough, his bloodshot eyes telling a sorry tale. While Bast was sure the alcohol was no longer leaking from his pores, he knew he looked as bad as he felt.

"How's it going?" Spoken at a protect-Bast's-poor-head volume.

"It's going." He liked Fitz, who was a tough but fair negotiator, and had taken a chance on him when no one else would. "I'm sorry about this."

"Hey, now, not your fault."

Meaning it was Pepper's? Sounded like that was the party line. "Yeah, I just want to get this over with."

Sophie appeared, her bright eyes taking him in and exuding a mix of sympathy and satisfaction for his fallen state. She probably lived for these kinds of disasters.

"Okay, a couple of things. Coach will also be present, so feel free to defer any questions about team strategy during your absence to him. And if it gets to be too much, just look my way and we'll wrap it up!"

He squinted at her.

"Hmm?"

"I'm giving you the signal that it's all too much. Can we wrap it up now?"

She chuckled. "Oh, you'll be fine! The press loves you, so it'll be soft balls all the way."

The press might love him, but he still didn't want to answer any of their obvious questions, which could easily be parried by, oh, anyone else. Coach, the medics, even Sophie knew as much about his injury as he did because privacy was an afterthought when it came to a pro's career.

But as Mando would say: This is the way.

He briefly closed his eyes, then opened them, turning

the switch in his brain to "on." *Bast Durand, Activate.* Only, as he approached the press room, someone caught his eye, a person he didn't expect to see.

Pepper.

She stood off to the side, arms crossed, looking like she wished the ground would swallow her up. Something fierce in his chest sparked at the sight of her. It should have been anger—and there was plenty of that to go around—but this was a strange instinct to squirrel her away to a closet to keep her out of harm's way.

And maybe finish what they'd started that night in Jimmy's Tap.

"Is Pepper going to be out there?"

Sophie slid a glance her way. "No. She's—I'm not sure why she's here."

He was already surging forward to find out. "What's going on?"

"Are you okay?" Genuine concern filled those stunning hazel eyes, set off by dark circles beneath them. There was no doubt that she hadn't slept much.

"I'm as fine as I can be under the circumstances. You shouldn't be here."

"Why?"

Because if the press got wind of her presence, they'd crucify her. "I don't want to have to worry about you."

"Why would you—I don't need you to worry about me."

"Bast, we're ready for you," Sophie called out.

As if he wasn't feeling bad enough about his injury and the likelihood he was out for several weeks at a minimum, now he had to worry about Pepper being a target. He did not have time for this.

"In case you haven't noticed, people are pretty pissed at

you, and to be honest, there's only so much I can do to protect you."

Wide-eyed and flushed, she asked, "Protect me?"

"From the press. But don't worry, I'm not planning on talking about you in there. It was an accident."

He could be magnanimous. It was one of the things that made him so well-liked. He was generous in both victory and defeat.

She stared at him for a long beat. Finally she said, "I appreciate you saying that."

"You made a mistake, that's all."

She nodded a couple of times. "Sure. Except the replay tells a different story."

"The replay?"

"The replay showed you weren't paying attention. At least not to anyone but the buxom blonde in the front row, the one with the 'I love you, Bast!' sign."

That *may* have been a contributory factor, but he wouldn't be addressing it now. "I barely remember that." *Excellent defense, Durand.* He had never sounded more guilty.

"No? It looked like you were making eyes at her. In fact, you were barely moving, so something in the crowd snagged your attention. Probably those Double-Ds, which on closer inspection had your name tattooed on one of them. Ring any bells?"

Christ, just when he thought they might have reached an understanding. So maybe it was partly his fault. Must they hash this out now?

"Bast!" Sophie placed a hand on his arm. "We really can't wait any longer."

He sent one last glance at Pepper, his gaze drawn to a clump of blue glitter in her hair near her cheek. "We'll talk later, okay?"

She blinked in that way women got when they were trying to hold back tears, and his heart cracked right there and then. He wanted to tell Sophie to screw the presser and just let him take care of his woman.

Christ on a puck, where had that come from? He and Pepper were not connected like that. Except every time he ran into her—sometimes literally!—something shifted inside his chest. Something tearing open and knitting back together.

Dazed, he walked into the press room and took a seat beside Coach Calhoun.

"How's it going, son?"

He mustered a smile. "Can barely feel it to be honest. Not sure what all the fuss is about."

Coach patted him on the back. "That's the spirit."

It was true. It would heal much more quickly than before, but as for his ability to work future magic with a stick, he had no idea. This might be the end of the road for him.

The questions started, the first one from Jordan Cooke, who also happened to be married to Bast's new teammate, Levi Hunt.

"How's the wrist feeling, Bast?"

Holding his braced arm up, he flexed his fingers. "Not bad. I've had worse."

Everyone chuckled in commiseration and in appreciation of good-natured Bast who always managed to put on a good show.

"Any idea when you might return to practice or even play?"

"We're looking at a few weeks."

A few more toothless questions followed about recovery times, what this meant for the line-ups and the early part of the season. Coach handled most of those, which gave Bast time to let his mind wander and dwell on how he might have screwed up here. Sure, that blonde in the front row had caught his interest, but it was still the mascot's responsibility to not collide with the players. Mascotting 101!

Bast clawed his attention back to the press conference, where the air was thick with foreboding. Maybe he'd missed something, but he suddenly felt more on edge than usual, like he was waiting for a bolt of lightning to strike.

Thunder rolled before the flash.

"Coach Calhoun, how's your daughter?"

The question came from the back in a voice Bast hated. Curtis Deacon, the *Sun-Times'* hockey reporter and one of the team's harshest critics.

"My daughter is fine," Coach said gruffly.

"Only, it's strange that she would be on the ice. What kind of training does she have?"

"There was a miscommunication about going on. She knows how to skate. Usually."

Usually? What kind of backhanded shit was that?

Deacon wasn't finished. "Some people are saying that she shouldn't have been out there at all. Why would your daughter have that job?"

"She doesn't any longer."

Even the usually cynical press corps looked shocked at that. Did the man just fire his daughter in front of the whole wide world of sports?

Screw this. "The all-important mascot job—is that what you're asking?"

That got their attention.

"Are you saying it's not important?" Deacon asked Bast, digging in his heels and dropping Bast into the bad books of mascots everywhere.

"I'm saying that Pepper Calhoun knows how to skate." He supposed she did. *Usually.* "It was an accident."

"One that's cost this team dearly." The asshole was *not* letting up. "The fans would like to know that there are consequences."

"Like what?" Bast snapped. "Are we going to put the mascot in the stocks so you lot can throw rotten vegetables at her? Maybe just accept that shit happens"—groan from Sophie—"and that the world doesn't have to end."

Or maybe that groan was from Pepper. He slid a look to the door through which he'd entered, and sure enough, she was standing there, her big eyes wide and watching.

It *was* an accident, but maybe it was also for a reason. The first time he'd injured his wrist had led to strengthening his relationship with Reid. Who was to say there weren't some greater forces at work here? The universe telling him something he would never have given credence to before it happened.

He couldn't believe Coach's thundering silence. This was the man's daughter they were sharpening their pitchforks for.

Bast shot him a look of *nothing to say, man*?

Coach returned the stare, then faced the press once more. "Any other questions?"

All hands shot up.

"That aren't about my daughter's clumsiness?"

All hands descended, while a few people laughed.

Bast shook his head in disbelief. "You've got to be kidding me."

Jordan leaned in. "About what, Bast?"

"I can't believe you—all of you—are being such assholes about a person who stepped in to help out at the last minute." He turned to Coach Calhoun. "And you should know better."

"Now, Bast—"

"Nope. Done here." He stood, a little too violently as it happened because a water bottle turned over, fell on the ground, and made a sad roll to the front row.

He was sick of it all. The press, the team, the NHL, the whole wide fucking world. He was sick of taking it all in his stride and being the nice guy.

Things were going to change, and that started right now.

12

Pepper was slap-bang in the middle of a nightmare.

She had been declared the villain when it came to this "accident" involving the star hockey player. Familiar territory for her, of course. Pepper Calhoun, a walking disaster-piece!

Compounding the catastrophe that was her life, father had fired her in front of everyone and Bast was talking back at the press conference, giving her father the evil eye, and staring squarely at her in what could be best described as a "determined" manner.

He looked awful.

Of course Bast could never look truly awful because the man was gorgeous, but relatively speaking, he had the cast of a man who had tumbled out of a vat of gin. Maybe his hungover state was why he was so not himself. Usually he was the nicest guy in the room. What had happened to him?

Oh yeah. *She did.*

She had only come by to tell her father in person that she was going to lay low at Bridget's. Foolishly, she'd briefly entertained the notion that he'd gather her in his arms, apologize for being so rough on her, and beg her to stay.

But no. Her father's behavior in that presser made his attitude clear. *My clumsy daughter is at fault here.* It was true, but it still hurt to hear it from her father's lips.

Just as Bast gave a final glare to the open-mouthed peanut gallery, she made a quick exit. In the restroom, she splashed cold water on her face and assessed the mess of her reflection. She looked tired, drawn, like her world had imploded.

But she needed to remember that it was worse for Bast. She'd been through this before with Kent, and while she wasn't to blame for his career collapse, she could see why people might see the correlations. One minute, he was happily engaged and on top of the world. The next his fiancée had left him, seemingly for another player (all lies, of course). Kent looked like the victim, helped along by the Denver Diamonds' PR, and when his career went into the toilet, the Pepper curse was born.

Now she was adversely associated with another star, the wrecking ball for another athlete's career. They would be tied together forever in gifs and memes that would be played over and over for eternity.

Yet for some reason he was defending her—publicly. And getting snappy with her father. She didn't need that. She didn't want to feel grateful to him for accepting his role in all this. And she sure as hell didn't want this warm glow in her chest, the feeling that maybe this mess could be salvaged.

That she could be salvaged.

After ten minutes, she grabbed her purse, stepped outside, and breathed a sigh of relief. All clear.

Until she turned a corner and walked right into a pack of

reporters, hovering like murderous crows. Hopefully they didn't know what she looked like. After all, she couldn't be more different than her previous incarnation as a Diamond WAG.

Her hopes were quickly dashed the moment that ass, Curtis Deacon, shoved a phone under her nose.

"Pepper, any chance we could have a word?"

"Uh, no comment." She took a practiced step back.

"Really? You're at the center of an important event that affects the welfare of a player and the progress of the team. I would think you'd like to tell your side of the story."

"I don't have a side. It was an accident."

"Your father said you were clumsy. There's also word going around that you have a gripe with Bastian, maybe some history. Is that true?"

"Of course not. We hardly know each other."

Someone else chimed in. "So you *do* know him?"

"Not at all." She hated lying, but any nuance would be lost. "It was an accident."

"What kind of skating experience do you have?"

"Should the mascot position be given to someone more qualified?"

"How's Kent doing?"

"Leave her alone!" A very deep, very growly voice cut through the peck-peck of chatter. Bast had appeared behind Deacon and shouldered him aside.

Deacon's eyes flashed, an animal sensing prey. "Just trying to get to the heart of the story. People are curious."

"There's nothing to see here, Deacon. Move along."

More reporters approached, phones held high, obviously recording. Deacon wasn't letting go, his expression avid as he sensed a story, even though there was nothing to see here.

Pepper slid a look toward the latest acquisition for the Chicago Rebels. She had never seen him so animated. So angry. Except for that night at Jimmy's Tap when he discovered her identity.

She was the reason this man was on the cliff's edge.

She touched his arm. "We should go."

He blinked and looked at her, his expression almost uncomprehending, then seemed to shake himself. "Right."

But Deacon was too committed to his take. He moved toward her, his phone at the ready. "Come on, Pepper, give us something better than 'no comment'."

Two things happened at once.

Bast yelled at Deacon, "She told you once, asshole!"

At the same time, someone pressed Deacon from behind, placing him a little too close to Pepper for comfort. Bast stepped between her body and Deacon's, responded with a shove, and the reporter went down.

Pepper rushed forward to help him. "Oh, are you al—?"

The words were snatched by the wind whizzing by her face. Bast had grasped her elbow and was moving her toward the exit, like they were speeding toward the blue zone.

"Move. Now."

"But—" She threw a look over her shoulder. Deacon was back on his feet, looking none the worse for wear, while several of the other reporters were ... darn, following.

"Wait, what are you doing?"

No response.

"Bast, I need to talk to my father."

"That's not a good idea. He's not exactly your biggest fan right now."

The press was on their heels, nipping like yappy little hounds. Memories of the last time she'd been in this position flashed through her short-circuiting brain. The shoving, the accusations, the invasive questions.

Today wasn't much different.

"Pepper, did you push Bast on purpose?"

"Pepper, have you spoken to Kent lately?"

"Pepper, did you know your father was going to fire you?"

Oh my God, this was ludicrous. Bast was still holding her elbow with his right hand—because his left, dominant hand was in a sling. And why the hell were the questions still about last night? Bast Durand had just assaulted a reporter (was that what happened? She *thought* that's what happened) and was now whisking her away from the scene of the crime. A shove and run.

"Bast, where are—"

"Get in." He opened the passenger door of his car.

She took a glance over her shoulder. The hordes were still coming, like the infected in *The Last of Us* video game. Into the car she went and watched while he circled, his face grim and unyielding, and clambered in.

"Should you be driving?"

"No." He slipped his hand out of his sling—this could *not* get worse—started the car and peeled out of the player lot.

A good thirty seconds went by before he spoke.

"So what's the plan, Pepper?"

"The plan?" She cut a sharp look to him. Thankfully he was keeping his eyes on the road, driving to—she wasn't sure where, and right now, she didn't care.

She just wanted to get away. From the press, her father, her brother, this life that felt like a too-tight skin. She should be including Bast Durand in that litany, yet strangely, here, beside him didn't feel *wrong*.

Ignoring his question and the weird feeling of security

that had wrapped around her, she circled back to what had just happened. "You pushed Deacon over. He could sue you!"

"Let him."

Let him? Was this what it took to break a man? So maybe a guy like Bast had the resources to withstand whatever shit-storm was inevitably coming his way, but Pepper certainly did not. She'd barely survived the last onslaught. Again, she was at the center of a scandal, where people would inevitably place the blame on her.

"I need to get out of here."

Bridget's was close by, but there wasn't a place far enough away on this planet to escape her feelings. "My friend lives in Evanston. I was planning to stay with her for a few days."

She shot another look at Bast. He looked furious and a shiver shuddered through her because it was unbelievably attractive.

"Thanks for what you did back there."

"Deacon's a bully. Has always rubbed me wrong."

Her gaze strayed to his long fingers, peeking out of the wrist brace as they rested on the steering wheel.

"Maybe I should drive?"

"Maybe. But first ..." He pulled into the parking lot of a KFC.

"Some fried chicken?"

He turned to her. "Listen, I'm not very happy with you right now, but neither am I prepared to let people beat you up over what happened. If anything, that privilege belongs to me and me alone."

His mouth was scrunched up, every word out of it clearly an annoyance to him. He hated having to defend her, but some innate decency in him made it necessary. She hadn't forgotten his part in it—Flirty Eyes as Tara labeled it —but she recognized that she was at least 75% responsible here.

She whispered, "Okay."

"Okay what?"

"Lay it on me." He narrowed his eyes, so she explained further. "Scream at me. Get it all out. Say your piece."

He tapped the steering wheel with his fingers, assessing her. A minute passed. Two. The silence stretched to a tautness that twanged her nerves.

Finally he spoke. "You'd like that, wouldn't you? You'd like to be absolved of your guilt in one fell swoop. It's not that easy."

"So you're planning to stay mad at me forever?"

"I don't know yet." He looked out the window and after a few tense seconds, seemed to come to a decision. "Wait here." He opened his car door and stepped outside.

As if she had anywhere else to go. She watched him pacing alongside the car while he spoke to someone on the phone, maybe his brother. He must've been telling him about the press conference and its aftermath.

Her phone buzzed with a text.

CONNOR

What the fuck, Pep? Durand is in MORE trouble because of you?

That didn't take long. She put her phone in Do Not Disturb mode. She just couldn't deal with this now. Outside, Bast was walking back and forth, and at that moment their gazes clashed, flooding her brain with the memory of that night in Jimmy's Tap, before it all went horribly wrong. Flushing her blood vessels with warmth in this already too-hot car.

She looked away before he did, wishing that felt more like a victory than it did.

He got back in the car and passed his phone over to her. She mouthed "What?" and when he didn't respond, she said, "Hello" to the screen.

"Pepper."

She glared at Bast, who held her gaze levelly. Probably why he was such a good player.

"Hey, Dad, what's up?"

"What's up? We're in the middle of a PR crisis here, that's what."

Nothing new, then. "I'm sorry, I didn't mean to—"

"Durand explained about Deacon. What an asshole. Are you okay?"

"Yes, I am. Bast got me out of there and now I'm going to head to Bridget's for a few days. To stay out of your way."

He growled. "Is this because I fired you?"

"No, Dad. I don't even want that job. Mascotting isn't my life goal." Though it was embarrassing to be sacked by your own father in front of a rapacious press corps, she would be fool to think it wasn't coming. She slid a glance at Bast who was making no effort to hide his interest in her conversation.

She stuck out her tongue at him.

His lips turned at the corners and his brows rose. Oh, goody. She had amused the great Bast Durand.

"Anyway, I'm on my way back now to pick up my car. I'm guessing the press have probably dispersed."

"They have not. And Pepper, you're not coming back. Durand needs you to drive him to Michigan."

She snapped her gaze to Bast, who was watching her with an impenetrable expression.

"Michigan? That's miles away."

Her father sighed. "Yes, and Durand should not be driving with that wrist."

Then maybe Durand should not be going anywhere that required driving for, oh, *hundreds of miles*.

"I no longer work for the Rebels org. You fired me, remember?"

"Independent contractor, Pepper. You will do this for me, for the team, and for Durand."

"What about the NHL, Chicago, and my country?"

"That, too. Call me when you get there." *Click.*

13

—————

PEPPER STARED AT THE PHONE, then turned to face Bast.

"Where's this place in Michigan?"

"It's Reid's cottage on the lake. Belhaven Harbor." He pointed at the GPS. While she'd been talking to her dad, Bast had helpfully inputted the location.

"That's over 400 miles!"

"You said you needed to get away, and I need a driver. Two birds, one puck."

She checked the GPS again. Six hours from Chicago. Six hours from the noise and invasion ... but she couldn't spend any more time with Bast. It would be good for neither of them.

"I'd be stuck there."

"I'm not supposed to drive long distances with my wrist." Which didn't address *her* concern at all—because it was all about him.

"Then hire someone."

"I'd rather it was you."

"Well, you can 'rather' all you want. I'm not going."

"You owe me."

"I don't owe you a thing! You said back there it was an accident. You defended me." A foreign warmth pervaded her chest when she remembered exactly how he'd done that. She didn't hold much truck with violence, but then no one had ever defended her so physically before. It should not be attractive, but apparently those caveman tactics were when utilized by one Bastian Durand.

He glared at her, clearly not as happy to recall today's disaster of a press conference and the events that put them together in the same car. "Yes, I did. And now you need to do me this favor."

"That's not enough to make me your driver to the middle of nowhere. I'd be stuck on that mitten pimple."

"Mitten pimple?"

She gestured at the GPS. "It looks like a pimple on the Michigan mitten."

He exhaled noisily. "Get me there, and I'll hire someone to take you back."

She shook her head. "I have somewhere to be."

"You have somewhere to hide. And remember, Coach asked you to do it."

Ordered her, more like. Of course John Calhoun had told her to drive Mr. Superstar wherever the hell he needed to go, to be his slave because he was an invaluable asset to the Rebels organization. Pepper's wants wouldn't rate.

She turned to him. "Did you call him and say you wanted me to drive you?"

"Maybe."

Maybe? What the hell kind of answer was that?

The air felt strangely charged. She didn't like the mood that now pervaded the car, like she was in the presence of a man hovering on the edge.

"Why would you do that?"

"Because you and I have unfinished business."

That sounded vaguely threatening, but also kind of ... sexy.

"Are you okay? Because you don't sound okay."

"No, I'm not okay. I just want to get some sleep and wake up in a different place, far away from all the shit." He leaned in close, his mouth slanted in a cruel slash. "So, how about you do as you're told and drive me to where I need to go?"

"And people say you're nice. You're not nice. You were never nice!" She poked a finger in the well of his shoulder.

"Ow."

"Oh, sorry."

He growled. "Listen, I don't want to do anything drastic —" What did *that* mean? "—but I do need a ride. I'm asking for your help here."

"This good cop/bad cop thing you've got going on is bordering on ridiculous. Which is it? Blackmailer or victim?"

"Whichever works to get what I want."

Her hormones did *not* respond favorably to that last statement, uttered with such clarity that it heated her in places that were frigid and action-free of late.

"You are really pissing me off, Durand."

He placed his forehead on the steering wheel and murmured, "Right back at ya."

She needed to remember he was the truly injured party here. His career had blown up, and while she wasn't taking complete blame for it—no more fall girl for Pepper Calhoun —she recognized she had a considerable part in all of this.

What the hell, it wasn't as if she had anything better to do.

"Okay, let's switch."

His relief was obvious, maybe even a little knowing. She held up a hand.

"If you're going to be a smug dick about it, you can find some other idiot to be your lackey."

"My lips are sealed. Promise you won't turn the car around. I really don't want to go back there."

He sounded so miserable that her heart keened for him. Thing was, she didn't want to go back there either.

"I promise. I'll drop you off, and then we'll figure something out. You can hire a driver to get me back. You can afford that."

"You can have anything you want as long as you get me to Belhaven Harbor."

Belhaven Harbor. It sounded nice, like an escape from reality.

But she wondered if the escape was truly better than the disaster she was leaving behind.

PEPPER KNEW she had to focus on the road, what with her precious cargo in the passenger seat. The sky was dark and threatening, though it was barely three o'clock. This wasn't the time to let her mind wander, yet she couldn't help thinking of her situation and how it had gone from bad to worse.

Two years ago, she'd been on top of the world. Four weeks into her internship as a preschool teacher at Melrose Prep in Denver, six months from graduating with an early childhood education degree that she'd worked her ass off for, a life she'd crafted with friends and hobbies she loved. So her parents' marriage was in trouble and her dating life wasn't anything to write home about, but she had friends and a burgeoning career.

Then she met Kent.

Her brother Connor had just been signed with the Denver Diamonds, and while Pepper had hoped Denver would be hers—like a city of almost three million people could belong to one girl—she recognized that her brother's pro-athlete presence would change its vibe. Suddenly, her friends wanted invites to games and VIP events, and Connor was always willing to oblige. A notorious party animal, his college years were legendary for their outrageousness, and now she was caught up in it, too. That was how she met Kent, one of his teammates.

She should have realized then and there that it wasn't a good match.

She slid a glance sideways, checking on Bast. His head had fallen gently against the window and he was snoring lightly, which was good, because she needed him to have some flaw. Some reason to place him at a distance.

There was a small scar above his eyebrow. Good, good—what else? His nose had been broken during that on-ice incident last year when he also broke his wrist. There was a slight crimp at the bridge, so you'd hardly know it had undergone any sort of damage. But she'd compared before and after photos one night and saw the change. It should have diminished him, but of course it hadn't.

Neither did the scar, really.

So back to the snoring. She clung to it, a touchstone of boorish male reality that kept her sane. Kept her from thinking of how his beard had felt when she touched it that night in Jimmy's Tap—why had she done that?—and how his eyes had darkened with a smokiness that consumed her.

Warmth flooded her veins, turning them to molasses as

she imagined what might have happened if Bridget hadn't shown up and shouted her name ... If the next logical step to feeling up a man's beard was tasting his lips.

The car wobbled a little as she straightened the steering wheel. Thinking about kissing Bast was dangerous. Better to recall the worst of those days with Kent.

A whirlwind romance, the press called it. Her friends insisted she do her best to get a ring on it. Maybe a hole in the condom, one of them had said, then laughed heartily as if it was all a joke. But they weren't joking. She'd somehow hit the motherlode and every one of her friends were green with envy.

If only they knew that a hole in the condom wouldn't do the trick. That their sex life was not all that amazing, at least nothing like Pepper had expected with a man as attractive and seemingly virile as Kent.

Tired of the pointed questions and barely suppressed jealousy, she found herself making new friends after introductions to Kent's teammates and their wives. Women who were in the WAG world, who had already achieved some status and wouldn't have weird expectations of her. Unlike her friends and co-workers who knew the team's schedule by heart, winked at her after every game, and looked pointedly at her fourth finger.

Not yet, eh?

Suddenly there was pressure. To lock him down, get it done, plan the life. She had no intention of pushing, but when he finally asked, it was a relief. No more expectation. No more sly winks and nudge-nudge. And the Diamonds WAGs accepted her fully into the fold. She was no longer a transitory figure in the group. With this ring, she'd acquired a trusted status.

"You're one of us now," Becca, wife of Dustin Marsh, the

team's goalie, had told her as the girls gushed over the two-carat diamond. Older and experienced, she'd taken Pepper under her wing—*I've been dying to fix those eyebrows!*—and gave her a makeover.

Pepper frowned to herself as she sped up on the highway, escaping Chicago. Escaping her latest screw-up. But there was no escaping the past. At the time she'd thought she needed to be more glamorous. After all, she wasn't as slender as the other WAGs. She didn't have designer dress sense or know how to wear heels. She worked with little kids, all sticky hands and streaming noses. Hoodies and jeans were more her thing, with the odd, cute dress found in the bargain racks at Marshalls for work.

Kent had loved the transformation. *I dig you as a brunette, but I want to fuck you all the time as a blond.*

That should have been her first clue. Or maybe her tenth, especially as the makeover still didn't improve things in the bedroom. Who had he fallen for, exactly? But she knew who she had fallen in love with, or thought she did. This amazing man—a pro athlete—who could have anyone at all wanted *her*. Pepper. And suddenly the pressure was back. Because nothing was truly locked down until the wedding day. Or maybe a kid.

She started dieting, after Becca told her that the designer dresses would look better if she lost a few pounds. *Not that I'm fat-shaming you. You should have seen me after the birth of the twins. But we have to keep the boys on their toes, hun.*

Pepper had taken all the advice, tried her best to be what Kent needed. Until she found out that she wasn't what he needed at all ...

She re-focused on the drive as they left the interstate for a two-lane highway, then a more rural road. Her ass was sore, but she didn't want to stop until they were closer. Until she put as much distance from her last screw-up as she possibly could.

The skies had turned dark as the snow steadily continued its fluttery descent. Had this been in the forecast? She hadn't thought to check. But then she hadn't expected that she'd be leaving Chicago on a multi-hour road trip.

The sign for Belhaven Harbor appeared, thirty miles out. That was about twenty-five minutes, or closer to forty-five with the way the snow had become denser. She was used to this kind of driving, having lived on the East Coast and in Denver. But she was conscious of her charge, of how she needed to get him to Reid's place safely.

What was this lake house like? Something idyllic and romantic, she supposed. Not that she was looking for romance. But if no one had been there in a while, it was probably low on supplies. That would be her first task when they got to town.

Belhaven Harbor was smaller than she'd imagined. All towns seemed to be so built up these days, especially if they were on the edge of a lake, but this one had retained an old-fashioned quality to it. She strained her eyes for hints of civilization as she drove through the main drag. A diner, a post office, a library—there, a general store. She pulled into the single parking space outside and considered waking Bast. But he looked so peaceful. Best to let him sleep.

She looked around. There was a Hawks ball cap in the car's drinks well, so she put it on and pulled it down over her eyes. Belhaven Harbor might be a small town, but the Internet was everywhere. She had been too nervous to check whether the press conference and the altercation (if she didn't call it an assault, maybe no one else would?) had made it online, though they must have. She was in the eye of another media hurricane, once again a magnet for shitstorms.

Upon stepping out of Bast's car, she realized that she was in more trouble than merely being a pariah in the world of hockey. The snow was falling heavily in large clumps that were sticking, building inch by inch.

Inside the store, she nodded at the old guy behind the counter, picked up a basket, and started to shop. Milk, coffee, bread, burger buns, frozen chicken, ground beef, cheese, bananas, tomatoes, eggs, Pringles (salt n' vinegar, yes!), a six-pack of IPA. She raised the basket and placed it on the counter.

"Pretty nasty out there," he said as he eyed her haul and inputted numbers into a cash register older than him.

"Sure is."

"You headed to the lake?"

"I am."

"Figured as much. You'll need to get a move on."

Unease wriggled in her stomach. "Could we get stuck?"

"Not if you get out there now. Which place is it?"

She didn't know if it had a name, and she'd rather not say "Reid Durand's place, y'know, the hockey player."

"Not sure, it's plugged into my GPS. Owned by a friend. I think it's on Bullfinch Road?"

"Right. The old Morton place. They sold it last year. Nice couple renovated it over the summer."

She breathed out a sigh of relief. It sounded like this guy didn't know who owned the place now or was just wonderfully discreet. She was determined this place remained the hideaway that Bast needed.

You too, Pepper.

Paying up, she grabbed the box he'd loaded the groceries into. "How's the phone signal down there?"

"Weather might affect it, but we got signal. This ain't Mackinac." The addendum almost came with a spit-take on the store's floor.

"Okay, thanks."

14

Bast woke up alone.

Lately, this was not that unusual. Over the last year, he'd been rather down about his injury, which had a net effect on his sex life. He didn't feel like going through the motions, playing the game of flirtation—not that he needed to employ that much in the way of gamesmanship to get someone into his bed. But he had not been as active in that area since he broke his wrist.

Or, not active at all.

At first, it was because he didn't want to risk hurting it. Protecting it was key. Then he just got out of the habit. Until the night he met Pepper, and then suddenly, *hello, libido, where ya been?*

Lately he'd been feeling on edge and could have done with a night of sweaty sex before his season started. But something had held him back. He'd gone the entire spring and summer without trying, all because—well, he wasn't sure why. The yips, he supposed.

So waking up without a warm woman wasn't so unusual.

But waking up in an empty car with the windscreen covered in snow was unexpected.

The car was parked, the engine off, the driver nowhere to be found. He fumbled for his phone, wondering where they were. Wondering where Pepper was and hoping she was safe.

He had several messages from Reid.

Are you okay?

Have you checked the weather?

Text me when you get in.

When had his brother become such a mother hen?

The trunk opened, bringing with it a blast of cold air and a thump as something was dropped in it. Ten seconds later, Pepper was back in the driver's seat.

"Where were you?" he barked.

"A little cranky when we wake up, are we?"

"You weren't here." He didn't go to the trouble of rescuing her to have her fall down a damn gorge or something. "You should have woken me."

"You needed your rest. We're a few miles out, so I stopped for supplies."

"Reid has the place kitted out for the Apocalypse. We'll be okay."

"You needed fresh milk and coffee and fruit. And there's no 'we' here."

He could say powdered creamer, instant, and Trader Joe's dried apricot shit, but he didn't. Instead he picked up on the other thing.

"What do you mean there's no 'we' here? You'll be staying at the lake house tonight. It's too late to go back, and I haven't had a chance to organize the return trip for you."

"Or yell at me properly."

"Yeah. Mustn't forget that." Once he was more awake, he planned to break it all down.

How she'd ruined his comeback with her terrible skating.

How she'd almost ruined his signing onto the Rebels with her lying.

How those hazel eyes and luscious lips haunted his nights.

Maybe not the last one.

He took another look out the window, which was now completely covered.

"Did you really think you were dropping me off and skedaddling? Not in this weather."

"It's not that bad," she said, her tone more hopeful than confident. The windscreen wipers strained mightily to remove the heavy, wet snow that was clinging barnacle-like to the glass.

"I'll drive the last few miles," Bast said. "You've done enough."

"It's okay, really."

But he was already out and around to the driver side. The snow was falling consistently now, crunching like broken glass underfoot. "Just climb over the stick."

"I can walk around—"

"Now, Pepper!"

With a peel-his-skin glare, she clambered over to the passenger side, and he made sure to help himself to a good eyeball fill of her most excellent ass. All curves, the perfect roundness for his hands.

She settled in the seat with an *oomph* and turned to catch his ogle.

"Really?"

"Yeah, really."

He'd had the hots for her in that bar and now desire was rearing its head again. Which was inconvenient because she was the last woman on earth he wanted to think of like that.

Were the rumors about her and Gallagher true? That she cheated with his teammate, broke the guy's heart, and ruined his career? Connor hadn't said so outright, but he blamed Pepper. Said she was a jinx. The press were of the same mind. The focus of the media was on what had happened to Gallagher, but what about the effect on Pepper?

So many questions.

He adjusted the seat back a couple of inches, started the car, and checked the GPS. Five miles out. "What's the forecast?"

Pepper was on her phone, her eyebrows crimping in that way he really enjoyed.

"This can't be right. It's now saying that the snow is supposed to fall for thirty-six hours." She passed her phone over as if he might interpret it differently.

This was not what he saw this morning. "I checked the weather coming up, and it said two inches. This is projecting a foot or more."

"Are you kidding me? How the hell am I supposed to get back to Chicago in this?"

"We'll assess tomorrow and worry about it then." He nudged the rearview mirror, not that anything was visible. "Let's just focus on not dying on the way to the lake house, okay?"

She looked over her shoulder. "Maybe there's a hotel in town. They'd be better equipped for an easier exit tomorrow."

"Maybe. But we're a few miles away from the house. Let's

stick to the plan instead of pulling a Jesus, Mary, and Joseph and looking for an inn."

She folded her arms. "Drive on, Mr. Bossy."

He put the car in Drive and inched out onto the road. Shit, it was coming down hard, but this SUV had four-wheel drive so he wasn't too worried about getting stuck.

Five miles took forty minutes, but soon they were turning into the driveway down to Reid's place. He'd bought it last summer and Bast had seen a ton of photos. Right on the lake with its own dock, a hot tub, room for a pony.

A wave of tiredness hit him, the last twenty-four hours finally catching up. The excitement of his return, the soul-crush of failure. He just wanted to sleep and wake up in a world where his wrist was healed.

Instead he'd created a world where he was stuck with *her*.

Six hours ago, he needed to get away, and having Pepper drive seemed like a smart idea. Give his wrist and brain a break. While he agreed the crash was an accident, that didn't make everything better. She needed to suffer and atone somehow; driving four hundred miles out of her way seemed like a good start.

He hadn't reckoned on a snowstorm, or how his dick pulsed with life every time she leaned in close. Neither had he reckoned with how her scent filled the car, or her ass looked perfect enough to take a bite from. He especially hadn't reckoned on still wanting her despite their complicated history.

Now the smart idea didn't seem so smart.

Now it seemed kind of stupid.

Because he was pretty sure that Pepper wasn't getting out of here tomorrow. Or the day after that.

Which meant the only person likely to suffer here was him.

15

Pepper couldn't catch a break.

They were in the middle of nowhere, caught in a snowstorm. With how it was raging, there was no way she'd make it out tomorrow, which left her stuck. With Bast Durand.

The thought sent a shiver down her spine, not completely related to the frigid temperatures.

At least the place looked a decent size—from the outside anyway—so hopefully they could avoid each other. Once inside the house, Bast input the alarm code and fumbled for the switch. Light came on. What a relief.

The living room was all white oak beams and Nordic-inspired comfort with a huge fireplace and comfortable looking sofas. The art was eclectic and the huge picture window fronted what must be the lake—if they could see past the falling snow.

"Wow, this place is something else."

"It's all my sister-in-law. For someone who used to hate letting the grass grow under her feet, she's sure found a way to put her stamp on her living spaces."

Pepper had met Reid's wife, Kennedy, a couple of times

and had always been impressed by her bohemian style and free-spirited approach to life.

"Pity we can't see the lake. I bet it's pretty." She placed the box of groceries on the kitchen table. "How about I make us something to eat?"

"I'm not hungry. I'm just going to crash."

"Oh, okay. I'll set something aside for you."

"Sure."

Huh, why was he suddenly in a bad mood? He'd been cranky before, but she'd have thought the five-hour nap would have helped. Probably decided he was mad at her again.

"Before I do anything, I'm just going to freshen up. Where's the bathroom?"

"It's ensuite with the bedroom."

Something pinged. "Bedroom? As in singular?"

He shot her a dark look but remained silent, leaving her to draw her own conclusions. One bedroom, with, she had to assume, one bed. She looked around, anxiety building.

"You'd think a multi-million dollar athlete could afford an extra room."

"This is their place away from it all, for the two of them. So they're not thinking of extra, unwanted guests."

Gotcha. "I'll take the sofa," she said cheerfully. "And I'll knock before I need to come in and use the bathroom."

His gloom seemed to increase in direct correlation to her efforts to be positive. "Suit yourself."

"I'll go now if you don't mind."

Like the rest of the cottage, the (one) bedroom was lovely, the furniture tasteful, quality pieces with clear nods to Kennedy's sense of style.

The bathroom had a nice big shower, a clawfoot tub, and

Moroccan style blue and white tiling. So pretty, but ... they had to share. For how long, she wondered?

After washing her hands, she considered next steps. Miraculously she had a signal on her phone—not being in Mackinac and all—so she shot off a message to her dad.

PEPPER

Made it! The asset is secure. Might need to stay overnight because of the storm, though.

DAD

Glad you arrived safely. Check in tomorrow and let me know how Durand is holding up. He's bound to be feeling a bit down about this latest setback.

Pretty clear who was the priority here. Next, she sent a text to Elle.

Hey, I'm sorry, but I won't be able to watch Hatch tomorrow. I had to get away for a few days.

The response was immediate.

ELLE

Please don't worry. I saw the press conference and what happened afterward. Take all the time you need, and remember, I'm here if you need to talk.

Sweet of her, but confiding in the wife of one of Bast's teammates seemed like a bad idea. How could she trust anyone these days?

She texted back.

She hoped.

What had she been thinking when she agreed to drive Bast all the way here? He was the last person on earth she should be holed up with.

Several texts had come in from Connor, all variations of "da fuck, Pepper?" and "call me."

She dialed his number. "Say what you have to say."

"Dad said you drove Durand to some secret fucking location! What the fuck, Pep?"

"I'm just following orders. And what happened was an accident."

"Jesus, Pepper, what the hell is going on here? You know he's had a shitty year with his injury. The last thing he needs is more—"

"What? Drama?"

"Well. Yeah. I would've thought you'd be trying to keep a low profile after Gally."

"That was the plan. But sometimes plans go off the rails."

Her brother scoffed. "Or are driven there."

For once, she'd like her brother to act like the protector she needed. "I so don't need this right now. As usual, you don't have all the facts."

Connor took a breath, like he was aiming for calm. "I wish you'd tell me what happened with Gally."

She swallowed back tears. "Can't you just accept my word that I'm not to blame?"

"What am I supposed to think if you don't confide in me?"

They'd been circling the drain of this argument for

months now. "And why the hell would I when you just assume I'm the problem? Go to hell, Connor!"

Gah! She almost threw her phone against the mirror. Connor was the golden child in the Calhoun family, the one with a tangible talent, an instant connection to Dad, while Pepper existed on the periphery, her achievements never on par with her brother's. Of course he was going to take Kent's part in all this.

Her stomach rumbled, angry with her for forcing it to survive on a lone cinnamon-raisin muffin, which she'd eaten at 8 a.m. She would feel better when she ate. If Pepper knew one thing, it was that food would be her savior during this difficult time.

Walking out of the bathroom, she was greeted by a flash of strong chest. It took all her willpower not to stand and stare.

Bast was peeling off his shirt.

"Oh, sorry." Averting her gaze, she headed to the door.

"Pepper?"

"Yes?" Still with her back to him, she stood in place waiting for him to speak.

"I need a hand."

She turned to find him with his T-shirt bunched up around his neck, revealing most of his broad chest and one strong shoulder. Bare, golden skin that would probably be very smooth under her fingertips.

Not that she would ever know.

"A hand?" she repeated.

"Yeah. If you can do so without inflicting further damage."

Ouch. Okay, he was still hurting—everywhere.

"Sure, let me ..." She curled her fingers under the neck of his shirt. "If we could get this over your head ..." She moved in closer, now mere inches from his body, and stretched the fabric. "It might be easier if you sit?"

Sitting on the bed, he grunted.

"Sorry, am I hurting you?"

"No, just ..." He seemed to grit his teeth. "Do it."

Moving the material over his ear, she murmured, "Just bend your head—okay, there." The tee was now in a puddle over his left shoulder. Gently, she worked it down over his brace. It felt warm in her hands, so she quickly folded it and placed it on top of a dresser.

He stood before her, shirtless and cranky, the evidence of her crime covering his wrist.

"Do you need your sling?" She looked around for it and spotted it on the bed.

"I'll deal with it." He pushed his sweats down, giving her an eyeful of an intriguing bulge wrapped in black cotton. When she didn't look away, he shot another glare at her. "I'm taking that nap now."

"Oh, of course. Let me know if you need anything."

His answer to that was to turn away.

Bast lay on his back, his wrist resting on a pillow, and fumed.

He was being a dick. He knew it. Pepper knew it. After that press conference and his scuffle with Deacon, the whole fucking world knew it.

After sobering up, he should have reverted to his normal, cheerful self. His wrist wasn't broken, it was merely sprained. This shouldn't be the end of the world, yet he couldn't help the doubts churning in his brain. What if this meant it was always weak, forever prone to re-injury?

His wrists were crucial to his future!

Crucial wrist. Good name for a band.

He should have managed his T-shirt removal by himself. He had a ton of experience in pulling a shirt off while his wrist was wrapped like this, so why the hell had he asked for Pepper's help?

He'd overheard her in the bathroom, upset at someone. Maybe her dad or Connor. Maybe Gallagher, though Bast couldn't imagine she would still be talking to him after all they'd gone through. But hey, what did he know?

He wanted to, though. He wanted her story. He wanted to delay her exit from the bedroom so he could find out what made her tick, so he asked for help he didn't need.

Only, the slightest proximity to her was torture.

Up close, her scent had infiltrated his nostrils, curled into his lungs. That floral memory from all those months ago when they first met cut a path through his lizard brain.

The swell of her breast had brushed against his shoulder, and apparently that, combined with his lack of action for a year, had sent his hormones into a riot. It was all he could do not to place his hands—okay, hand—on her hip and drag her into a straddle over his lap. His cock twitched with the image that presented. Pepper's thighs over his, her pussy flush against his rock-hard erection, her breasts smashed against his chest. Would her nipples be hard? How would they taste? Tangy? Sweet? All he'd have to do was swirl his tongue around them, get those nubs of candy pebble-hard. Then suck on her tit until she—

Stop.

He ran a hand over his cock, straining against his briefs, and let out a brief moan. Fuck, that felt good. But he couldn't do a thing about it, not with her so close.

He shook his head, desperate to restore reality. The one

where he was still mad at Pepper and should not under any circumstances be thinking of all the sweet ways he'd like to fuck her.

Just breathe, man. Fucking breathe.

He checked his phone. More texts and messages, everyone wanting a piece.

He shot a quick one to Reid, telling him he was okay and was about to take a nap, then another in the same vein to Hudson.

One drew his attention above the others. A message from an unknown number but with a photo he recognized: a tattoo of his name with a puck zipping through the "a," followed by an image of a flame.

UNKNOWN

Hi, Bast! I hope you don't mind me reaching out. Dex gave me your number. I just wanted to check in on you. I'm Kylie, btw. Lol!

Kylie, the cute blonde from the game. Like she needed an introduction with his name etched on her body. This might be the boost he needed, after a rotten day.

A rotten year.

His fingers hovered over the message. It wasn't the first time he'd sexted with a fan. That's how it started with Marina—Marina, who moved on to better and brighter prospects when he was at his lowest point. Kylie would be the perfect diversion, but then he remembered that she was exactly that: if he hadn't been so distracted by her, he would've seen Pepper coming.

A growl of frustration erupted from his throat.

He shouldn't have brought her here. It made no sense, and because he couldn't figure it out, he needed to not do anything stupid like respond to a flirty text from a woman he had no real interest in.

He had at least six calls from his agent, so Bast decided to move the man up his list of who needed his attention right now.

"About time you called," Kit said. "Where are you?"

"Reid's place in Michigan. Belhaven Harbor."

"Where the hell is that? Never mind, I can Google it. So. Care to share why you went ballistic on a member of the press this afternoon? Or why you got pissy with your new coach in front of the entire world?"

Would you believe I felt like someone had to protect the woman who supposedly royally fucked me? Nah, I wouldn't believe it either.

"I don't like bullies."

"That's it? You don't like bullies. Jesus, put it on a fucking T-shirt or chat about it on Insta."

"Kit, how about you tell me how bad it is?"

He offered that world-weary sigh that agents seem to have a lock on. "Deacon and the *Sun-Times* are assessing their options, which is code for they're talking to lawyers. I figure we can get this fixed with an apology and a donation to Deacon's favorite charity, which is probably Assholes-Not-So-Anonymous. Some of the sponsors have been on—"

"Who?"

"Under Armor. Gillette. T-Mobile. Just check-ins asking if you're okay that quickly segued into 'about that press thing'."

Kit had done a Herculean job of making sure Bast kept his sponsorships while he was injured, even going so far as to have some of them re-up for a couple of years. But anything with violence—off the ice—would give them a reason to reconsider their support of him.

Which is why he should have said: *Right on it!*

Instead of this gem: "I won't apologize. Deacon was a complete asshole to Pepper."

Kit sighed and asked the billion-dollar question. "And since when is it your responsibility to defend her?"

Since everyone told him he shouldn't.

"Told you, I don't like bullies." His father was one. Reid had been one until Bast became strong enough to fight back. Things were different now, but something in Bast's brain triggered whenever he encountered similar behavior.

"Well, as your agent, I'm advising you to play nice with Deacon and his massive news organization. And do it soon, so we can soothe the ruffled feathers of the people who pay the big bucks."

"I'll think about it," he said begrudgingly because it was what Kit needed to hear.

"Good man." Kit gave a significant cough. "Another thing I need to ask. What's with you and Pepper Calhoun?"

His pulse spiked. "Nothing. I don't like—"

"Bullies. Yeah, got it. But there's footage of you two leaving Rebels HQ together in your car. Where is she now?"

One wall over, driving him insane.

"No idea," he lied.

"You just left her at the side of the road?"

He should have. Because now he was stuck with her in this too-small luxury lake house-slash-cottage.

"I dropped her off at a friend's place. She's not my responsibility."

"Good. Keep it that way. Need I tell you that messing where you eat is not a good idea? She's your coach's daughter, never mind the rest. And why you'd want to say a kind word about the woman who tanked your comeback is beyond me. Haven't you heard what happened with her and

Kent Gallagher? Stay away while we get the Bast train back on the tracks."

Sure, sure. "I'm trying to take a nap. Check in later?"

"Yep. Rest up, and I'll keep you posted on any news."

Kit would kill him if he knew Pepper was here, so best to keep that nugget to himself. He assumed Pepper would be discreet as well, but he really shouldn't assume anything. Best to verify. He grabbed his sweats, struggled with his sling, and headed out to the living room.

She was in the kitchen with her back to him, headphones on, humming along to something. Every now and then she burst out with a few words.

"I could never take the place ... of your man!"

Ah, classic Prince. He stood back, watching as she sliced something on a cutting board. Then sliced a dance move with a shuffle of her feet and a wiggle of her ass.

God, she was a curvy thing. She moved silkily around the kitchen with the kind of grace she had not exhibited in the crash seen around the world. Mesmerized, he watched her until she turned and jumped.

"Oh! I didn't see you there."

"Obviously."

He needed to stop being such an ass, but he couldn't think of a way back to the nice guy he usually inhabited. That version was frozen on the Rebels ice.

"I was just making something to eat. There's frozen chicken and ground beef, which I'm defrosting in the fridge for tomorrow. At least, if I can get back to Chicago, you'll have something for the rest of your time here. For tonight we have pesto—jarred, of course—and pasta. Also I bought tomatoes at that general store, so I could make—"

"Have you told anyone where you are?"

She bit her lip. "Ah, no. Well, except for Dad. No one else knows. Neither would they like it."

"Good." His brain rewound over what she said. "Why wouldn't people like it?"

"Because I already damaged your career and they'd think it strange that we're ... together like this. They probably think it's strange anyway, what you did back there. But that we're still ..." She gestured between them. "No one's going to like that."

"Why?" He knew, or thought he did, but he wanted to hear her take on it.

"Look at what happened."

She wasn't talking about him—or not only him. It was all that stuff with Gallagher, of which everyone was quick to constantly remind him. He hated being forced into a pen with the rest of the cattle.

"What's for dinner again?"

"You're hungry?" Her face lit up, and Christ Almighty, that lit something in him. This small chink in his shield ...

"Yeah. I can't sleep, so eating sounds like the next best option." Well, sex did, but that wouldn't be happening. Kylie and her tattooed tits were burning a hole in his pocket.

"Great. Have a seat and let me work my magic on these ingredients."

He watched as she went through the steps of filling the pot and setting it on the stove. Even though he liked to wait until the water was boiling to throw the salt in, he didn't complain when she added it to the cold water.

"That'll take a few minutes. Would you like a drink? There's beer."

"A beer would be good." He sat at the farmhouse table.

She headed to the fridge and took out two IPAs, cracked them open, and set one before him. She stood back at the

kitchen counter, like she was moving away from an unex-
ploded bomb.

"How's your wrist?"

"Throbbing a little but otherwise not much to report."

She blinked those big storybook eyes at him and took a
drag from her beer.

"What did you mean earlier?" he asked. "About people
not liking the idea of us together?" He quickly amended,
"Here."

"Haven't you heard? I'm bad news." She said it with a
touch of challenge.

"I might have read something in the *New York Times*."

"Oh, nothing so lofty. But I certainly made the grade on
TMZ, the *New York Post*, and various other fine
publications."

She turned back to check on the water, which had yet to
make any meaningful progress in the last ninety seconds.
Her shoulders had stiffened, and it took every inch of his
willpower not to reach out and run a soothing hand over
her back.

"You looked different back then. Skinnier. Blonder. It's
why I didn't recognize you at Jimmy's that night."

Picking up her beer, she took a sip and turned to face
him. "The WAG makeover. Didn't suit me."

He agreed. She looked better now, filled out, more
natural. Stunning, if he was honest.

"You didn't like being a player's fiancée?"

"Not really. It felt suffocating. Like I was always on and
couldn't be myself. But alone, with Kent, it was different. We
were different. Until we weren't."

"Until you broke his heart and tanked his career." That's
what Connor had said. It was a load of crap—of course it
was—but he wanted to hear her say it. To defend herself.

She held his gaze coolly for a moment. "Yeah, poor Kent."

"You sure did a number on him. Or so the press said."

Her chest rose with a quickly drawn breath. "That's me. Career destroyer."

"Bullshit."

Her lips twitched. She turned to check the water, but he saw it: the exhale, the shoulder roll, the stiffening of her spine. Like she was getting ready to do battle.

"Watch out, Durand. You've already fallen afoul of the Pepper curse. You don't want it to get worse, do you?"

He laughed, a dark sound. "I don't believe in curses or bad luck or that one person has the capacity to inflict that much damage. Maybe you screwed over Gallagher and broke his heart. Maybe he deserved everything he got. But what I don't get is why you don't stand up for yourself when the world says you're the bad guy here. Why the hell, Pepper, are you taking it lying down?"

16

The million-dollar question.

While she thought of a suitable response, she added half a box of shells to the pot. When she turned back, he was staring at her intently.

Feeling brave, she stared back.

And why not? He was both perfect and shirtless. He'd come out here to ask whether she'd blabbed to the world about her whereabouts, and she'd managed to hook him with the promise of dried pasta and pesto from a jar.

What a siren she was.

Taking another sip of her beer, she let her eyes run over his shockingly painful beauty. He wasn't overly muscled like Kent. Bast was more naturally sculpted as if the gods had carved him in one blockbuster session from human marble. She'd read about his routine online, or lack of it. He liked to run and swim rather than do excessive gym work. All part of his born-with-it gift set. He was smooth, too, which had her fingers tingling with the need to touch him.

Would his nipples pop under her fingertips? Would his stomach muscles clench if she ran a hand over them? A throb started up between her legs, and she took another slug of beer to cool herself down.

"Maybe I just prefer a quiet life," she said in answer to his question.

His look was incredulous. "If this is you preferring a quiet life, Tequila Girl, then you are going about it all wrong."

Tequila Girl. He'd come up with a nickname for her. *Swoon.*

He gestured with his hand toward her. "So the online stuff about you and Gallagher was all garbage?"

"Sure, but I don't see why I have to confirm or deny. It's no one's business but mine and Kent's."

"So you don't mind people talking crap about you?"

"Of course I mind." It came out sharply, belying her cool-girl-don't-give-a-fuck attitude. Then quieter, she added, "But people are going to say whatever they want. Make up their own narratives. I can't change that."

"Like the Pepper Curse."

"That's what they called it. Which is why I ..." She paused, unsure how to phrase it.

"Why you what?"

Ran from you that night in Jimmy's Tap. She was trying to save him, not from any actual curse, which was ridiculous, but from the sheer negativity that seemed to follow her like a bad smell. But just like those *Final Destination* movies, the Grim Reaper always found a way. Or Lady Bad Luck.

"Could we talk about anything else but my sordid tabloid history?"

"Sure, how about mine?"

She laughed. "You don't have one. You're Mr. Nice Guy, never a bad word. In fact, you choose carefully, don't you?"

"Women? Well, I don't do drama, so that kind of dictates my sex life. Except for the last woman I dated."

She was surprised he'd volunteered that. "What happened there?"

"She moved on."

"After you were injured?" She had suspected as much. Marina Morgan had dated an NFL player quite soon after Bast.

"Women are fickle," Bast said. "They like winners, and anything less than that has them looking for the exit."

"Not all women. Some will stick around, trying to help even if it seems pointless." Heat rose to her cheeks. She turned away to stir the pasta water.

The heat didn't stay on her face. Her whole body warmed with the weight of Bast's stare on her back.

Finally he spoke. "Injuries weren't what Marina signed on for."

"That's horrible. Whatever happened to in sickness and in health?"

"We weren't quite at that stage." He looked thoughtful. "So you're the kind who would stick around when the going got tough?"

Yes, she was loyal to a fault. Just ask Kent. She could tell Bast about her ex, how she tried to get him the help he needed, but it would open about ten cans of worms.

"I like to think I'm not all that fickle. I talked to you in that bar, didn't I?"

Now that surprised him. He wasn't expecting a wry call back to their first encounter. Not only did it surprise him, it pleased him.

"Yeah, you weren't fussy at all." But a second later, the air changed. "But you were in a hurry to leave. I'm guessing you weighed your options and decided I wasn't such a good bet."

She tried to parse that. "Wait, you think I left—or tried to leave—because I thought you weren't a … winner?"

He shrugged, took another sip of beer. Hurt rolled off him in waves. This injury had really messed with his head.

"Not at all, Bast. I was really enjoying talking to you, but letting it go on any longer was leading you on. Once you knew who I was, it would—"

"End the way it did. With me being a jerk and you feeling ashamed."

She nodded.

"So if I was any other guy, or reacted any other way, you might have stayed?"

"I wished you were someone else. Just like you wished I was someone else."

That was either the best thing or the worst thing she could say. His nostrils flared in … anger? Or something else?

She stirred the pasta, keeping her eye on him. "I didn't ruin your life that night, but it came around again."

There was that look of incredulity again. "Wait, do you actually believe this Pepper Curse business?"

"No. But I'm not the luckiest person."

He squinted at her. "Connor said you were always breaking things."

"You spoke to Connor about me?"

He tapped a finger on the table. "I wanted to know what happened with Gallagher."

"Why?"

"Because …" He seemed to change his intent mid-sentence. "I didn't like seeing people pile on, and I needed some background. Connor was less than informative, and I see you're not much better. Which is fine. It's none of my business. If you want to play the martyr, then go ahead."

Now hold on. "I'm not playing the martyr."

"Sure you are. You say you're trying to keep your head down, looking for a quiet life. But you're doing the worst job of it. You've already taken out Gallagher with his dump in the minors. How did you manage to cause all that?" He held up a finger. "Oh, right, you broke his heart and he went on some sort of bender, then you refused to defend yourself."

"I'm not saying it's my fault—"

"Just enough to feel like you're the victim here."

"I don't feel like the victim. But the press *is* being unfair to me. And so are you."

"Oh, really? Well, here's some news, Pepper. You're getting some shit from the press, which is going to blow over. You know what won't blow over?" He held up his arm. "This. This is now a serious fucking issue. This could be my life going forward. There might always be a weakness here and that's something I have to live with. Something real that affects my career, not some hokey black cat, spilled salt, walking under a ladder shit curse that doesn't exist."

"I'm not asking you to believe it. I'm asking you to stay away from me."

"Now she tells me!" He stood and approached her, his uninjured hand thrown in the air to make some very important point, she was sure. "You think I want to be here with you, stuck in this too-fucking-small cottage with one bed and you shaking your damn ass? You think that I don't for a second regret stepping in like some ridiculous white knight, telling off your dad and the press? Or shoving Deacon over so now my sponsors are wondering about ditching me?"

"I didn't ask you to do that! I didn't ask you to send dirty looks to my father, or talk back to the press, or push Curtis Deacon over like a skittle. And I certainly didn't ask to be driven to this pimple town in the middle of nowhere so I can spend all my time looking at you and your dumb muscles and your too-handsome face. It's not fair, Bast. None of this is fair."

She gestured wildly at his chest which was mere inches from her, and of course that out-of-control motion resulted in her grazing his skin. Later she would analyze this moment and think: *I flapped my hand around on purpose, hopeful of touching hot, bare skin and hard, unyielding chest.*

"You want to talk about fairness?" he yelled. "Your hips, your ass, your ... lips." He was right on top of her, against her. Still not touching, but the air between them was a whisper's worth. "None of it is *fair*."

His gaze dipped to her lips, and she snatched a breath inside them. She was certain she would need that oxygen intake for what came next. But her lungs refused to fill, and her shallow inhales turned her desperate.

Lusty.

His last words about none of it being fair were spoken harshly, yet low enough that she could hear the pounding of her heart, the rapid blink of her eyelids, the thunderous throb between her legs. Or maybe she only felt that, an overwhelming need rushing through her.

That need had to find an outlet. Touching him, then pushing him away, seemed to be the next best step.

So she did.

She touched his chest and felt his juddering exhale.

Push him away. That was what was supposed to come next, but Pepper's rotten luck was working its magic. Reeling another victim in.

"So unfair," he murmured just as his mouth crashed into hers.

He tasted of beer and anger, a dangerous combination. She was stuck here with a guy who hated her and apparently wanted her despite that inconvenient lust.

But he didn't have a monopoly on high emotion. Turned out she wanted him, too.

Inconveniently so.

He continued his assault, sucking on her lips, twining his tongue with hers, and then he added his good hand to the equation, holding her hip steady when all she wanted to do was grind.

Feeling powerless was the worst, and she was sick of it. All that bare, tempting skin called to her. She moved her hand over his chest, found a nipple, rubbed, and yielded a throaty grunt that went right to her core.

He drew back, stared at her with more of that scowl that was so strange on him but was working a treat for her. Her fingernail scraped across his nipple, and he shut his eyes. Then pushed his body into hers, poking his erection into her stomach. And it didn't seem to be flagging, not like Kent's.

She'd never been able to make him happy in the bedroom, or anywhere else she tried when she hoped variety might make it better. But with Bast, there wasn't any sense that she was doing it wrong. Probably because she wasn't doing anything at all.

This was all him. His mouth, his hand, his erection butting against her stomach with delicious friction.

But she didn't want to be some passive participant. She coasted a hand down his chest between their bodies. "I can—"

"No," he gutted out.

That left her hand trapped in no-man's land at the waist of his sweats. So he didn't want her to touch him. She wasn't sure she'd ever understand what men wanted. Maybe this was some odd way to punish her.

Except what he did next had her rethinking that theory

entirely.

He nudged her feet apart, separating her thighs, and dropped his body a few inches so—ohhhh! *There.* His cock strained against his sweatpants, but its hardness rubbed where she was soft, sensitive, and increasingly wet.

"Take 'em off," he said, inserting a finger into the waist of her jeans.

As things now stood, they hadn't crossed a line. They had kissed. They had petted (if it was possible to "pet" someone with their cock). Once they got naked, it would be game over. She should stop, draw a line under it like she had the night in the bar.

Yet she needed this. If she could give this man pleasure, maybe she wouldn't be a complete failure. Everyone hated her, and even though this wasn't real affection, it amounted to something she could hold onto. Something tangible.

She unbuttoned and unzipped her jeans.

"Down." His blue eyes, so warm and friendly that night they'd first met, were now hazed over with something less ... amicable. Something dark and dangerous.

She pushed her jeans down and kicked them off. Her panties remained, and she held onto that last vestige of cotton like it was a symbol for her dignity.

"Just do it," she managed to utter.

His lips twitched, the slightest smirk. "Do what?"

"Get your payback."

"Oh, no. That's not how we're playing it, Tequila Girl."

"But—"

He shut her down with another kiss, so consuming it made her dizzy.

She had one more chance to cut this off. Make a stand. But his lips were her Kryptonite, the fatal flaw that was going to determine every move going forward. She had already lost the moment she kissed him back.

She waited for him to pull his sweats down, take himself in hand, finish what he'd started. Use and punish her.

So it was a shock to see him fall to his knees.

She gasped as his palm cupped her, the heel of his hand rubbing a stroke of possession over the damp material.

His eyes darkened as his face moved closer. His breath puffed hot and heavy on her mound while his thumb worked the seam, on the outside of her panties. She jerked against his hand as he brushed over her clit.

He froze. "Is this okay?"

"Is this ...? Yes. It's ..."

He inhaled between her legs, his nose deep against the fabric. Curling a finger along the edge of the elastic, he peeled her underwear down over her thighs.

Her panties had made it to her feet, and with a gentleness that shocked her, he lifted one foot out of the elasticated hole. Then, as if annoyed with that display of tenderness, he pushed her thighs apart roughly.

"*Ohhh*," she moaned, willing him on with sounds because words were weapons that hurt. Best to keep them sheathed.

One wicked finger ran along the length of her exposed seam, working its way through the folds.

"Oh, God, that's ..." She halted, worried the sound of her voice would somehow annoy him. Remind him of who she was. Suddenly fearful, she dropped her gaze to find him staring up at her.

"It's what?" He grunted.

"Amazing. So good."

Another grunt as if to say, *of course it is. I'm Bast Fucking Durand.*

"Put your foot on my shoulder."

"What—I don't want to hurt you."

He lifted her foot and placed it on his right shoulder, the one not connected to his injured wrist. His groan at seeing her further exposed, deliciously accessible, had her close to coming.

He thumbed through her again and then—finally—his tongue gave one long, ice-cream lick that sent shudders of pleasure through her. His free hand gripped her thigh, pushing it apart to give his greedy mouth better access. He lapped and lapped until the shimmery sparkle of an orgasm started to thread through her.

But before she could reach the frothy peak, he stopped.

She groaned at the cool air that hit her where his tongue had been. His mouth was wet, his lips shining with the taste of her. So this was his plan after all. Take her to the brink and leave her hanging?

"Open up for me."

"Wh-what?" She was as open as she could be, rudely exposed in the most embarrassing way.

"I've only got one good hand. I need you to open your pussy lips for me. Use your hands."

Use her ... *Oh my God.*

He took one of her hands and placed it over her damp center. "Do it."

Dazed with the fog of pleasure, she did as he demanded. Using both her hands, she thumbed her folds aside. Surely it wouldn't make a difference, except it did because she'd followed his very erotic order. She was touching herself, working with him for her own pleasure. An active participant, just like she wanted. As if he knew.

The power she felt as she watched him take his finger and insert it was immeasurable.

"More," she whispered. "Please."

Another finger slipped inside her, now two, stretching her. Helpless to resist the overwhelming sensation, she started grinding on those fingers. She needed to come so badly, and her clit was right there. Her thumb shifted, but he second-guessed her move.

"No. That's mine." His tongue pressed against that bundle of nerves, while his fingers curled inside her walls. And then he was sucking on her clit, all while she spread herself for him like some wanton thing.

Finally it hit, the wave of body-wracking sensation. He remained in place, hungrily taking as if it gave him as much pleasure.

Even more.

Only when she placed a hand on his head and ran her fingers through his dark locks, did he pull away. As if he'd been in a dream world and she was reminding him of the reality with her touch.

Of who she was. Bad news.

He leaned back on his haunches, giving her the perfect view of his erection still poking through his sweats. Feeling exposed while standing panty-less in the kitchen, she knelt and reached for him.

"Let me. I owe you this."

The glare he sent her way was enough to chill the hell out of the afterglow.

"Bast—"

He stood and loomed over her. "I can take care of myself."

And then he walked away.

17

BAST WOKE UP, confused. Scrambling for his phone on the bedside table, he touched the screen.

2:13 a.m.

Instinctively, he blinked, waiting a few seconds to adjust to the darkness. On one side was the pillow on which he'd placed his arm so he wouldn't accidentally roll over on it. On the other ...

Where was Pepper?

You never figured out the sleeping arrangements, idiot.

Instead he'd sucked on her sweet pussy, brought her to climax, and fucked off back to the only bedroom without a kind word. Some might say he'd been kind enough taking care of her and forgoing his own pleasure, but Bast didn't agree with that line of thinking. For him, sex wasn't quid pro quo, I-got-you-off, now-it's-my-turn.

Though she had offered. Knelt before him, her hand outstretched, those big hazel eyes pleading with him to let her put him out of his misery. Take him in hand and rub away the pain, not just of the last twenty-four hours but the last year.

Let me. I owe you.

But he didn't want her to feel she had to reciprocate for what had happened in the Rebels arena. He hated that she might think that about him.

This dynamic between them had morphed into something he'd never experienced with another woman. His relationships were usually casual, fun, low stakes. But with Pepper, so much had gone wrong for him to worry if right was truly possible. He was a different person around her. A beast off the leash.

The sight of her, pink and pretty under his tongue, had been hotter than the sun. The way she responded to his gruff orders, the way her body's muscles worked his fingers, sucking them in deep. Greedy and grasping.

For the second time in twenty-four hours, he turned into the pillow to bite back his aching lust.

Another groan as the thought of her coming on his face had his cock straining against his briefs, aching to be touched. He'd gone to bed, furious with himself for losing control. Anger was not a typical emotion for him. He rarely let anyone rile him in this way, and he never let it fuel his sex life. Sex was an outlet, but he didn't use it as a power play.

But Pepper had pushed him with her stupid theories about bad luck and unfairness and her wish that she was anywhere but here. That he was anyone but him. Well, he didn't want to spend time with her, either, not when he was so dangerously attracted to her.

And especially not now when he knew the sounds she made when she came.

And the taste of her slick, hot folds under his tongue.

And how her eyes flashed with hurt when he told her he'd take care of himself, thanks very much.

He ran a hand over his cock and cupped it hard. Another muffled moan had him leaning into his uninjured side to avoid the pain. Or he could just suffer this case of blue balls until he was rid of her.

He pushed back the cover, which is when he realized: the air was unusually chilled.

Did that mean—he switched on the lamp. Nothing.

The power was out. Where the hell was Pepper?

Quickly he pulled on his sweats and grabbed his phone to use as a flashlight. In the living room, he saw her silhouette on the sofa, and as he approached, he found her huddled under a thin throw blanket.

Shivering.

Of course, where else would she have slept after he stormed off in a blue-balled huff? Could he be any more of a jerk?

"Pepper," he whispered as he hunkered down beside her. "You awake?"

"Of course I am. It's an icebox in here."

He chuckled.

She turned, the light of his phone catching her annoyance perfectly. "What's so funny?"

"Me. Because I'm a jerk, and I left you out here."

"Well, you're the big shot asset who must be catered to. Of course you need your precious sleep."

He sat on the sofa and placed his phone on the coffee table so it could cast some light over the living room. "The power's out. I'm going to check the generator and see why it didn't switch on."

"That's somewhere outside." She shook her head. "I'll check it. You need to protect your wrist."

"We can do it together."

"Okay, but I need to use the bathroom first. I'll be out in a second."

He foraged for winter jackets and boots and suited up as best he could. He found flashlights in the mudroom, and while waiting for Pepper, he pulled at the door to the patio.

Stuck.

Next he tried the front door, only to find a waist-high snow bank blocking his exit.

"Damn," he heard behind him in Pepper's whisper.

"Yep. I'm not sure this is the best option at night. We can figure it out tomorrow."

"While we freeze to death?"

"No one's freezing to death. Didn't you notice all the firewood? We have a fireplace in the bedroom, which is where you're sleeping tonight. With me."

"Not sure that's wise." She folded her arms defensively.

"I'm talking about sharing a bed, Pep. Shenanigans-free. You're not going to be comfortable out here, and neither would I be, so you're in with me."

She looked doubtful, so he continued making his case.

"The bed is big enough, and I'm sure I could create a sufficient barrier to keep you on your side in case you start creeping over trying to steal the warmth of my body."

"I would not—"

He passed over her objection. "I know you won't allow me to sleep on the sofa—gotta protect the asset and all that —and I'm too much of a gentleman to allow you to sleep out here. In fact, if I hadn't thrown a hissy fit earlier, I would have known you were out here already. I'm sorry about that."

Color had risen to her cheeks. After the intimacy of earlier, surely she couldn't be embarrassed, but this was a different kind of intimacy. They were talking about sleeping together without sex.

"I don't know."

"I do. After what's already happened between us, you're drawing a line here?"

"What if I touch your wrist by mistake and hurt you again?"

"You a thrasher?"

"Not usually."

"Prone to nightmares?"

"Only the one I'm living in right now."

He grinned. "I think we can risk it. We'll both be a lot more comfortable in there."

What a fucking liar he was. Sleeping less than a foot from Pepper was going to be the opposite of comfortable. But he'd go with it for now because he really didn't want to sleep on the sofa. When he broke his wrist last year, he'd mistakenly napped on the sofa once—and woke up on the floor.

Not nice.

So for the sake of the body that paid his bills, he'd sleep in the same bed as Pepper Calhoun.

As for the body that had a permanent hard-on for this woman, he'd deal with that later.

18

How could a luxury lake house feel so *small*?

Pepper almost preferred when Bast wasn't talking to her. When he was just mad and taking it out on her with his tongue. That she could deal with (well, not really, but she could learn to appreciate it). What she couldn't deal with? This gorgeous, charming version with apologies and kind words.

The sexual tension should have been a thing of the past. Orgasm provided, check. Forgiveness dispensed, check. That should have been enough to move them past the thick sizzle of want that was coursing through her in his presence.

However, it had only intensified. She knew what he could do, how his mouth felt between her thighs, his tongue licking and delving, the evidence of desire slicking his lips—

Damn Reid and Kennedy. This place was gorgeous, but couldn't they have added a guest room? Then again, they probably didn't want any guests. Reid had always struck her as the surly, anti-social type. He wouldn't want to share Kennedy.

There was something appealing about that, even if it was

caveman behavior. Not unlike Bast's defense of her earlier. Maybe he and Reid were more alike than she'd previously thought. They seemed so different, yet there had to be some deep bond there as brothers, some affinity in values.

With all this swirling in her head, Bast came out of the bathroom, his mouth twitching at seeing her sitting stiffly on the side of the bed. He had already set the fire, and it was crackling away, providing light, heat, and romance.

"I don't have anything to wear to bed. My overnight bag was in my car at Rebels HQ." Also, she needed to call someone to make sure it didn't get towed.

With one hand, he grabbed his duffle bag and hauled it onto the bed. "Could you ...?" He gestured to it.

"Oh, right." She unzipped it.

"There should be a T-shirt in there. Also, there are spare toothbrushes in the bathroom."

She grabbed a tee without even looking and headed into the bathroom, where she used her phone to provide light. The T-shirt had Bast's number at the Hawks on it. Number 10.

God help her but she sniffed it, hoping against hope that the top note was laundry detergent. But it wasn't. It was the scent of Bast, and it was divine.

She pulled it over her head. It was extra-large, but not *that* roomy because she wasn't a Barbie doll. Her thighs looked—well, strong. Not slender, Pepper was fit and healthy, especially since she'd put on weight after her failed engagement. No more dieting or pressure to be WAG perfect. She didn't miss it.

Rummaging around in a drawer, she found a blister-packed toothbrush. Business done, she hauled in a deep breath and opened the door.

He was already under the covers on the right side of the

bed, with his braced wrist propped on a spare pillow on the opposite side of his body. As she closed the bathroom door, she felt his eyes on her.

She pulled back the covers, trying not to pay attention to the fact (a) Bast was clearly shirtless and (b) he was closer to the middle than he should have been because he needed more room on the edge for his arm.

And she had thought the lake house was too small. Was this bed a full-sized one? Maybe any bed with Bast Durand in it looked minuscule.

"It's a queen," he said.

"What?"

"You seem to be measuring the bed, so I'm telling you that it's a queen. You getting in? Not that I'm objecting to the view."

His tee, which was very soft after multiple washings, stopped at the top of her thighs. The strong ones she'd been admiring earlier but didn't feel so proud of now. Was he making fun of her?

Quickly, she climbed in and pulled the covers up to her neck, noting he'd added another comforter.

Reality was settling into her bones. He was too close, impinging on her side, and she was about to sleep in the same bed as Bast Durand after he'd given her a wonderful orgasm and she hadn't returned the favor. How in the eff did they get to this point?

She checked her phone. 3:30 a.m. and she was now wide awake. Where was all that yawning when she needed it?

She made a point of fluffing her pillow, anything to distract her from looking his way. When she settled, she found him focused on her, his eyes gleaming in the firelight, though now he'd put his uninjured arm behind his head. A tuft of underarm hair that should not have been erotic made her mouth dry. Then water. Then dry again.

She swallowed, looked at the ceiling.

"I thought you were tired," he said.

"I am." Or she was, but now every nerve was strung tight.

"You seem tense."

If tense meant turned on, then yes, she was exceptionally tense. She'd already had one mind-blowing orgasm today, and now she was wondering about him. About how she wanted to return the favor. Touch him, bring him pleasure. But he had already refused.

She closed her eyes and tried to ignore the presence beside her, tried to pretend his steady breathing wasn't driving her insane with desire. How could standard inhaling and exhaling be sexy? She couldn't even see him, so that should have helped her get past this.

But it didn't because she knew what he could do. How, even one-handed, he could bring her off because she had been oh-so-helpful, spreading herself like a buffet for him—

"Could I ask you something?" she said to the firelit dark.

"Shoot."

She turned her head slightly. "Why were you at Jimmy's Tap where people might recognize you? Probably the worst place to be an incognito superstar hockey player."

His smile was rueful in the half-dark. "It was Reid's suggestion to meet there, and I actually thought my disguise was top notch. I wasn't in a great place that night, and I just wanted to be in the mix. If I couldn't play, I could watch with people who love it."

She understood that need to be part of something greater.

"Except for one person," he added.

That made her lips curve. "What torture for you, sitting beside the one person who couldn't appreciate your art."

"Right?" He grinned. "Of all the girls in the world. Anyway, I still had a good time."

Left unspoken? Until he found out who she was.

"You said you weren't in a great place that night. Because of your wrist?"

"Yeah, feeling a bit sorry for myself. I'd just found out I had to get surgery."

"Oh, wow. I bet that was a shock."

"First of many."

He meant her, but he didn't sound annoyed. If anything, his tone was amused. But she wasn't sure she could let the guilt go just yet. Earlier in the kitchen, he'd gone off on her about the possibility of his wrist never being fully healed. How that might be his life going forward. That was where his head was at, and she needed to acknowledge it.

"It must have been so frustrating. Being out so long."

"Yeah, of course. I love hockey. It's what I'm meant to do, so when you're not doing what you're built for, you tend to feel … diminished, I guess."

She understood that. She was supposed to be doing something else.

The thing was she didn't think she'd ever make it back—and to be honest she wasn't sure what she was trying to make it back to. That world in Denver, the one where she finished her degree and got a job with little kids? That life seemed so out of reach now. She was lucky to be able to spend a couple days a week with Hatch.

"What would you do if you couldn't play hockey?"

"I'd be a fucking mess, Pepper."

She blinked, not expecting such honesty. "This last year has been hard on you. Harder than you've let on, I think."

"It has." He wiped his eyes, suddenly looking tired. "I haven't really wanted to admit that."

"Have you talked to anyone about it? Reid, perhaps."

"Reid blames himself for the original injury, so it's hard to bring it up and not make him feel like shit. My dad's not one for the heart-to-hearts."

"What about your mom?"

"She's awesome, but I don't like to worry her. She's always been able to trust I can cheer myself up. Reid gives her fits, so understandably she needs to carve out space for him."

"You shouldn't have to miss out on her maternal wisdom."

He smiled. "I'm a self-propelling pump-myself-up machine. It's been a rough year, but it's also been good for my relationship with Reid. We haven't always got on."

It sounded like there was more there. She turned to say something soothing about how it would all work out and he'd be back on the ice before he knew it, but the sight of his face—that gorgeous, handsome face—dried up her speech. Trying to avoid staring at him directly, her gaze dipped lower. A man's shoulders shouldn't be so sexy. They were just joints covered in hard muscle and smooth, golden skin.

There it went again, the telltale throb between her legs.

"You can talk to me. Or get mad at me. Whichever works to help."

"Thanks. But I'm not really one for grudges, no matter how hard I try."

"You were pretty mad at me when I offered to reciprocate." She waved a hand toward the kitchen. "Earlier."

"I hadn't intended to let it go so far. I"—he paused—"I didn't want you to think you owed me because of what happened on the ice."

She let out a breath. "So it wasn't because you didn't think I could."

He frowned. "Why would I think that?"

Because I've never been good enough before. "You didn't seem interested."

"Oh, I was interested. But I was pretty annoyed at how much of a jerk I've been to you over the last twenty-four hours. And maybe I wanted to make myself suffer."

"Martyr to your penis?"

He chuckled, but it sounded pained. "The dynamic here is kind of messed up. I'm not used to fighting with the women I want. I'm not used to this much … friction."

The dynamic might have been messed up, but that could be fixed with a little honesty. She saw no good reason why Bast should have to suffer any more than he already had.

She leaned up on her elbow. "Then let's not fight."

LET'S NOT FIGHT.

It was as simple as that. "So if we're not going to fight, what should we do?"

Her lips curled, which was the first time he'd seen her smile since the night they met. There they went again, those firecrackers in his chest.

"Maybe you should take care of yourself like you promised. Unless you already did."

Did she mean …? The saucy smirk on her lips assured him that yes, she meant exactly what he thought. That was unbelievably hot.

"I didn't. Martyr to my penis, remember?"

"So you really need it, don't you?" Her eyes dipped to where his cock was covered by the comforter, and that bad boy immediately responded. "Go ahead, Bast. Whatever you need."

He pushed back the covers. They were impediments to his hand, and frankly, he wanted her to see him. To witness the damage she had wrought.

Her eyes flared in the fire's glow on seeing him tenting his briefs. He pushed them down, so now he stood proud and ready for her.

"It won't take long," he whispered. "Just keep looking at me."

She swallowed, her tongue darting out to wet her lips, the effect so sexy it had him groaning. Gripping his cock, he started to stroke. Slowly, because even though he'd said it wouldn't take long, he wanted it to last more than ten seconds. He wanted her to watch him with those gorgeous eyes forever.

"Just look?" she murmured.

"What?"

"'Just keep looking at me' is what you said. Is that all you want?"

He'd refused her offer earlier, so she sure as hell shouldn't be so generous as to propose it again.

Evidently sensing his need, she leaned over and placed a hand on his chest. Just that one, simple touch sent a surge through his cock. Pre-come was leaking over his hand, and he wasn't sure how much longer he'd last. He stopped for a moment, to let the beast subside.

She ran a hand over his stomach. The muscles bunched, craving her touch. She asked permission with her eyes, and he nodded. Desperately.

Her hand dipped lower. Pushing his legs apart, she

traced a finger over one of his balls, which felt heavy and sensitive.

"Tell me what you like," she whispered.

You. More than I realized. More than is good for me.

"Cup them. Fondle them. And then ..." As she did that, she moved a finger along his taint.

"Jesus, that's amazing."

"Yeah?" She sounded breathless. "Can I taste you?"

He could barely get the words out. "You-you sure?"

She nodded and inclined her head, but before she could get there, he released his cock and cupped her jaw.

"Pepper, you don't owe me anything. I mean, for what happened. Don't ever feel you do. I've been a jerk."

"You've a right to be."

"No. I don't. I can be angry, but I shouldn't take it out on you. And you should never feel this is a way to make me feel better." At her wry smile, he loosed a chuckle. "Of course it will make me feel better, but that's not your responsibility."

"So I should leave it to you. Let you be responsible for your own orgasms."

Hell, no! "Maybe. But it seems helping each other out makes it so much better, don't you think?"

A lovely blush overtook her cheeks, her mind evidently returning to that moment earlier when she held herself open for him. It also had the effect of toggling a switch, resetting his brain to Bast, the decent guy. He wasn't an asshole, not usually. He wanted to be the man she'd met before he turned into this gloomster.

"It was so hot," she whispered. "What you did. What you ... said."

All that awe in her voice made him feel like a king. He curled his fingers from her jaw to the nape of her neck and stole a kiss of those gorgeous lips. A whimper escaped her throat, followed by a moan, and his neglected cock almost exploded at the sound.

She ran her tongue over her lips, touched them where he'd crushed them.

"I might have been mad, sweetheart. But that doesn't change how goddamn sweet you tasted. And watching how your fingers stretched that pretty pussy wide for me ... never seen anything so sexy."

"Really?" She sounded disbelieving.

"Really. Now use those magic fingers on me. Stroke my dick while I tell you how good you tasted on my tongue."

Her mouth was close to his, brushing against his lips as she took his cock in hand and tugged in a way that had him moaning to the heavens with pleasure.

But neither was she some passive participant. She had questions.

"How good did I taste?" she asked as she jerked him so damn sweetly.

"Oh, sweetheart, so good." He nipped at her lower lip. "Like the sweetest candy with the perfect tang. But—"

More pre-come dribbled over her hand, sending her gaze to his dick, raw and engorged in her grip.

"But what?"

"But better than that, and you were so wet for me. I loved that." Just as he loved what she was doing to him now. He had to kiss her more. Every part of him needed to be rubbing and touching and sucking on her.

"A little faster. Yeah, yeah, just like that." He kissed her again, this time deep and slow. "Now I need you to touch yourself."

"W-what?"

"You've got a free hand, so put it to use. Inside your panties, where you're all slippery and wet for me."

She whimpered. "I-I can't do both. Your cock and ... me."

"I'll help. Go ahead now."

After a few seconds hesitation, she adjusted so she was kneeling beside him and moved her hand down, squirreling it away inside that clean white cotton.

"That's my girl. Now tell me how it feels."

Nothing, not a word, just her eyes fluttering closed.

"Pepper," he moaned. "If I can't do it, I need you to talk me through it."

"I'd sound ... stupid."

"Never, sweetheart."

She shook her head. "I can't." He heard it in her voice. Shame.

Someone told her it wasn't hot. Anger reared up in his chest. Who had messed with this girl's mind? "Fuck that guy. The past doesn't matter. All that matters is how we're making each other feel. How good this is."

"Bast," she whispered.

"Does it feel slippery? Hot?"

"Yes," she panted as she continued to stroke, one hand on his cock, the other inside her panties. "It does."

"Need more than that. You aching for me?" His gaze drilled into her, and his hand cupped her jaw and held her in place while he sipped at her lips. "'Cause I'm aching for you. Want to fill you. Want to fuck you so badly."

"Oh, oh ..." Her stroke inside her panties became more agitated.

"That's it. Bet you're soaked. I want to drink you down, get my tongue in there and lick that gorgeous pussy clean. Can't wait to get back there. Taste you again."

That did it. She shuddered, her hand stilling around him as her orgasm hit her.

It didn't take long for him to follow. Too quick, to be

honest, but it had been building all day. Since the night he met her eight months ago. He never would have dreamed it would happen this way, and when it did, he wasn't sure why he'd ever been mad at her.

Spent, he collapsed back on the bed, meaning to pull her down beside him, but she slipped his grasp, standing quickly, and went into the bathroom.

Damn. He'd upset her.

But when she came out, she was carrying a washcloth.

"Shall I?" She gestured to his abs.

He nodded, thinking he'd never refuse an offer of care from her again.

She rubbed the warm cloth over his stomach, stripping away the mess. Not just the come, but the cobwebs of his brain.

This is the real Pepper—vulnerable, giving, sweet. Not what those fuckers out there think.

"Thanks. For everything."

"Everything?" She chuckled softly. "Don't answer that. I know it's too soon."

He lay his head on the pillow. "Fuck, yeah it is. Christ, what a twenty-four hours."

Her smile faded. Obviously it was too soon for her, but he wasn't about to let her get down on herself about it.

"You're going to have to get over it. Time for us to move on."

Sure, that was easier said than done, and no one knew better than him how hard it was to get over something that was mired in the mud of guilt.

"Just like that?"

"Just like that."

"But you're Bast Durand, and I'm the woman who might have damaged your career."

For the first time in his life, he hated being that guy. "So pretend I'm not me."

She snorted. "Right. You're impossible to think of as anyone else."

"Listen. Here we are, snowed in, miles from civilization, hidden away. No one but my brother and his wife truly know where we are. We can do anything, be anyone."

She considered it, then responded in a small voice. "Start over." The way she said that was filled with a hope that tugged at his heart.

"Start over," he repeated, liking a little too much how those two small words created a weird *th-thunk* in his chest. This last year had been about crawling back, starting anew, but there was still stuff crowding the path forward.

For both of them, he suspected.

He pulled the covers back. "Come to bed. It'll look better in the morning."

19

THE LAST FEW times Bast had opened his eyes after a fitful sleep he'd not liked any of the worlds he woke up in.

A world where he was still injured.

Or a world where he was alone in his car and Pepper was off doing her hunter-gatherer bit.

Or especially the world where his balls were bluer than one of that Picasso dude's more famous artistic periods.

Yeah, he'd hated that particular wakey-wakey, though it hadn't lasted long. No, Pepper had saved him with her hot hands and gorgeous smile.

This time when Bast woke up, the world was different. First off, the air was as chilled as Zamboni-fresh ice, but he was warm as toast, buried under the covers. It reminded him of those early mornings back in Grenville when his dad would yell at him to get up for practice. (Reid was already first up, naturally.) Bast would snuggle into his pillow, trying his best to retain the heat built up inside the duvet, hating practice because he didn't think he needed it. Reid might, but as Bast was naturally gifted—or so everyone kept telling him—he shouldn't have to be up so damn early.

His father wouldn't hear of it. *No son of mine is going to skate by on his good looks.*

Now, he was not only warm, but he was wrapped tight by a woman blasting enough heat to power the lake house's generator. Sometime during the night, Pepper had curled her body around his and he'd shifted so his uninjured arm had her in its embrace. One of her legs was locked in between his, her thigh in a sensual nudge against his morning wood. She'd buried her face in the crook of his neck so his nostrils were being tickled by her hair.

God, she smelled good.

Which only made him harder.

Last night was the hottest night of his life, and he hadn't even gone all the way with this woman. But as sweet as that was, he had to say this wake-up moment might be close to it. Pepper in his arms, her body seeking him out for comfort in the night.

She lifted her head, one mad curl over her eye. "Hi."

"Hi," he murmured back.

She blushed and moved back, but he held on.

"What are you doing?" she whispered.

"Enjoying the first morning in a while where I don't feel like the world is ending."

Her lips parted, closed again. She returned her head to that warm spot where it had been resting.

"You can say something, y'know," he murmured against her hair.

"I don't want to ruin your day when it's been going so well."

He chuckled. "Speaking would ruin it? Nah. Unless you say something silly about bad luck or how sorry you are."

She raised her head again. "Don't athletes have special morning routines that crave silence?"

"Not me. I'm kind of chatty."

"I noticed." She squealed because he'd lightly pinched her butt. "Hey!"

"That's for your cheek. Literally." He kissed her forehead. "And if you're referring to the fact I like my sex communication on the dirty side, I didn't hear you complaining. In fact, you seemed to be getting into the spirit of things there once I warmed you up."

"Well, dirty talk is not really my forte."

Someone had made her feel foolish about it. He took an educated guess. "You and Gallagher didn't talk dirty to each other?"

"Oh, I tried, but he laughed at my efforts."

"What a jerk." The more he heard about this guy, the more he reckoned Pepper was done wrong.

Her laugh was nervy. "Let's not talk about that. I'd much rather live in the present for a while."

He understood that. But he had a feeling Pepper's past, especially with Gallagher, had her all up in her head. Also the immediate past—Bast's and Pepper's—was hard for her to just blindly forget.

This was a woman who was stuck.

He was getting to a better place, though. It wasn't in him to hold a grudge or dwell on the painful, at least not where Pepper was concerned.

Which was a strange thing to settle on.

"Guess it's hard for a preschool teacher to think like that."

She gaped. "Now wait a second. Do you think preschool teachers don't have dirty thoughts? Or can't do spicy talk? I did my best!"

"I know you did," he soothed with fake condescension.

She must have realized that he was yanking her chain

because she exploded. "Ha, ha, hilarious. So maybe I'm not the most sophisticated when it comes to sex communication"—she finger quoted that last bit—"but I've never not tried. It's not my fault I haven't had a whole lot of practice."

"Why, just the one careful owner, was it?"

"Not even."

Not even? What did that mean? Blinking, she seemed to realize that she'd given herself away.

While he parsed her words, she pushed back, using him for leverage, and tried to escape the bed. But he already had the warm cocoon going, and no way was he letting her bring cold air into this heated bubble of perfection. He circled her waist and gently pulled her back while the import of that exchange washed over him.

One careful owner ... not even.

"Hey, I want out of here."

"No, you don't." He rolled over her gently, pinning her down. She struggled, but he could tell her heart wasn't in it. "Are you saying what I think you're saying?"

She growled, and it was so damn cute, but not enough to redirect this conversation to anything other than what he'd heard.

"Pepper, was Gallagher your first?" He was still hung up on the meaning of "not even."

She turned her head away from him. "Sort of?" At his confused expression, she added, "It means we never—look, I can't talk about this, about Kent, without violating his privacy."

"Okay, but you can tell me about you, right? Were you a virgin before you met Gallagher?"

She nodded.

"And after?"

Another nod.

Fuuuck. "And now?" But he already knew the answer before she moved her chin, ever so slightly.

"You guys were engaged, but you didn't have sex?"

"Like I said, I can't go into it. Just know that I'm not expecting anything here. You're off the hook."

He'd practically forced himself on her, and she was a ... virgin?

He rolled away and off her.

She was looking at him carefully, probably thinking what an asshole he was for practically goading her into hand jobs and touching her so intimately.

"I had no idea," he said. "All that stuff yesterday and this morning—I went too far."

She shook her head. "Do not for one second take away my agency here, Bast Durand! I knew exactly what I was doing. Exactly what I wanted to do. I begged you with my body to touch me and taste me and ..." She swallowed and restarted. "I've never wanted to touch someone so much. To give them all the pleasure that's in my gift to give. I know I came off as inexperienced, and that's because I am —in actual terms. But I've done things. Watched porn. Admittedly not as filthy as some of the things we did, but ..."

She placed a hand on his chest. "I loved every second. Please don't think you pressured me into it. I've never felt that good before, and it confirmed for me that maybe I'm not as bad at this as I thought."

Protectiveness reared inside him, that rampant need to slay everyone who'd told this woman she wasn't good enough.

"And you think you're bad at dirty talk? You just knocked it out of the park this second with the recap of our lusty history."

Another blush that was so adorable. "You have low standards."

"Nope. Is that what happened with Gallagher? He said you were bad at it? So bad you never even got to the finish line?" He was so confused.

"Like I said, Kent's off the table as a discussion. But I do want to thank you for making me feel sexy and wanted." She gave him a soft kiss. "For everything."

And then she slipped out of bed and headed to the bathroom, leaving a cold influx of air.

AT LEAST THREE feet of snow were banked against the large picture window in the living room. Pepper's weather app said the area had been blessed with fourteen inches; the wind must have blown it into a frigid wall against the glass.

Just over a foot wasn't too bad. She would dig a path through to the driveway, but they'd need a snowblower for the rest. Fortunately they didn't need to find the generator. About an hour ago, the power had come back on, just in time for them to heat water for much needed coffee.

Something furry interrupted her sightline. A squirrel, perhaps? It moved along the snowbank, burrowing every few inches as if looking for something it had lost. Pepper could've sworn it made eye contact with her as it padded over to the window.

On closer inspection, it looked like a chipmunk. It raised a paw—claw?—to the window in a friendly wave. Or maybe it wanted to eat her.

Pepper drank her coffee and reflected on the events of the last twenty-four hours. She hadn't meant to let her inexperience show so obviously. Add that to the list of other things she hadn't meant to happen.

Let Bast Durand kiss her. Lick her. Bring her off twice.

She could have lied and said that she wasn't a virgin, but his joke about "one careful owner" had set her off. Kent had his reasons for being unable to perform in the bedroom, and Pepper sure as heck would not be spreading those around. His career was already in tatters. Rumors like that would finish him.

Instead she'd let the paparazzi machine steamroll her. Took the blame because it was less embarrassing than telling the truth.

My fiancé's performance-enhancing drug use didn't help him in the sack.

At the time, she'd assumed she was the problem. Kent could only go so far before a de-rection situation occurred. She'd tried everything—a makeover, new clothes and lingerie, toys, even getting the advice of her new girlfriends (in as discreet a way as possible)—but nothing seemed to work. Only later, when she discovered his PED use did she understand that maybe she wasn't the problem after all. Maybe the drugs' side effects were to blame.

After they broke up, he begged her to keep his secret. He wanted to get help and if word got out about his drug use, he'd never recover and get back to his peak in the game. So she didn't say a word.

Loyal to the last.

No one cared about the demise of their relationship until Kent got into a fight in a bar with his teammate Dustin Marsh. The tabloids exploded, looking for dirt. The team's PR jumped into overdrive, crafting a story that blamed Kent's personal issues on his recent breakup.

Enter the villain from stage left.

The gutter press ran with every rumor. Pepper was cold-hearted, too busy flirting with Kent's teammates, only interested in the WAG life than the real work needed for a relationship. Poor broken-hearted Kent after Pepper abandoned him!

Several of the rumors had Becca Marsh's stamp on them, a woman Pepper had once considered a friend.

She couldn't win. And while she knew it was counterproductive to keep Kent's secrets, especially as they made her look like Cruella, she wasn't the kind of person who would throw someone in pain under the bus.

Her phone buzzed with a text from Elle.

Hey, can you talk?

PEPPER

Sure.

But instead of texting or even calling, Elle initiated a FaceTime call. Pepper couldn't ignore it, so she took a seat on the sofa and answered it.

"Hey there!" Pepper offered in her cheeriest voice. "How are things?"

Elle's lips twitched. "I should be asking you. I saw what happened at Rebels HQ after the presser—what's going on?"

Orgasms. So many orgasms.

"Just keeping a low profile. How's Hatch? Did his little sniffle clear up?"

Elle smiled. "Oh, he's fine. That's why I'm calling." In the background, a baby voice yelled out, "Peppa!"

"You hear that? I know you're usually on duty only a couple of days a week, but he's like this every day you're not here."

"I didn't know that." Now she understood the need for video.

"Why do you think his next word after 'mama' and 'dada' was 'Peppa'? You're a big part of his life." That made her feel warm, but Elle's follow-up brought the chill back. "Hey, nice shirt. Wait, isn't that Bast Durand's old numb—"

"Oh, this old thing." Subject change needed stat. "Can I say hi to my favorite guy?"

"Yes!" Elle laughed as Hatch appeared in the frame, close enough for a nose-hair count.

"Hey, buddy, I miss you."

"Peppa!" With his cute little fist touching the screen, he muttered some baby babble that could have been "I miss you too."

Pepper spent a minute or so talking to him, asking him about his puzzles and if he got any snow. She wasn't expecting answers, but it was comforting all the same. The last couple of months working with the Kershaws had grounded her and given her hope that she might make her way back to doing what she loved, working with kids in a more structured capacity.

"Hey H-man, let me show you something." She took the phone and switched the lens to take in the snow and her new chipmunk friend, who was on another digging mission. Poor thing, his food sources must be covered up. "Isn't he cute?"

"Oh, most definitely," Elle said, which is when Pepper realized someone else was in the frame: Bast.

He must have used the mudroom entrance off the kitchen while she was on the phone. He had a shovel over his back and was contemplating the frigid landscape like some frontiersman of old.

"Idiot," Pepper muttered as she quickly switched the lens direction back to her.

Elle chuckled. "So *that's* what's going on. You and Bast are what? Sorting out your differences?"

"He needed someone to drive him to the backwoods of Michigan, and we got stuck under a couple of feet of snow. And now he's ..." Bast had started digging, but it looked to be slow going with one hand. "I don't know what he's doing."

"But you two are friends?" Elle sounded hopeful.

"'Friends' is a stretch. He's not mad at me anymore, or at least he isn't today. He really shouldn't be doing anything that might exacerbate his injury."

Elle scoffed. "You can't tell them what they can and can't do. Theo had a groin injury last season, and do you think it stopped him?" She leaned in. "It only made him more determined, if you know what I mean. It's as if they have to prove they can do all the things."

Pepper rolled her lips in. "Kershaw is kind of stubborn."

"Wait, who's taking my name in vain?" The man himself appeared, plopping down on the Kershaws' comfy sofa.

"Name taken in vain implies you're a deity," Elle said, and when Theo opened his mouth, his wife shut it down with, "You're not a god, babe."

"Not what you said last night, Elle-oh-Elle." With a cheeky wink, he gathered Hatch on his knee and faced the camera. "Pepper, you're alive! We were worried about you."

"You were?"

"Of course. If Baby Durand thinks the press are so dickish he needs to push them over in your defense, then maybe you're not such a menace after all."

"Theo!" Elle glared at her husband. "Pepper is not a menace. It was an accident."

"Yeah, I know that, honey. But people are gonna have opinions. It helps that BD is taking her side."

That made Elle smile impishly. "It sure does. In fact—"

"I'm so sorry for leaving you guys in the lurch," Pepper cut in, hoping that was enough of a warning to Elle not to spill the beans about her current living arrangements. The last thing she needed was another rumor mill grinding away about Pepper and her latest hockey player victim. "I hope to be back in the city in a day or so."

Elle nodded in understanding. "It's okay. Things are a bit quiet here, except for Hatch screaming for you and Theo getting under my feet because the plane couldn't take off for the New York away game."

"You love that I'm here." He turned to Pepper. "You should see the sexting when I'm gone, Pepsi Cola."

"Theo!"

"And when I'm not." He winked at Pepper, which made her giggle. Out of the corner of her eye, she saw no sign of Bast. Maybe he'd collapsed behind a snowbank, which would serve him right.

"Can I say goodbye to my best buddy?"

Theo kissed his son. "Wave to Pepper, H-man."

"Peppa!" He waved, and in doing so, brushed the screen and hit the end call button. Perfect timing because Bast had just come out of the kitchen wearing sweats and a T-shirt that made his guns look spectacular.

Her mouth watered, but she managed to say, "What were you doing out there?"

"Digging a path to the dock. Thought we might take a walk later."

Not likely. "You're supposed to be resting your wrist."

Shrugging her criticism off, he sipped from the coffee

mug he'd brought with him and peered outside. "Making friends?"

She followed his gaze. The chipmunk had returned and was scrabbling around, probably looking for food. "That's Chester."

"Chester?"

"He looks like a Chester. I wonder if we have any nuts or seeds."

He growled (not Chester, but Bast). "Do not feed it. It'll come back with its entire family. Speaking of families ... were you talking to Kershaw and his kid just now?"

"Yeah. Elle called because Hatch wanted to say hello."

"You're pals with the Kershaws?"

"I babysit for Hatch a couple of days a week."

Bast looked like he had a million questions. "You used to go to school for that, didn't you? To teach little kids. How come you're not doing the preschool teacher thing?"

"I never finished my degree. When I broke up with Kent, I got off track."

He nodded in sympathy. "Got the yips?"

"You could say that. I've been looking for daycare jobs, but people run searches on me and the whole thing with Kent is all they see. Sometimes they'll pull me in for an interview just to ask personal questions about what happened."

He looked horrified. "With no intention of hiring you?"

"People have to get their kicks somehow. But I love watching Hatch. He's such a character."

His lips curved. "You're a woman of many talents." The cheeky grin implied that some of those talents were sexual, which should have made her feel objectified but strangely pleased her. Perhaps she wasn't completely useless.

"So, what are the chances of getting out of here today?"

"Slim to fuck no. I took a look down the driveway. It's impassable, but the thaw should set in tomorrow." He sounded confident. As he sipped his coffee, he eyed her over the lip of the mug. "You have somewhere to be?"

"You know I don't. But you came here to get away from it all, so I can't imagine you want a reminder of what happened staring you in the face."

Listen to her! She sounded so mature. Orgasms were the cure.

"Let me worry about that. The question is how we're going to spend our time." He looked like a mischievous schoolboy thinking dirty, dirty thoughts.

"Maybe you can do some reflection while you're here."

"Not sure I need to reflect on anything. Relaxation is the goal."

Said as if the only way to achieve that was with *more* orgasms.

She really needed to stop thinking about orgasms.

"Why are you here, Bast? Really?"

He opened his mouth and closed it quickly. When he spoke, it sounded measured.

"I told you, I needed to get away."

She understood that instinct, being a champion runner-from-trouble herself, but she wasn't sure it was good for him to be separated from the team right now. He was new to the Rebels, and bonding in those early days was probably important.

"But shouldn't you be staying close to the medics?"

"I've been here before, so I know what needs to happen for my recovery." His gaze slipped away toward the window. "There's a lot of expectation hanging on my move to the Rebels. I haven't played for a while and people have been building this up ever since the acquisition was announced.

I'd rather not be in Chicago while they tear me apart." Facing her again, he cocked his head. "I think you know how that is."

"I do. But it doesn't seem like your style. I would've thought you'd ignore all the haters, and anyone you can't ignore, you'd give 'em the bird."

"Maybe I'm a sensitive little flower who needs a break. Ever think of that?" He flashed that blinding grin, which she interpreted as "back off." Funny how she knew that.

His phone vibrated, and he checked it and returned it to his pocket.

"Who's that?"

He gave a slight grimace. "My brother."

"He must be worried about you."

"He doesn't need to be. I've got this." He sounded a touch impatient. "It's just weird between us at the moment. It's always been me getting the accolades, winning titles, hitting records, and now it feels like I'm starting over while Reid's got his shit together and everything's working out for him. I can't help being a bit envious of him and his life right now."

"And you preferred when it was the other way around?"

He considered that. "I didn't prefer it. I'm not used to being second best, especially where Reid's concerned. Which probably makes me the biggest asshole."

"Maybe not the biggest."

He gestured with his finger and thumb. "This big?"

"More like ..." She stretched her hands apart, measuring his assholery to more suitable proportions. "It's okay to be envious, especially when your life has been upended like it has. Things are bound to be tricky given his part in your original injury." She took a chance. "What happened there?"

"Just some family stuff spilling onto the ice. Reid told me

later that he'd just found out Kennedy was leaving the country soon, and it pissed him off. Also, my father came to town for the game, which wasn't unusual, but he rarely went to see Reid play. He only came to Chicago because we were both playing in the same game."

"You're his biological son and Reid's his stepson?"

"Yeah, same mom. And that difference colored our lives growing up. Dad was kind of a dick to Reid, and Reid was kind of a dick to me." He quickly added, "Just the usual older brother hazes younger brother stuff. We're good now. But we had to have that clash on the ice last year for us to get there. Reid feels terrible about it, and I told him we were good. All was forgiven. But lately ..." He shrugged. "Now things seem kind of muddy again."

Well, they would be. The dynamic between these brothers sounded complex.

"Eventually, you probably should get it off your chest. With Reid. It's not his fault that he's on a peak while you're in a dip."

"I know that. I had hoped we'd be on top of the world at the same time."

She touched his chest and peered up at him. "That'll happen. You're too good not to come back from this, and then you and Reid can go out there together and mop the ice with the competition. No one expects you to get over this in a couple of days."

He placed a hand on her hip and pulled her close.

"You're good at this," he said.

"What? Offering unwanted opinions?"

"Soothing supersized egos." His eyebrows rose, his mouth kicked up in a cheeky grin.

"Which of your supersized egos are we talking about?"

Leaning in, he nuzzled her nose. "All of them."

20

BAST WAS a firm believer in boundaries.

It had taken him a while to get there—only last year he was delivering unwanted groceries and sex life advice to Reid—but he liked to think he'd established some rules with how to deal with people, especially his father.

It was why he'd finally called his dad on his bullshit attitude toward Reid. Henri Durand hadn't liked it one bit. His whole life post-professional hockey was dedicated to ensuring his legacy lived on in his sons. And while Bast was happy to go along with that because it aligned with his own goals, he now understood that his father's influence was unhealthy. The man had played Reid and Bast off one another for years, and now that they'd pushed back against that narrative, the relationships between all of them were much better.

Except he had just let Pepper into a dirty little secret: he was still kind of pissed at Reid for how things had gone down during that on-ice clash last December—and maybe more. He shouldn't feel this way. While he understood that the accident that broke Bast's wrist had brought them closer, it had uprooted stuff that Bast thought he was over.

Their childhood competitiveness that turned dark for a while.

After the injury, Reid, the most taciturn, moody guy on the planet had wanted Bast to shout at him, tell him he was a dick, unload all the trauma.

While Bast wanted to keep calm and carry on. Just a different way to approach things. So there was the niggling sense that something wasn't quite settled between them. Bast would have preferred to let their play on the ice and the same team bring them closer.

His father had called at least three times since Bast had left Chicago. In olden days, that would have been thirty times, so the push-back against the assholery was working a treat. Bast decided to put the old man out of his misery and call him back.

"Hey, Dad."

"Don't 'hey, dad' me! What the hell is going on?"

"Not much. I'm taking a few days away from the city to relax."

His father sputtered like a stroke was imminent. "Relax? You need to be in physio every day, and if you can't be playing, you need to be in the gym, keeping up your fitness levels."

Bast had some ideas about that, all of them involving Pepper under and over him. He was right where he needed to be.

"Dad, what did I tell you about trying to Monday night quarterback my career? There's nothing you or I can do right now. I need to rest and think about next steps—"

"Na-uh. That's the last thing you should be doing. There's too much reflection in the game these days. Psychologists and well-being shit—we had none of that back in my day, and we all put in the best years of our lives."

Said the man who retired when his body collapsed at thirty-one, was three times married, and about to put a ring on his fourth bride.

"It's okay to think for a bit, Dad." Maybe even talk about stuff like he just had with Pepper. That had felt ... good. Maybe he should be more honest with Reid, like she suggested.

"What do you have to think about?"

"Stuff. My career. What's next."

Henri exploded. "You're twenty-six years old! This is just a hiccup. What do the docs say?"

"A month to recover, then another month to six weeks of rehab. It's a sprain so not the end of the line, but my wrist is weak since the break."

"And it'll stay that way if you don't get into rehab. Now's not the time to turn soft, son."

"I'm not—it's just there's always the possibility it won't ever be completely right." Having to endure another extended break away from the game while the sword of doubt hung over his head terrified him.

"You're going to be fine," his father insisted. "I don't want to hear any of the negative talk."

Right. No losers in the Durand family.

His father moved on quickly. Anything to do with "feelings" made him uncomfortable. "I can't believe Calhoun has his daughter in that job. What the hell is that about?"

There it was again, the beast in his chest. "It was an accident, Dad."

"She shouldn't have been there."

"I have to take some responsibility here. I was kind of preoccupied."

"It's not your job to get out of the way of the freakin' mascot, Bast. And what the hell was going on at that press conference? Sure, I've wanted to punch a journo or two in my day, but pick your battles. And defending that chick after she fucked over Gallagher's career?"

"You don't know anything about that." Neither did he, but right now, he trusted Pepper more than Gallagher. "Could we talk about anything else? How's Shona?"

"Driving me nuts. But a woman planning a wedding will always be as bad as a chick on the rag." *Jesus, Dad, did female equality and basic respect really pass you by?* Before Bast could push back, his father spoke again. "You ready to stand up for me?"

Bast rubbed the bridge of his nose. "I can't believe you're going for a big ceremony." Most people in his dad's position would go a little more low-key.

"Shona wants a big day. You know how women get."

"I was best man at your last wedding. Maybe you should ask Reid." Who would tell him where to go. Reid had eliminated the toxic elements from his life and only spoke to Dad when absolutely necessary.

"What's the deal, son? You don't want to see your old man happy?"

"It's not that—"

"Because you don't always find the right woman on the first try. You'll know when it happens. Thunderbolt."

"Fourth time's the charm, I suppose."

His father sighed. "I know you're not in a good place right now. Too much time to think over the last year, and now a few more months to dwell on it? Not good for you. Better find yourself something to occupy your thoughts. A hobby. A woman. You haven't been yourself since Christina."

"Marina. And I don't need a woman, Dad. I just need some peace."

Henri made a noise of blatant disagreement.

"Right," Bast said. "Signing off now."

"Think about the wedding. We're doing it in Montreal."

"Okay, Dad." He hung up.

Henri wasn't the easiest person to get along with, and Bast sympathized with every woman who'd taken the plunge with him. At his heart, his father was desperate for the adulation he no longer got in hockey and had replaced that with seeking affection in all the wrong places.

Was that what Bast would be like once he'd left the game behind? Looking to substitute the high of hockey with the buzz of a new relationship? Was that what he'd been looking for that night in Jimmy's Tap?

He scrolled through his messages. There was one from Gwen, so he called her back.

"Hey, Gwennie, how are things?"

"Bast! You didn't have to call. I imagine everyone wants to talk to you. Are you okay?"

"Yeah, just laying low for a while. How's my girl?"

"She's sleeping with her teddy bear. The game took a lot out of her, and she was worried about you. How are you? Really?"

He took a deep breath. "Feeling a bit down, to be honest. The great comeback didn't go quite how I planned, and now I'm not sure what the next steps are." He leaned back on the bed. "I can't believe I'm moaning about this to you."

Gwen chuckled. "It's fine! This must be quite the blow. And poor Rowdy, too—though maybe you're not ready to hear that."

That made him laugh. If she only knew. "Nah, I agree. People were pretty hard on poor Rowdy. But all is forgiven."

"Oh, that's good to hear. Cecy is a huge fan, especially when she heard he was a she."

Look at that. Rowdy with her own fan base.

"I could set up a meet, if she'd like. If I'm gonna be replaced in her affections, I'm happy that it's Rowdy doing the replacing."

Gwen gushed that he could never be replaced—exactly what he needed to hear—and they finished the call with promises to connect when he returned to Chicago.

21

"Earth to Pepper?"

She looked up to find Bast with the remote in hand pointed at the screen. The Netflix carousel was up, and he was obviously asking her something while she'd been daydreaming about all the wicked things he'd done—and encouraged her to do.

"Say 'gain?"

He smiled. "Any preference for your viewing? Looks like it's already logged in on Reid's account."

She took a closer look, her eye immediately drawn to Reid's Watch Next list. Pretty sexy stuff. *365 Days, Sex/Life, Lady Chatterley's Lover* ...

"Didn't figure Reid as a classic lit kind of guy," she said.

"I think he's a gardener-bangs-the-lady-of-the-house kind of guy. Like us all. What's this *365 Days* about?"

"Some sex fest." Which she had watched more than a few times last summer, especially that montage on the yacht.

"Any good?"

She shrugged. "Heard it's kind of plotless. Man kidnaps

woman, takes her to a remote location, bangs her senseless, and makes her fall in love with him."

Only then did she realize that it sounded like the plot of *this* movie, the one she was living.

At least that last part would never happen. "Or so I hear. I haven't seen it."

"Cool, let's watch it."

Damn. She should have said she'd already watched it, but the thumbnail was super sexy and she didn't want to admit it. Even after what they had done together, she was still shy. Now she was going to have to sit there squirming while Massimo banged Laura on every surface of his super yacht.

"Better get some snacks in." He moved to stand, but she jumped up first.

"Let me! Popcorn? Chex mix?" *Me?*

"Sure, whatever you can find. I'm off my diet."

About ten minutes later she was back with fresh-popped popcorn, the salt n' vinegar Pringles she'd bought at the general store, a bowl of Lays (baked ones, which was probably a Reid thing—she'd heard he was meticulous about his diet), and a fun-sized bag of Twix (that must be Kennedy's influence).

"Oh, and we need drinks. What do you want?"

"Maybe we should open some wine? Think I saw a nice Pinot on the rack."

She used the rabbit corkscrew to open the bottle while Bast grabbed glasses. He poured the wine into one of the large bulbs before stuffing a handful of popcorn in his mouth. "Shit, this is good stuff. I always forget how good it tastes."

"The no-popcorn regimen? Is it really so hard to be a hockey playing superstar?"

He narrowed his eyes at her teasing. "I wanted to be as fit as possible for my return. Took a leaf from Reid's book. Now he's the one who's eased up—all Kennedy and Bucky's influence—and I'm watching everything that goes into my body."

"Who's Bucky?"

"Reid and Ken's dog. About a year ago, they rescued him together from the lake."

"Oh, that rings a bell. It was all over social media."

He took out his phone and scrolled through his photos. "Here he is. Such a dork."

An ugly-cute mutt, wearing a Santa hat, grinned at the camera.

"Aw, he's adorable."

"Yeah, he is. Funny how people can be changed by the simplest things."

"What do you mean?"

He looked thoughtful. "Reid's life was turned upside down when he met Kennedy. They rescued Bucky, and he needed someone to look after the pathetic little pup while he was away, so Ken moved in. Changed everything for him." He shook his head. "I've only been trying to get him to lighten up for years."

Ah, she understood—or thought she did. "He started with the Rebels last season, yes? So all this change coincided with coming aboard."

He nodded. "Yeah, for a while there, he was always the new guy on every team. Scrabbled his way up from the AHL, was shunted around a lot, didn't really stick anywhere. But he always made it seem like it suited him. He didn't want to get too close to anyone or anything until—" His shrug was filled with hurt. "I'm thrilled he has Ken and Bucky, thrilled that he's more open now. But we wasted years when we could have been, I dunno, closer. He was kind of a jerk for the longest time. Not that he's Mr. Sunshine now, but he's improved."

"You wished he'd changed for you. Instead it took a woman and a cute dog for him to get his hockey stick out of his ass."

He looked relieved and maybe a touch embarrassed that she'd figured it out. "I sound like a jealous idiot. He's happy, and he truly deserves it."

Sounded like there were some unresolved issues. "Has he apologized?"

"For breaking my wrist? Yeah, he feels terrible."

Bast had hinted that Reid was a bully to Bast when they were kids. His behavior in defending her was starting to make more sense. She supposed she should be glad to be the beneficiary of that protective streak, but she hated that it might remind him of a painful period in his life.

She moved closer and lay a hand on his arm. "Sounds like the feelings of hurt and resentment remain, about the wrist injury and some things from your childhood. And the fact it coincided with a rise in his fortunes and a dip in yours has got to be tough." If she recalled correctly, Bast was supposed to head to the Olympics on the Team Canada roster but missed out. Reid went in his place and came home with the gold. Ouch.

"I forgave him. For everything."

"Okay."

He leveled a serious gaze at her, and for a moment, she wondered if he'd rebuff her efforts to dig deeper. When he spoke, it was measured.

"It's been a rough year for me, but I don't want Reid to feel guilty about it. He's got everything he ever wanted, and me whining about my injury is just going to bring him down."

"That's generous of you. But for your own well-being, you might want to be more open with him instead of bottling it up."

"There you go being all wise again." He passed a glass to her, then picked up his own. "To the Great Unfestering."

"Ugh, sounds awful, but let me try this wine and—hmm, this is good!" She took another sip. "To the Great Unfestering. May we all feel so unburdened."

"Okay, serious talk out of the way. Now for the bang-fest!" He winked at her and grabbed the remote.

Damn. She would have to keep her mouth full of popcorn and try not to get turned on.

"So, could you sit over here?" He patted the seat on the other side of him.

"Er, okay." She moved around him, her legs brushing against his, and took a seat.

"Just need you closer to the best arm so I can try my sneaky make-a-pass move." He stretched his right arm over her head and gave a fake yawn. When the arm came down again, it was along the top-edge of the sofa behind her.

"Smooth," she said, enjoying this new vibe between them. He was so easy to be around when he wasn't spitting mad at her. "But telling me about your move kind of defeats the purpose of the sneakiness, doesn't it?"

"Just keeping you in the loop, sweetheart. I'm all about the consent." He pressed play and put the remote down on the coffee table.

Oh, right, the movie. *The sexy movie.*

She could handle this. After all, she'd had real-life almost-sex with the guy beside her, and she handled that like a boss. Told him how good she felt, how hot it was. Nothing had to happen here. Once they dug themselves out or the snow thawed—whichever came first—they could move on with their lives, no fuss nor muss. She would take some lovely memories with her ...

She shifted on the sofa, and to cover, she reached for her wine and took a healthy gulp just as Bast made a funny noise in his throat.

"What?"

"This guy is the worst."

"He is?" She knew he was—the guy was a Mafioso kidnapper with a very violent streak who was about to do any number of illegal things to the heroine in the name of obsession—but she wanted to hear Bast's opinion.

"That 'baby girl' business is ridiculous. And this dialogue is terrible."

Agreed. Bast grabbed some popcorn and munched on it.

Twenty minutes later, they'd come to some seriously sexy shower business.

"You okay?"

She turned to find him staring at her. The wine was gone, the popcorn reduced by 90%, and Pepper was tensely waiting for Laura to realize just how much trouble she was in.

Kind of like the heroine in this room.

"Yeah, I'm fine."

"Would you rather we didn't watch this?"

She chuckled nervously. "It *is* kind of stupid."

"But sexy."

"But sexy."

He smiled. "Only you don't want sexy right now, do you?" He was staring at her with serious intent.

"I-I wouldn't say that."

"It's just you're sitting so stiffly over there, and I'd much rather you were sitting stiffly over here."

She edged closer, then realized she was quite close already. Any more and she'd be on top of him.

"Yeah, I can't stop thinking of us either," he murmured. "Come here."

Us. Why did that sound so good?

Her breathing had picked up, and she realized that it was always like this around him. This effect he had on her was electrifying.

"Bast—"

"Just want to hold you. Is that okay?" He picked up the remote and muted the movie. Who needed that when she was living her fantasy right here?

Her answer was to sink into his side. He put his arm around her. And it felt nice. More than nice.

It felt like she was wrapped in a cozy sweater, except the sweater smelled like citrus-cedar wood body wash and had an impressively hard chest, which she knew because her hand was splayed against it, her fingertips sizzling at how unyielding his body was.

So the sweater analogy was all wrong. This wasn't cozy. It was a potent combination of sexy and comforting, and God knew she needed that. Both those things.

He was suddenly closer, and she was finding it hard to catch her breath. Her mouth had gone dry, and she could feel a hot puff of air—his air—on her lips.

The same lips he was currently stroking, ever so gently, as if worried he'd spook her.

Oh, that super yacht had sailed. She was spooked, but also frozen with lust.

"Bast," she whispered, her voice sounding like desperation in audio form.

That word was permission, an invitation to cover her mouth with his.

Which he did.

It felt so good to be kissing him again. He tasted good. No, better than that. He tasted right, and she didn't know if that was more wishful thinking on her part. Anything to justify why this was okay.

What had happened between them in the last twenty-four hours, all the hunger, should be enough to tell her this was a bad idea.

Yet she couldn't pull away. Perhaps it was how he was able to temper the hunger with a shocking gentleness. The kiss vibrated through her, not in a sexual way, or not only that, but in a way that told her he cared.

What an incredibly desperate, stupid conclusion to draw, but she felt as though she was in no better hands—or hand—right now.

She pulled back, her eyes locked to his, needing a moment to breathe. To assess.

He watched her, all blue-eyed intensity. "Tell me what you're thinking," he finally said.

"That thinking is overrated. And ..."

"And?"

"I want you."

His nostrils flared. He didn't speak. Was that good? Bad?

He seemed to be waiting for her to continue, so she did.

"I'm guessing there are no condoms, but I'm on birth control. An IUD because I wanted to be ready for ..." She trailed off. "But I understand that you barely know me, never mind trust me."

"It goes both ways. What if I told you I had all the check-ups when I came onto the Rebels, and I haven't been with anyone in over a year?"

"That would be interesting information to have. But

would you want to be ..." *Here goes nothing.* She finished in a small voice. "My first?"

He looked a little shell-shocked. Perhaps he'd forgotten their conversation from earlier, but he managed to recover enough to respond.

"I'd be honored, Pepper. But we don't have to do anything at all. I know the close quarters and sexy movies with bad dialogue gives this a certain inevitability, but we don't have to give into it just because the universe is telling us to."

Alarm skittered through her. "Okay, I understand." She moved away, but his arm was still in a lock-grip around her shoulders.

"Not sure you do."

"You think it would be an 'honor' to relieve me of my technical virginity, but neither do you want to fall in line with what the universe is instructing you to do. Got it."

This time she managed to slip his grip and push herself to a wobbly stand.

"Lunch?" Or perhaps it was time for dinner. She may have drunk too much wine, so meals no longer had meaning or set times.

"Oh no, you're not running away from this, Pepper." He grasped her hand and pulled her down, roughly, so she had no choice but to straddle him. All so she wouldn't crash into his arm.

"Bast, I heard what you said."

"And that was me telling you that you shouldn't feel pressured to give into the crazy fucking lust between us. What you don't seem to be hearing is that I would love that. The idea of being buried deep inside you and without a condom—Jesus, have you the slightest clue how hot that thought is?"

She couldn't respond, so he answered for her.

"Very, exceptionally, God-tier hot, Pepper. But I've been kind of jerkish and pushy and in-your-face these last couple of days, and that's not what you need. You need someone to guide you through it gently. Not sure I can be gentle with you. Not sure I even know how to do gentle. Not when I want you so badly."

Oh, wow. That was quite the declaration. While he spoke, she'd been holding her body above his thighs, desperate not to connect. But now she felt herself lowering to meet him and shifting forward a touch.

"I don't need gentle, but you might need gentle yourself."

"I—" He dipped a quick glance to his arm in a sling. "Maybe? But I want it to be good for you." His free hand, previously resting lightly on her hip, dug into the flesh there, then moved down to grip her butt and squeezed. That move brought her closer to his erection, so hard and perfect between her thighs.

"It's already been amazing," she said. "How could anything we do not be good?"

And then she kissed him, letting him know with her lips and tongue how much she needed this. Whatever he could give her. In a day or so, the snow would clear, and they'd be back in the real world.

But today? She would live in this moment, and for once in her life, count herself lucky.

22

———————

AFTER THE INTIMACIES they'd shared so far, Bast shouldn't have been nervous. Yet the responsibility he felt to make this perfect for her almost overwhelmed him.

"Ah, there it is," she whispered.

"There what is?"

"The reality bump. It's just hit you. Maybe clobbered you over the head."

"Kind of, but not because I don't want to do it. Or you. Because I want it too much. And there's a good chance I'm gonna fuck it up and make your first time the worst time."

She drew back to look at him, those whiskey-hazel eyes narrowed slightly in suspicion. "Good strategy. Play down your skills. Keep the expectations to a minimum."

"That's me. Bast 'Low Expectations' Durand. Keeping women dissatisfied since 2013."

"You lost your virginity when you were ..." She did the math. "Sixteen?"

"Fifteen actually, but that first time—and year—didn't really count because the skills took a while to develop."

"So there *are* skills to speak of?" She ran her hand over

his cheek, a soft gesture that had him leaning in. He was turned on, but happy to talk to her for a while and settle her nerves.

Sure, *her* nerves.

"There are skills. I think you've been on the receiving end of some of them."

That made her blush, which was so delicious it turned him warm all over.

"How did it happen?" At his querying look, she added, "How did you lose your virginity?"

"Georgina Hanigan, in the hockey equipment room at Grenville High."

"With a rope or a stick?"

He chuckled. "Not quite, but it did feel a bit criminal. She was the sister of one of my teammates, and if he'd found out, there would have been hell to pay."

And this woman before him was the sister of another friend. He could see her thinking it over, maybe over-thinking it.

"Connor and I aren't that close. And even if we were, I don't make sex-related decisions based on what other people think or how it affects them. There are only two people in this room. Only two people who matter here. I'm not going to talk to anyone about it, and that includes Connor."

Her expression was one of relief, but maybe something else? A weary acceptance that this would remain a secret between them. Because he'd have to be crazy to tell a soul that not only had he defended this woman from all comers, not only had he whisked her away to keep her safe from the hordes looking to tear her down, but he had also slept with her.

The enemy.

Of course it could be explained with any number of reasons, couldn't it? Forced proximity, a need for body warmth, revenge …

"And if anyone found out, you could just say the cabin fever got to you."

That she was already coming up with the PR narrative pissed him off. Or maybe he was annoyed that she had said exactly what he was thinking.

"You think I need an explanation for this?" He gave her ass an angry squeeze. "Or this?" Moving his hand through her legs, he stroked her sweats-clad pussy.

She closed her eyes and shivered, then opened them again, her stare direct and honest.

"I just want you to have some plausible deniability should it come to that."

Plausible deniability? Was this high school where you ignored whoever you were forced to kiss in a closet for seven seconds of heaven because they wore glasses or something?

"You're really pissing me off, Pepper. You think I wouldn't want to tell the world about what happened here? About how sweet you tasted and how good you are at hand jobs? Okay, maybe not the last thing because that would be very unclassy."

Her tongue darted out to wet her lips. "I'm trying to give you an out in case people ask questions."

"Well, don't! Let me worry about it. Hell, this started out as me trying to keep your private business private, and somehow, it's devolved into you thinking I wouldn't want anyone to know because of what? A stupid accident?"

Never mind that it had crossed his mind for the briefest second. Strangely, this dynamic only turned him on more, accessing the resentful, needful part of him. Blood was pumping to his cock, swelling it to the point of pain.

"It's okay to be mad at me," she said, while she ran a thumb over his bottom lip. "I completely understand."

It felt like she did, though not because of the accident and the rest, but because she knew it tapped into a hidden vein of desire.

"Time you made up for it, then," he muttered.

A slight turn at the corner of her mouth told him she was in on it, though he wasn't entirely sure what "it" was. A joke? A connection unique to this moment? To them?

Christ, that turned him on even more. She supposedly had little experience, yet she'd figured out something he hadn't even realized about himself: He was sick of being the nice guy.

She shifted a touch, enough to remind him that he was harder than he'd ever been for any woman. "How should I start making it up to you?"

"Take that shirt off," he said, low and rough.

Fuck knew how she'd remained a virgin for so long with the way she unveiled that seductress smirk. Gripping the hem of the tee—his Hawks tee—she peeled slowly, revealing pale skin and a flash of lilac lace. Her tits were as spectacular as he'd imagined: smooth, creamy swells spilling over the edges of her bra.

She threw the shirt behind her and let him look his fill while her chest rose and fell on shuddering breaths. A slight squirm of her body reactivated the pulse in his cock.

"Not yet, you witch."

She licked her lips. "Then what?"

"Pop them out of the bra. Show me how pretty they are."

Rolling her shoulders back, she pushed her breasts out and closer. Fuck, his mouth watered with the need to taste, and when she slipped one gorgeous teardrop-shaped mound of flesh from its silken cage, he almost lost his mind.

He moved a hand up her spine, splayed between her shoulder blades to inch her forward.

"Tell me what you need," he murmured, needing to give her agency in this. Needing to slow it the fuck down.

In her eyes, he saw desire mixed with trepidation.

"You can't say anything wrong. I need to know what you want." It was her first time—or would be when he finally drove his cock deep and true—and he needed her complete participation. The anger he felt had faded, and while some friction remained, it was mostly aimed at the world that had failed to appreciate this woman until now.

And that included him.

"Your tongue on ..." She plumped her breast, offering it to his mouth. "Here. Please."

Yes. He flicked his tongue in a tease, then unable to wait longer than three seconds, he blew cool air on her peaked nipple and followed up with a languorous lick. She must have been feeling braver because she squeezed that beautifully formed flesh and fed his greedy mouth.

He spent a couple of long, lovely moments sipping and sucking until her nipple was swollen and she was rocking into his body, her hand curled in his hair.

"Oh," she moaned as he nuzzled his lips past the barrier of her other bra cup and gave her left breast the same treatment. Drawing back, he unhooked her bra and let it fall behind her.

She opened her mouth to speak, then closed it again.

"Tell me," he urged.

"Could we take off your shirt?"

He liked the "we" there. "I'll need your help."

She nodded and together they worked his zipped sweatshirt off his good arm first, then carefully over the brace. She let her hands wander over his chest, and he returned the favor, even getting the fingers of his injured wrist involved. There was pain, but it was so fucking worth it.

She was worth it.

Exploring each other with a slowness that drove him wild, he tried for calm. Had she done this with Gallagher, but he didn't bite? What the hell was wrong with that guy?

He fucked up, that's what. And Bast was here, unwrapping the gift that idiot didn't want.

Instead of making him happy, the thought made him bad-tempered.

"Hey, you okay?" she asked, her hand back to a soothing sweep of his cheek.

"Yeah, just..." He shook his head. "Pissed off at the people who've disrespected you, and that includes this idiot right here."

"You don't have to say that."

"But I do, Pepper. I don't know what happened, but I do see the woman before me. She's kind and generous. Funny and warm. Sexy and real."

She looked a touch shell-shocked, like no one had ever told her any of this. Bast could feel the anger rising again.

"That's so—I don't know what to say."

"Don't say anything. Just be here in the moment with me."

With a nod, she leaned up and away from his dick—no! —and stood.

"What are you doing?" *Get the fuck back here where you belong, woman.*

She was wearing a pair of his sweats, thin ones, rolled over at least three times at her waist, and now she took both hands and pushed them down to her ankles.

Commando. Okay, all was forgiven.

"I don't have any clean underwear," she said, like he cared for the details.

"What a shame." His gaze focused on the neat triangle of curls nestled between gorgeous thighs. He'd already been there, but he couldn't wait to repeat the visit. "Strip me."

Slowly, she pulled on his sweats and removed them, her eyes widening on seeing his cock jutting toward her. She seemed frozen.

"You've already seen it."

"Yeah, and it's still beautiful."

No one had ever called his dick beautiful, but the awe in her voice warmed him through. He patted his thighs. "Back up here, sweetheart."

Straddling him again, she nudged close to his erection and placed both hands on his shoulders.

"This okay?" she whispered.

"Closer."

She moved in, the softness of her curls brushing against his rampant cock.

"Closer," he repeated, but this time he moved a thumb between the cleft and watched as her face transformed with eye-rolling desire. Catching on, she rocked over his thumb, then the extra finger he added, already so wet for him.

"Can I touch you?" she gasped, her hand coasting down his chest heading for home.

"If you don't, I might get very angry."

"Oh, couldn't have that. You're already so mad at me."

He was when this started, though he wasn't sure when or what *this* was. But not anymore. Now, he was just loving the feel of her wrapped around his fingers, the slick evidence of her arousal, the fullness of her ripe body.

Not wanting to examine the change-up in his attitude, he decided that kissing her would be the best way forward out of this quagmire. His lips claimed hers, and she sighed into him, all sweetness and acceptance.

His thumb glanced over her clit, and she jerked. "Oh, I-I can't."

He stopped immediately. "Okay, we don't have to do that."

"No, I mean I don't want to come that way. I've done that, and I need it to happen the other way."

"The other way?"

"Inside me. With you—your cock inside me." She blinked, waiting for him to criticize or laugh, he supposed.

He smiled against her lips. "You can come like this and still come in any other number of ways. Maybe we should give it a shot."

She panted a little as she ground her body into him. "If there's a chance it'll only happen once, I need it to be all the way. This ..." She gave a hard, glorious stroke of his cock. "I need this."

"You'll get it," he said on a groan. "You'll get it so deep, sweetheart, but you can trust me here. I know what I'm doing."

"That's good. I need that. Someone who knows." There was a slight melancholy about that statement. She'd really been screwed over when it came to sex.

"Okay for me to touch you?"

She nodded.

"Get you wet? Or wetter?"

Another nod, accompanied by a gasp as he circled that taut bundle of nerves with his index finger. As a left-hander, he usually stroked a woman with his dominant hand. But having to switch had him thinking on her pleasure more. No rote moves here, all delicious intention.

Continuing, he focused on listening to her body. Before,

he'd partaken of the buffet on offer without too much heed to the nuances. *If you lick it, she will come.* Now, he needed to ensure she was getting the best experience, no rock of sensation left unturned.

Eventually it became too much for her, and her eyes fluttered closed. After a couple of minutes, she made a keening sound and froze, her face overcome with a pleasurable agony he knew very well. Shudders followed while she came down on a long exhale.

"Oh, wow," she said, her forehead leaning against his.

"I think you're relaxed now."

A dreamy smile touched her lips. "Very. But you can't be. This must be torture for you." She moved her wet pussy along the length of his cock. Up, then down.

"You're a quick learner, Tequila Girl."

"And now I want to graduate." Lifting her body, she hovered over him and took him in hand, nudging his cockhead against her opening. "Is this alright?"

"Fuck, yes." Just the sight of her notching him into place, where he needed to be, had him leaking. "Don't stop."

She took him inside her a couple of inches then halted.

He groaned, needing to keep going, but this was her show. Her timetable.

"You okay?" she whispered.

"Never better," he gritted out. True and not true.

She sank down, gloving more of him but still not enough. So tight, her muscles working to pull him deep. He wasn't exactly shrimping it in the dick department, and suddenly he was worried that he might be too much for her.

"Am I hurting you?"

She shook her head, then rocked up in a sensuous slide that trip-wired every nerve ending in his body. Then she stroked down again until he was seated all the way inside her.

Fuck, so good.

Grasping her ass, he encouraged her to ride him into a steady rhythm while her gorgeous tits bounced close to his mouth.

"Yeah, that's it. That's perfect. You're perfect."

Encouraged, she continued sliding up and down, with each stroke pulling him deeper and gripping him harder. Watching her expressions as he fucked her was a revelation. A combination of softness and pride, like she'd finally figured out what it was all about.

He was so glad to give it to her.

That familiar sizzle was building in his balls with an added spark of "fuck yeah, I've missed this." But there was something else. Something new.

Not just for Pepper.

He'd promised that this wouldn't be a one-shot deal for her, so he thumbed between her folds and found her clit. There it was, that perfect shimmy, and this time, he was inside her, so it felt amazing as her muscles milked him, triggering his release and wringing every last drop from him.

Jesus.

She slumped against him, or maybe he slumped against her. Either way, they were collapsed in a joint heap of sated pleasure. Her chin rested on his shoulder, and he stroked her hair while feathering light kisses at her temple.

"How we doing?"

A little moan of satisfaction was his reward. She burrowed into his neck more, then shot up suddenly.

"Oh, I'm sorry. I should have asked if it was good for you."

He chuckled. "Sure, that's nice of you, but you aren't obliged to ask. You could, like all guys, assume it was amazing."

She grinned. "You mean, assume I'm so damn good at The Sex that afterglow check-ins are unnecessary?"

"Exactly. I asked if you were okay because it was your first time, but really I don't care. I'm a guy, and like all guys, I'm a hundred percent positive that I rocked my girl's world."

Her grin stretched wider. "Hell, she's lucky to even get a look at your dick, never mind touch it."

"True, the lady is blessed," he agreed, which sent them both into a laughing fit. After a couple of moments, they quietened down and settled into looking at each other. Her cheeks were a rosy blush, her eyes a burnished gold, those lips of hers still pink from his kisses.

"Seriously though, how are you?"

There was that gorgeous smile, still shy but a lot more knowing. *I did that for her.* "I'm wondering what all the fuss was about."

He swatted her ass. "Oh, are you now?"

Her giggle lit up the room. "Yeah. I mean sex is good and all, but—"

He kissed her again, drawing her in deep. "But?"

"But nothing. I don't want to joke about it. Thank you."

"Any time." He blinked as a movement caught his attention over her shoulder. "So, don't look now, but we have company."

A statement guaranteed to make anyone look. She squealed with joy on seeing the damn chipmunk peeking in through the window.

"Chester, you naughty boy! Cover your eyes."

And you know something, Chester did as he was told.

23

AFTER A SHOWER, because sex without a condom was sort of sticky, Pepper checked out her body in the mirror. Fully devirginized at last.

She erupted in a naughty giggle. So *that* was what it was all about. She had sort of hoped she could shrug and think "whatever."

That it wouldn't feel so important. That she wouldn't feel so different.

But it did. *She* did.

Of course she could never tell Bast that. He'd think she was clingy or wanted a relationship, neither of which applied here. It was just nice to have it over with without *feeling* like she'd had it over with. He'd been so patient, so in tune with what she needed. Her hope was that she'd given him something in return. She had the impression he was in a weird place with his injury and career, and that sex helped him feel closer to the god he assumed he was.

Her phone buzzed with a text from ... oh my God.

KENT

You okay?

She shot a quick look around, searching out cameras. Did her ex know that she'd finally thrown off the shackles of her virginity, a job he was incapable of doing because cheating in his sport was more important than the woman he'd supposedly loved?

KENT

I saw what happened in Chicago. Just checking in. Here if you need to talk.

More likely he'd seen the new bout of negative publicity, and he was worried she'd feel an urge to be more vocal in her own defense. These hockey players were something else.

She checked the Mascot Mania text thread, which had gone on without her.

MUSTANG (DETROIT)

Heard that reporter is gonna sue Durand for assault.

TOMMY TOGA (NEW YORK)

It was barely a tap. Jesus, Deacon wouldn't last long in a game. Or a mascot costume.

TRIGGER (NASHVILLE)

Can dish it out but can't take it. Still, sucks for Durand, though. All because he was defending our Pepper.

This was not good. She'd practically ruined Bast's career, now she'd left him open to a lawsuit?

She headed out to the kitchen, where she found Bast toeing off snow-covered boots. The air was a little chill, which meant the sliding door to the patio must have been open for a few seconds.

"You went outside? Again?"

"Yeah, just to get some air."

"You really shouldn't be doing anything with your wrist in such poor shape. What if you slip out there?" Her gaze was drawn to the sliding door—and the furry being huddled on a cleared path outside the glass.

"Is that Chester ... eating something?" She moved closer and sure enough, the little guy was munching on what looked like a cashew. "Where did he—" Her mouth dropped open. "You fed him? After telling me not to?"

Bast was moving his boots to a mat in the mudroom. "I figured he worked up an appetite while creepily watching us banging."

"Uh, he had no idea what we were doing."

Bast grinned. "Oh, he knew. I could see his beady little eyes lighting up."

"I think it's sweet that you fed him." A closer look at the patio revealed more than she'd first seen: a maze of criss-crossed paths. "He has a little play area. So cute."

Bast stood beside her. "Just making it easier for him to come and go."

"You and Chester, BFFs."

He snorted.

She leaned against the counter. "So, I just heard from the mascots that Curtis Deacon is making a fuss. That he might sue you."

Bast had opened the fridge and was rooting around.

"Hey, did you hear me?"

He looked up. "Deacon. Fuss. Sue. Yep."

"Aren't you worried?"

He straightened. "It'll blow over. My agent says I need to apologize, and we're good."

That sounded manageable. "So you're going to do that?"

"Nope."

"Bast, you cannot get sued because of me!"

Quick as a flash, he backed her against the table. "That was my call. You can't take on the blame for *that* as well, you guilt hog. And I won't be apologizing because I was right and he was wrong."

"But—"

He kissed her, working his mouth over hers in a way that made her a limp noodle. "But, nothing. Wait, did you say you heard about Deacon from the mascots? Plural?"

"Yeah, we have a text group. They're a good bunch of people. They have my back."

That seemed to amuse him. "So, do you guys talk about the players?"

"Of course we do, especially the ones who are total dicks. Or crash into the mascots and make it all about them."

"Okay, I asked for that." He gave her a quick kiss. "I'm starving, so let's make dinner. And then after that, I have a surprise for you."

Dinner she could get on board with, but she wasn't a fan of surprises.

"Is my brother coming to visit?"

He frowned. "Uh, no. It's a good surprise. I promise you'll like it."

She had no choice but to take him at his word, and she wished now that she hadn't brought up her brother because that reality was impinging on the fantasy. Had Kent talked to Connor and found out she was with Bast? Is that why he texted?

"So what's for dinner?"

"Burgers. We have ground beef that's thawed—thank you—and some seasoning, Worcestershire sauce and the like. And luckily you had the foresight to grab those burger buns at the store."

"That's me, all the foresight. How can I help?"

"We have tomatoes and onions. Maybe some sort of salad?"

She could manage that. She started slicing tomatoes, and together they worked side by side, initially in companionable silence.

"About Connor," she said after a short time.

"What about him?"

"How friendly are you, really?"

"We knew each other in college, and we text each other a couple of times a month. The usual trash talk. Meet up when we're in the same town." He slid a glance her way. "Back in college, he mentioned you a few times. But I still had no idea who you were when we connected in Jimmy's Tap."

Connected. "And I didn't realize you guys were friends. Connor and I aren't that close."

He nodded. "Sibling relationships can be tricky."

"You and he seem—I dunno—different."

He chuckled. "Wondering why we're friendly, I suppose."

"I didn't mean to imply that you shouldn't be. College friendships, especially around sports, are sacrosanct. I get that."

"Sure, college makes for tight, fast friendships. Maybe not the deepest, but you're usually working together toward a goal. Brothers on a team, that kind of thing. It creates its own ecosystem. But that wasn't why we were friends."

She stopped chopping and turned to him. "Then what was it?"

He paused for a moment, as if carefully choosing his words. "He needed someone to temper his worst impulses. Kind of like my brother."

She blinked. "You were his friend so you could—cure him of being a jerk?"

"Sounds like it didn't work if he's ordering you around and sending stupid texts about your misfortune." He grimaced. "Forget I said that."

"He did? What did he say?"

"Nothing. It's just a gif that's doing the rounds."

"Show me."

"Pepper—" But she'd already grabbed her phone and was searching it out. There was only so much Bast could protect her from. She needed to face this kind of thing head on.

"Oh. Well, it's funny except for the look of pain on your face. That's just awful." She flinched as the hit came around again. This was never going to go away.

He took the phone out of her hand. "How about we not watch that anymore? I'd rather not hear this blow to my career with a Godzilla roar soundtrack."

"You're forgiving me because of the great sex, aren't you?"

He grinned. "Sex *always* puts me in a forgiving mood, but no. I forgave you before that. Well, sometime between the oral sex and the cheeky feel-up while I was trying to sleep."

"Hey!" She thumped him in his good arm. "I was the one trying to sleep."

Quick as a flash, he pinned her to the counter, though

she could have resisted. The man had only one good arm after all.

But resistance wasn't in her future. She just wanted to lose herself in these good vibes for as long as they lasted.

He inclined his head until his lips were an inch from hers. "Your hands. My cock. So hot."

His lips nuzzled hers. Kissing him back was all well and good when sex was the end goal, but this seemed different. This was cozy and a little too domestic.

"I like that you're here," he said, mind-reader extraordinaire. "I know you don't want to be, but I like it. We both need this."

He held her gaze, urging her to agree, perhaps. Sparks lit across her skin just from the way he looked at her.

It had never been like this with Kent. Sure, there'd been attraction—he was handsome, well-built, fit, and she enjoyed spending time with him. But he'd also been critical. Hinting about giving up her job, to get ready for all the kids he wanted (except he seemed to have forgotten the important part of the equation—the production of sperm in the vessel's presence!). And while she assumed kids were something she wanted eventually, she wasn't quite ready to give up her job just yet. But that was the lot of a hockey WAG. If Kent was traded to another team, a different city, she would have had to follow him.

She'd been fully prepared to do that at one time. Subsume her entire life to her husband. It was what her mother had done with her dad, and when he said he had no intention of changing up that dynamic, she decided to call his bluff.

This was her time, Mom had told him. *Let's travel and see the world.*

But her father placated her mom as long as she could

take it, then failed to live up to her expectations. Pepper hated to see her father hurting, but she understood her mother's side of it. When a man's career came before his family, or the woman he supposedly loved, it was hard to see a way through that.

That's what Kent had done. Put himself and his career first with his PED use.

"Hey, what's happening here?" Bast tilted his head.

"Just a flurry."

He looked pleased that she remembered. She shouldn't have done that call back, which implied a more complex history between them than they truly had. Yet it felt that they'd known each other for a long time. Might even be capable of becoming friends one day.

"Flurry be gone," he whispered.

"Flurry be gone."

24

THE BURGERS WERE A HIT. It would have been nice to grill them outside. But the charcoal grill—currently stored in the garage—would've taken too long to heat up. As it was, they made do with pan frying them and toasting the buns on a pancake griddle.

Bast had done his best mixing the ground beef with Worcestershire sauce and seasonings, but Pepper had to take over to form the patties, as that was definitely a two-handed job. Together they worked as a team to make dinner, and it was more fun than she'd had in forever.

After dinner, he took her by the hand and pulled her upright. "About my surprise."

"Right, the surprise." She'd hoped it was forgotten. "Is it … sexy?"

"Definitely."

Okay. "Do I have to strip?"

"Absolutely. But first, wait here while I check on some-thing." He headed to the mudroom and put on his boots.

"You're going outside again?"

"Just for a second. Gotta check on my boy, Chester." He

switched on an outdoor light, slid the patio door open, and stepped out, closing it behind him.

She watched him trudge through one of the paths he'd shoveled earlier—how had he done all that work with one good hand?—and vanish around the corner of the house. The lights shone, illuminating several feet of nothingness. There was a lake somewhere out there, but she couldn't see it, not with the snow blanket covering the immediate view.

He came back in, dusting snow off his jeans. "Okay, there's an outfit on the bed. You need to change into it and come back here. You've got two minutes."

"I have to change clothes?"

He held up his phone, a timer already counting down. "Don't make me chase you, Pepper. I'm fast and—well, you'd probably like what I do when I catch you, so that might not be the best threat I could come up with. Just hurry, okay?"

Alright, she'd play along. On the bed lay a fluffy bathrobe and a hat. She recognized the headwear—it was the beanie Bast wore the night she met him in Jimmy's Tap, the one she'd made fun of.

"You've got one minute," he called out.

Okay! Quickly, she stripped and put on the robe, then the hat.

"Fifteen seconds!"

When she returned to the kitchen, the timer was just going off.

"Lucky, but I'll allow it." He took a long hard look at her, his gaze straying to the hat. He had also changed into a winter coat that came to mid-thigh. He was clearly naked underneath. "Nice hat."

"I'm always cold. Hence the headwear."

He grinned. "Tough to be you. Okay, you can wear these snow boots."

"Are we going swimming in the lake? Some sort of polar plunge thing?"

"God, no. Boots, Pepper. I also have socks."

She slid her feet into the boots, which were a size too big, but the thickness of the socks helped.

"Ready?"

"No."

Adding a fur-flapped hat to his head, he chuckled and opened the sliding door. "Come on, sweetheart. I won't steer you wrong."

She took his offered hand and stepped out into the night. It was cold but not nearly as bad as it had been yesterday. Snow crunched under her feet and was a little slick in spots; luckily the boots had a good grip and Bast's hand wrapped around hers kept her steady. The thaw was already setting in, with mini-icicles dripping and forming along the edges of the patio, like a gallery of oddly shaped penises. Just seeing that—the thaw, not the ice penises—pinched her heart with sadness: this was about to end, the snow globe world she was living in was melting.

They turned a corner and came to a separate patio, a spotlight illuminating what must be Bast's surprise. Steam whorls rose into the night, creating a magical, misty haze.

"A hot tub?"

"Yep. It took about five hours to heat it, but it should be perfect now. The key is getting in quickly."

The tub was surrounded by slate and recessed in the ground. A cover lay to one side, along with the snow Bast must have brushed aside to clear a path. This is what he'd been working on earlier.

"So how do we do this without breaking our three remaining good wrists?"

"Teamwork." He stripped off his winter coat and hung it

on a hook, removed his wrist brace and did likewise, then pulled off his shoes. There he stood, gloriously naked, except for his fur-flapped hat. She couldn't help her giggle.

"Really?"

"You and the hat, it's quite the look. Wish I had a camera."

"Pepper ..." he warned.

Okay, okay. If he could be brave, not that a body like his needed confidence ... she turned away and slipped out of the robe. Was her ass a better view than her breasts? Who knew and at this point, who cared? When she turned back, he ran an appreciative gaze over her.

"Gorgeous," he whispered. "Off with the boots, it'll just be for a second. Best if you get in first."

She did as he asked then stepped into the tub, one foot at a time. The temperature was perfect. Reaching up, she curled her fingers around his uninjured hand and guided him into the tub.

Together they sank down onto the ringed seat with moans of pleasure.

"This is so good," she murmured as the heat of the water warmed her bones and stripped away some of the heaviness in her shoulders.

"Right?" He sank back and closed his eyes for a moment.

Unable to resist, she watched his handsome face as his dark lashes created a half-moon over his cheeks. The rising steam had already dampened the hair peeking out from his hat, reminding her of that first night they met.

Opening his eyes, he caught her looking. Embarrassed to be so obvious, she shifted her gaze to a bucket near his head. "You brought beers?"

"Always be prepared. Want one?"

"Yes!"

He reached up and grabbed one, already open because apparently, he was a Boy Scout when it came to hot tub session prep. He passed a bottle over.

"What should we toast to?" he asked.

She looked up at the night sky, the bright crescent moon, and exhaled. "To hiding away."

"To hiding away." He clinked her bottle and took a sip of his beer. "Eventually we have to come out of hiding, though."

"Right. But for now, this bubble is the only place I want to be."

"I'm liking it here, too." He placed the bottle at the side of the tub. "Come over here." His voice had changed.

"Why?"

"Why do you think?"

"Because you're getting a thigh cramp, and you need me to massage it out?"

"I need a massage alright, but not in my thigh. Besides, you owe me."

She rolled her eyes. "Thought we were even."

He shook his head. "Not even close, but not because of what you think. This isn't some payback for what happened on the ice two nights ago. You'll never owe me for that."

"Th-then for what?"

"For the last eight months of temptation. For being the cause of my wet dreams and nonstop hard-ons. For just being here and driving me into a frenzy."

He ran his hand under the water and stroked something. It was very clear what that "something" was. "For this."

He had been thinking of her all this time? "I can't be held responsible for any of that. You have to take some of the blame."

"Do I?"

She expected he would grin then. Like this would be a good point in the proceedings to showcase charming, devil-may-care Bast, the man who flirted and teased but was never serious.

But he didn't grin, and as the moment extended, it transformed into something deeper. Significant.

"What do you need?"

"I need you to ease the ache, Pepper."

She slid across the water and knelt on either side of him. "What about my ache?"

As soon as it came out of her mouth, she knew she meant more than the physical. She needed her soul to be soothed, her pain to be salved.

"I think more teamwork is needed."

She liked when he thought of them that way. Escaping the city together like Bonnie and Clyde, cooking in the kitchen, giving each other pleasure. These things could have happened alone, but together, they made it easier. It was what she'd always hoped for in a partner.

He was already hard beneath her, his cock nudging between her legs. He moved one hand around to brace her against him. Tighten the hold.

"Hold on a second," he murmured. "Let me look at you."

"In this silly hat?"

"It's a toque."

"A what?"

He smiled. "It's Canadian for a wooly hat, like a beanie."

"You were wearing it when we met."

"And you made fun of it, some crack about my grandma knitting it."

She dragged her lower lip between her teeth. "And you said a sick little girl gave it to you."

He rubbed soothing circles on her back. "Cecy. She's a

ten-year-old hockey fan from Chicago. She had leukemia, and I visited her a few times. Her grandma, Gwen, gave me the hat."

That sounded familiar. "Is that the little girl you raised all that money for?"

"I just got the GoFundMe started. The fans did the rest."

"And all you got was this stupid hat."

"Hey!" He pinched her lightly and drew her giggle. "That hat's special to me. I don't let just anyone wear it."

"I'm honored. Maybe I should show you how grateful I am." She rubbed her wet breasts against his chest, the slippery friction divine.

"Don't worry, you'll get your chance." Strangely he wasn't making any moves to forward this into orgasm territory. He seemed content to hold her close, hold her like she mattered. The quiet chill surrounding them made her feel like they were the only two people in the world.

"No one can bother you here, y'know," he whispered. "This is a safe space."

Now that was a lie. Nothing was safe about this. Not his fingertips grazing the side of her breast, nor his chest rising and falling gently, nor his scent curling inside her lungs and making it hard for her to breathe.

"It doesn't feel safe," she murmured.

He tucked a strand of her hair that had fallen from its topknot behind her ear. His hand hovered for a moment, as if he was unsure how to proceed, then his thumb absorbed the tears she hadn't realized were falling.

That care, its unexpectedness, made the tears come faster. She hiccupped like she'd eaten too much too fast, and then she sniffed. "I don't need your sympathy. If anything, I owe you all the care in the world."

A little hyperbolic, perhaps, but she couldn't bear his tenderness toward her right now.

He didn't speak. His thumb was still on her cheek, mopping up the tears, but his eyes had gone dark. She recognized that look. She'd seen it when the cameras did close-ups—somehow they were able to get in close enough to see the whites of his eyes—as he was headed to the blue zone. Like he had a mission.

And she was it.

His thumb brushed her lower lip, which wobbled—whether that was before or after the glide of his thumb-pad against it, she couldn't say. Not that it mattered. What mattered was he was touching her while looking like he wanted to devour her.

Yet he'd chosen not to do that. He still felt hard between her legs, but this connection between them had moved way past the physical.

"Thank you," she whispered.

"For?"

"For being the last guy who should have defended me, yet the first guy who did. You haven't demanded I justify why I'm worthy of that kind of care."

"You don't have to justify a thing, Pepper. I trust that you have your reasons for playing it this way."

Trust. How was it this stranger was the one who took what she'd said at face value when everyone else assumed she'd brought all this on herself?

She inhaled, though her lungs seemed to be on hiatus. "I do have my reasons, but there's also a chance I've made a huge mistake."

25

BAST HAD NOTICED Pepper's melancholy earlier, but the fun times in the kitchen while they'd prepared dinner seemed to cheer her up. It had only been a couple of days since the crash seen around the world, and with the way the press—and the public—were still covering it, it was bound to still bother her.

He knew that feeling, the ache in your stomach when you've made a mistake that people refuse to forget. Part of it was the injury she'd caused him, but more of it was whatever had happened in her past. What had happened with her ex was a millstone around her neck.

"I'm happy to listen, as long as you don't feel like I've cock-duped you into this."

"Cock-duped?" She giggled, the sound a musical tinkle on the cold night air. "Your dick's not that powerful, Durand."

"Take it back."

"Okay, maybe a little. Powerful, that is, not a little dick."

"Thanks for the clarification."

She turned serious again. He didn't want to push her. This was her show.

While she thought about it, he maneuvered her, so she was sitting between his legs, her back to his chest, his chin on her shoulder. Steam rose around them, encouraging them to sweat out their secrets.

He waited, giving her the space to decide how this would play out. Not facing him directly seemed to do the trick. He felt the moment she let go.

"I was living in Denver, in the last year of my degree when Connor was traded to the Diamonds. We hadn't lived in the same city for a while, and we've always had a weird dynamic. Not particularly close, but he would still go out of his way to warn off any guy he didn't like the look of as a potential suitor, the usual big brothers must protect little sisters schtick. Like it was a job."

"He was protective," Bast offered.

"Sure. But it meant I never really dated much, and you can see what effect that had on my sex life."

"So Connor did a good job. I applaud this."

"Oh, shut up."

He pressed his smiling lips to her neck. "Go on, sweetheart."

"Well, all that changed when Connor introduced me to his teammate Kent. Kent's a couple of years older than Connor, had been with the Diamonds for about five years, and Connor really looked up to him. I guess he felt this would be a good guy for his sister, one he could approve of."

"Okay." Kind of feudal, like "let's conjoin these great hockey dynasties," but whatever.

"Kent was just coming back from an injury. A ligament tear in his shoulder, and he had more time on his hands than usual. It was nice, how he wooed me. Long walks, candlelit dinners, full-court press in the romance department."

Bast made a noise of annoyance.

"Really?"

"I can be pissed at the guy."

"You don't even know what happened."

He touched his lips to the silky skin of her shoulder. "He hurt you. It's enough."

That seemed to relax her. "When he heard I wasn't all that experienced, he was pleased. Said that was perfect, and we could take it slow.

"I think I fell for him when he said that because he was so unlike other athletes, guys I'd known in college or Connor's usual friends. Don't get me wrong, he and Connor were alike in that they partied a lot, but I was happy that he was willing to wait. I also kind of put it down to his injury. He was working his way back to form."

That rang a bell. "He was back pretty quick."

He heard her hesitation and the weight of her next words. "Yeah, he was."

Bast's mind ran a million permutations, enough to blow Dr. Strange and his prognosticating out of the hot tub, and he came up with the most likely one.

It was bad and yet it explained so much.

"He was doping?"

She let out a breath and nodded.

Holy shit.

Hockey's attitude to performance-enhancing drugs was generally different than other sports. Doping wasn't as big in the NHL, and that was largely down to how an overabundance of muscle can be a negative in hockey. Grace, athleticism, and stamina were more valued than being totally ripped.

But an injury was a different story. A long time out of the game messed with a guy's mind. It certainly messed with Bast's. Though there were arguments made that if ever there was a time it should be okay to take PEDs, it was during the recovery period. There were even synthetic concoctions that could supposedly evade drug tests.

But it was a fool's game to even risk it. "So he was doing PEDs? For sure?"

"He was careful about it, went through cycles, whatever he needed to do to avoid tests. And the side effects can be tricky. I did research and it scared me. Heart conditions, organ damage, nerve disorders. But he said he had it under control."

Her body had gone stiff, so he tried to relax her by rubbing her arms until she softened again.

"Pepper, I'm so sorry you had to go through that. How long before you knew?"

"Once we were engaged, I told him I was ready to have sex. I thought it would probably be a good idea to make sure we were compatible."

"Smart."

Her chuckle was dark. "It didn't go so well. I thought it was my fault, that my inexperience was showing and I didn't know what to do to please him. He would get angry when he couldn't perform ..." Her blush was furious. "And tell me that I wasn't doing it for him."

Anger flared. What a complete asshole.

"So, that's why you broke up?"

"No—I mean, that would be a pretty shallow reason to break up with someone. I wanted to help him, but one day he yelled at me, and I could tell it was the drugs talking. Making him a different person. I told him to get clean or we were done. I said I'd be with him every step of the way. He promised he would, that it was just temporary while he came back from injury. And when I saw that he couldn't—that he wouldn't—I told his coach."

Wow, what a tough call. He wasn't sure it was the right one, but he wasn't living it like Pepper had. He tried to imagine how Gallagher felt when his fiancée reported him to the team org. Betrayed, of course, but then he remembered that the guy was cheating. Bast had gone through his own issues after injury, but not once did it occur to him to take illegal drugs to speed up his recovery.

"Why didn't you tell Connor or your dad?"

She shrugged. "I didn't want to make them complicit. Either they wouldn't want to do anything—which would have crushed me—or they'd feel a duty to report it—which was a hard burden to place on them. But if I was going to live with that, I needed to have some say in how it would all go down. I was worried he was hurting himself, and if he could get out from under it now, we could move on." Her shoulders hunched, and she turned in his arms. "Maybe it was a mistake."

"Pepper, you did what you thought was best. He made the mistake."

She clearly still had her doubts. "I said I'd help him get through rehab or whatever needed to happen. I wanted to be there for him. He was furious with me, saw it as a betrayal, and that's when I realized it was never going to work. The team org went to bat for him, told me to stay quiet. Even tried to pay me off. I didn't take their money. I just let them craft a narrative that made me look like I screwed him over."

"Sweetheart," he murmured.

Her voice was breathy, heavy with imminent tears.

"My so-called friends, the other WAGs, were talking to

the press, saying I'd broken his heart and that all he wanted to do was reconcile with me, and I refused to take his calls. I couldn't go to the preschool where my internship was without being hounded by the press. They told me it would be better if I took a break. And then I was so stressed that I couldn't finish my degree. The university suggested I take time off because I was failing my classes and ..." Her breath hitched. "It was just all too much. And I couldn't tell my side of it. If he'd cheated on me, I'd shout to the hilltops. But cheating the sport he supposedly loved ... I couldn't breathe a word. He was doing illegal things, and if I talked about them publicly, he could get into serious trouble. Sure, the team knew, but they were happy to cover. He begged me to stay quiet. Even though we weren't together anymore, I still cared for him."

Gallagher had *this* loyalty, and he threw it all away? "But he managed to fuck up his life all by himself."

"That's one way to look at it."

"That's the only way to look at it, Pepper. He's a grown man responsible for his actions. Did you tell him to take drugs?"

"No, but I wanted to help him. I wanted to be a good girl-friend and fiancée, and I think I probably handled it wrong. He was going through some bad stuff, and I wasn't as supportive as I should have been." She added in a lower voice, "All because I was horny."

"What?"

"If I hadn't pushed him to get busy, he wouldn't have had to get mad about not being able to—well, y'know—and it never would have exploded into this problem."

One way to look at it. Wrong, but he wouldn't say that yet. "How did you find out?"

"I came across a pill bottle in his toiletry bag when I was

looking for a bandage. I snooped and looked them up, along with the side effects. It was kind of a relief to know that maybe I wasn't completely terrible at sex, though he still maintained that wasn't it."

Meaning he'd rather blame this beautiful woman for his failings instead of the real culprit. "And you *still* wanted to be the good fiancée?"

Her nose twitched. "I wanted to help."

"But you knew you weren't the problem, right, Pepper? You knew that doing that shit changes a guy, not just physically, but makes him an asshole? Though sounds like he was one already if he's gonna go there."

"I know that."

"Do you? Because it seems to me you're taking on a whole lot of responsibility here. Too much."

She looked like she wanted to believe him, and if there was one thing he would do before their time together was over, it would be to convince her that this worldview of hers was all wrong.

Over. Why did the thought of that fill him with dread? Probably because he liked being hidden away where the world couldn't bother them. Just the two of them, figuring shit out.

She inhaled a steadying breath. "But my life had already gone down this rabbit hole, and there was no returning from it. No internship, no degree, no job. And I couldn't get a new one because one Google search reveals my sordid romantic history."

"Christ, this story does not get better."

She let out a mirthless chuckle. "And then Kent got into a fight in a bar with Dustin Marsh, one of his teammates. He was probably high, but again the team came to his rescue. Except they probably realized something had to be done, they could no longer give him the tap on the wrist, especially as his on-ice performance had gone downhill."

Probably because he was no longer getting the benefit of the PEDs or had come to rely on them too much. Working his ass off would not have been enough to get that needed boost.

"He got dumped into the minors," Bast confirmed with not a little glee.

"It's a wake-up call for him, I hope. I want him to succeed."

"Jesus, you're a saint. He screwed you over. Made you out to be the villain when you were trying to get him healthy. Everyone thinks you cheated on him or somehow broke his heart when really, he's the cheat. A drug cheat."

"What am I supposed to do? Go public with the real reason we broke up? How does that help? I've no doubt he's getting the assistance he needs from his team's org at last. Me blabbing is only going to screw his life over again."

"Yet, your life is a mess in service to his. How is that right?"

"It's not. But two wrongs and all that." She took a breath. "We're not going to agree, but I'm asking you to keep this to yourself."

He let out a low growl of discontent. "You've got to do something, though. A revenge dress like Princess Diana. Or maybe a revenge relationship. With me."

"Use you to show my ex I'm doing just fine without him?"

"I don't mind being used. You can use me all night, every night." He tried to make it sound like a fun, sexy way for her to get some measure of solace here.

When really the idea had him completely bewitched. Just as Pepper herself did.

This could work, right? He was falling for this amazing woman, and now he was trying to come up with ways to be with her back in the real world.

"That's sweet of you to offer," she said, but much to his disappointment, she didn't bite.

"Well, if revenge clothed or naked doesn't float your boat, there's always the name-a-cockroach strategy."

"The what?"

He grinned, while his heart tried to jump out of his chest. He wanted this to continue, and he had no idea how to do that without spooking her.

"You can have a zoo name a cockroach after your ex for Valentine's Day."

Her eyes went round. "You're kidding."

"I am not. Gallagher might have screwed you over, but you've got this in your back pocket."

"Kent the Roach. It has a ring to it."

"Right?" He tightened his grip on her and pulled her in close. "What I'm trying to say is that you don't have to accept the status quo. It's completely up to you how to make the change you want to see. I know that sounds kind of sappy, but I truly believe it."

In fact, he just needed to follow his own damn advice.

Her eyes were soft and shiny. "It doesn't sound sappy at all. Thanks for listening. It means the world."

She kissed him, then, her lips sucking on his in a way that made him lose his mind. He let himself be swept away in the heat of her, the sheer delight this closeness made him feel. The only possible response was hard and hungry, which he indulged in for several soul-searing seconds.

He pulled back. "Is that you saying you're done talking about this?"

"Kind of?"

"So you've figured out the sex as distraction thing pretty quickly."

She giggled, and just hearing her happiness, brief though it might be, filled his soul with joy. He wanted to hear that noise every morning and every night. He wanted to be the one person who made it happen.

"I know! I'm pretty good at it, aren't I?"

"The sex or the distraction?" he murmured as he brushed his lips over hers.

"Oh, both, Durand. Both."

26

PEPPER AWOKE, already aware that the world was different.

Brighter.

She'd told someone about Kent. For the past ten months, she'd held this secret inside her. It had wound her up and twisted her insides, coiled them as tightly as a spool of metal thread. To feel it unravel while she poured her heart out to Bast had been scary, but with each word spoken, her chest loosened and freedom beckoned.

What a gift it was to share your troubles. But no one else could have drawn her out like Bast. He hadn't been pushy about it, but part of her felt he needed to know. So she could put his mind at ease that he hadn't made such a bad decision in defending her.

Or sleeping with her.

If it came out that they were together in any way, he could say that Pepper wasn't as bad as all that. She'd been unfairly maligned. After all, a nice guy like Bast Durand, who could have anyone, wouldn't sleep with a girl who did a fellow hockey player so wrong, would he? No one wanted the world to know they're siding with the villain.

Maybe she was overthinking it. It wasn't as if it mattered. This was just a snowbound fling, nothing more.

And as it would be over soon, she needed to squeeze as much out of it as possible. She lifted her head a few inches from the pillow. God, he was beautiful. Those lovely lashes lying peacefully on his cheekbone, that shock of dark messy hair, the firm lips that healed every hurt.

One eye peeked open. "Morning."

"Morning," she whispered back as she snuggled into his neck.

"Sleep well?"

She exhaled a breath that told him all he needed to know. If it had been any other morning, she would be checking the weather, wondering if there was a chance she could leave today.

"Like a sexed-out lump."

He kissed her temple. "That's good."

It *was* good. All of it.

"I've been thinking," he said.

"Never a good idea."

His lips curved against her forehead. "About that night in Jimmy's Tap."

"What about it?"

"You didn't have to stick around. You knew it was me and that if I knew who you were, I would inevitably have some sort of opinion. But you stayed."

She lifted her head and faced him. "I liked how you made me feel."

"How was that?"

"Like I was worth your time. I should have left the second I figured it out, but you were so charming and direct, and I wanted to feel good for a few minutes. I knew who you were, that it couldn't go anywhere, but for that brief moment when you were blissfully ignorant, it was perfect."

"Yeah, it was," he agreed. "It is."

With his free arm, he pulled her into his body and explored her lips with his. She loved how he kissed, that languorous application of his skillful mouth that built in depth and pressure until it was just this. Them. Nothing else could intrude.

Except her rumbling stomach.

"Hmm, sexy," he murmured, which made her laugh.

A buzzing sound came from the nightstand on his side of the bed. He ignored it, even when it happened again.

"Maybe you should get that."

"It's just Reid or my agent or—"

"A pair of tits," she offered after leaning up to check.

"That description could easily apply to my brother *and* my agent."

She picked up his phone and showed him the screen. "Kylie says hi."

"What—oh, Kylie." He glanced at the X-rated photo on the screen. "She still hasn't apologized."

"For what?"

"Distracting me as I skated off the other night. Kylie and her big tits have a lot to answer for."

"Hmm, about time you accepted her tits' part in all this. So you and she have been texting?"

"O'Malley ran into her in a bar and gave her my number, the dick. I haven't answered. In fact ..." He went into the phone and ... blocked her number.

"You don't have to do that for my sake."

"I know." He smiled as his hand moved beneath the covers and captured her breast. "But I kind of have my good hand full right here."

"Salty or sweet?"

He pretended to think about it. "Both."

She rolled her eyes. "You have to choose one."

"Okay, probably sweet because I love ice cream. I don't think I could live in a world without it. You?"

"Salty. I'm a Pringles salt n' vinegar girl. But I probably should lay off them for a while."

"If that's a way of fishing for compliments about your curves, then I'll bite. Keep eating the chips."

She offered a silent fist pump. "Winter or summer?"

"Winter. A thousand percent."

She looked out the window, at the setting Winter sun, then back at him. "Me, too."

They'd spent the day watching silly action movies ("Nothing sexy," Pepper had insisted, "let's try to finish *something!*"), raiding the pantry (Kennedy had the biggest stash of Japanese KitKats in the Continental US), and playing this or that. He now knew that she would choose chicken over fish, Marvel over DC, mountains over beach, and smarts over wealth.

Now they were lying in front of the fire, living out some "apres-ski fantasy shit" as Pepper had coined it.

"Okay, here's one," he said. "Children or none?"

"You mean becoming parents?" When he nodded, she said, "Children. Definitely."

"Figured as much. You work with kids, so you must be crazy about them."

She got this dreamy expression on her face. He loved that look on her.

"I love watching them figure out stuff and how their little

minds expand when they learn something. It's such a trip to see it. There was one kid I used to work with during my internship who found out the size of dinosaurs—that they were as tall as buildings—and his little face was just the best."

"You miss it."

"I do. But I'm lucky to be able to watch Hatch for a few days a week."

He curled his fingers around hers. "Sounds like the Kershaws are lucky to have you, but it's not your dream, is it? You want to teach. Finish that degree."

"Maybe. It's just—I've lost my mojo."

He shook his head. "Know what that's like. When I was injured last year, I sort of assumed that it was just a bump in the road, something I could overcome with sheer force of will. People like to tell me I've never had to struggle—"

"People?" She raised an eyebrow.

"Okay, Reid. And the press, to a certain extent. Our paths to the NHL were so different that we've always been compared. It looked easier for me, but I still worked my ass off. And this last year was tough. My girlfriend dumped me. My team ditched me. I lost a couple of sponsors. But there were upsides. Closer to Reid, getting to know Ken. And I'm with a new team, which is an amazing challenge because let's face it: the Rebels need me."

"They do," she agreed with a chuckle.

"So, you thinking you've lost your mojo? That's completely understandable. But if you really want to teach little kids, to fill their spongy brains with knowledge purely so you can feel better about yourself—"

"Hey!"

He grinned. "Then you're going to have to pick yourself up, dust yourself off—"

"And start all over again." She was leaning in, watching him avidly.

"Well, maybe not from scratch. But you're not completely alone, Pepper. Anything you need, I'll help."

She ran a finger over his chest. "You've already done so much."

"Right, but we're friends, aren't we?" He liked to think they were more, but Pepper was skittish, given her history with Kent.

"Never thought I'd agree, but the Rebels arena seems really far away."

It did. Going back to that world didn't really appeal. Here it felt like he could fix someone else's problems instead of worrying about his own.

His phone vibrated with a FaceTime call from Gwen. "Sorry, I've got to get this."

"Should I ...?" She gestured toward the kitchen.

He held her hand. "No, stay. Hey, Gwen! Everything okay?"

"Hi, Bast! I'm sorry to disturb you, but Cecy was worried about you. Any chance you would say hi to her?"

"Of course. Damn—I mean, darn, I'm sorry I haven't called her before now. Is she around?"

Gwen beamed at him. "Just a sec. Cecy, Bast wants to say hello."

Cecy appeared, her eyes big in her face. "Hi, Bast, are you okay?"

"Fine, kiddo. Just a little setback." He raised his slinged arm. "Sorry if I gave you a scare."

"That's okay. Grammie said you probably know how to fall properly, like a stunt man."

He wished. "That sounds about right."

"And is Rowdy okay?"

He cast a quick glance toward Pepper, who was scooting away on her hot ass, but not fast enough for him. That Cecy was a huge Rowdy fan had completely escaped his mind.

"Rowdy? Oh, Rowdy's doing just fine. In fact ..." He leaned over to frame Pepper in the camera lens. "She and I are hanging out now. Hey, Rowdy, meet Cecy."

Pepper waved. "Hey, Cecy! So cool to meet you. Big hockey fan, huh?"

"Yes, I am. And I love Rowdy. She's my favorite." She tilted her head. "Are you really inside that costume?"

"I sure am. And I promise I can usually skate better than that. Also, Bast will be back in business before you know it." She reached for his hand and squeezed it.

Cecy giggled. "Are you guys together? Like a couple?"

Gwen could be heard protesting mildly at the nosy question.

"Just good friends," Bast said quickly, but he didn't let Pepper's hand go. "So, what else is going on in Chicago? Has the snow started to melt?"

Cecy spent a few minutes talking about the snow-woman she had built in the yard, which she had dressed in both Rebels and Hawks colors (he'd been hoping she'd get over the Hawks now that he was a Rebel, but she clung stubbornly to the old ways). It was hard to believe she was the same little girl with those dark circles under her eyes from months before, and the sight of her so cheerful made him happy.

After a while, Gwen came back on to tell her granddaughter dinner was ready, and they spent another minute saying goodbyes and promising to meet soon, including Rowdy, aka Pepper, aka his new friend who was definitely not his girlfriend.

"Gosh, that was so cute," Pepper said.

"Isn't she?"

Pepper grinned. "I mean, you with her, and how she absolutely adores you. That's the same little girl you raised the funds for?"

"Yeah, her insurance couldn't cover everything, and Gwen's her sole caregiver since Cecy's parents died a few years back. The money raised helped for Gwen's accommodations because they had to travel from Rockford while Cecy was getting treated." He didn't mention that he'd set up a trust fund for her education as well.

"Oh, the poor thing. What a tough life she's had in such a short time."

"Yeah, definitely puts my problems in perspective."

She looked thoughtful. "You probably do a lot of those hospital visits. I bet there are a lot of kids and families in the same boat."

He had no doubt. When he heard how deficient the financial support was for Cecy and Gwen, he'd been happy to lend his name to any fundraising efforts. Since he'd joined the Hawks, he'd received innumerable requests to donate to or boost a cause, and as wealthy as he was, there was only so much he could do.

"There's never enough, but there have to be more ways to help."

"Your name's very powerful."

"You think?"

She nodded. "Definitely. You could put it to anything, and it would be a success. But it's not just your name."

"No?"

"The name's a great start, but you need to have the right temperament to follow through on something like that. And you do. You're hard-working, generous, empathetic."

It had crossed his mind already: using his name for

something more than the odd fundraising effort. For something that might exist separately from hockey.

"I've been thinking about what might happen if my wrist never heals completely. If I don't make it all the way back."

"And what have you concluded?" Bast loved that about Pepper. She didn't rush in with a bunch of platitudes about how he needed to think positive and not assume the worst.

"All my life there's been one goal—be the best at this sport I'm crazy about. Crush the competition and win everything in sight." Time away from the game had given him time to think. "But maybe there could be a life outside of hockey."

A legacy he could leave if this hockey business didn't work out.

27

It's been four days since Bastian Durand was injured in his comeback game on Rebels ice, and both the player and the organization have been unusually quiet. Other than a fractious press conference in which Durand was uncharacteristically grouchy (more like his elder brother, in fact), and even going so far as to get physical with a member of the Sun-Times *news organization, there's been no word on when he might re-start rehab or return to practice. It's almost as if Bast Durand has disappeared off the face of the earth. Efforts to reach him and mascot Pepper Calhoun have been unsuccessful. Why all the secrecy? Is Durand undergoing another heartbreaking wrist-surgery? The fandom would love—in fact, deserves—to know.*

— CURTIS DEACON, *CHICAGO SUN-TIMES*

PEPPER AWOKE to a rumbling sound off in the distance. She raised her head from the pillow and listened, waiting for awareness to kick in. Her phone's screen said 10:23 a.m. Late, but then they'd stayed up most of the night.

The sound was louder now, closer to the house, and then it stopped.

Maybe one of Reid's neighbors was using a snowplow. Pepper wasn't sure how to feel about that. For four days, they'd been holed up in this snow globe world of their own making. Talking, cooking, hot-tubbing, more.

So much more.

It was safe to say she'd thrown that monkey off her back. She was practically a sexpert now! She could return to Chicago a changed woman, ready to date—or, maybe not that just yet. She needed a job first. And maybe somewhere to live. But those things seemed more attainable than they had four days ago. Mentally, she had shifted to a better place.

Yet she loved where she was now. Time was suspended here where the real world couldn't touch it. A momentary panic gripped her, an unwanted acknowledgment that this would end soon.

There was only one possible reason for this dread building inside her: she was falling for this good and decent guy who had fought dragons for her.

She moved her hand over his chest, feeling the rugged contours of his body, imprinting them on her memory. But it was more than just his muscles she wanted to remember.

In her mind, she set aside space for their conversations, how well he listened, how angry he got on her behalf. His funny hat and the way he rubbed the bridge of his nose when he was stressed. His sense of humor and cheeky charm.

Her favorite Bast muscle was the one inside his chest, but as she couldn't reach inside and hold it close, she went for the next best one. Her hand coasted south and gripped his hardening cock, enjoying the pulse of it in her hand, the power beneath her fingertips. That throaty moan he released as he rocked into her clasp.

Continuing her stroke, she kept her eyes on his handsome face. Those lovely lashes fluttered, then peeled open to reveal all that perfect blue. His smile on seeing her, that gorgeous, wonderful curve of joy made her so happy.

She stored it away with the rest.

"You've been busy," he said, his lips stretching wider.

"The early bird catches the worm."

"What a terrible thing to say about my cock."

She giggled and stroked harder, loving how he responded. The flush of his cheeks, the dilation of his pupils, the drag of teeth along his lower lip.

All filed away.

"Should I apologize?" she asked.

"Yep. Tell him he's nothing like a worm."

Moving down under the covers, she applied a kiss to the swollen head. "You're beautiful." Then a lick, which got a satisfying gasp. "Absolutely perfect." Followed up by a lusty suck that drew his moan.

"Sweetheart, that's—oh, fuck, that's so good."

"I've wanted to do this since our first night here. I asked to taste you, remember?"

"I-I do."

She swirled her tongue around the head until a splash of salty liquid emerged.

"But you wanted to kiss me instead. Maybe you didn't think I'd be any good."

"Never crossed my mind."

She smiled. "Tell me how to do it. What feels good."

"Pepper, what you're doing—ah, yeah. That. Christ, I

must have been dreaming about you before I woke up. Primed for that gorgeous mouth." His hips rocked, pushing him deeper between her lips. Faster, with more urgency.

"Gonna come, sweetheart. You might want—"

She sucked harder, needing this, needing him to lose control, and when he did, it felt like the sweetest victory.

Looking up, she saw him gazing at her with such affection it made her want to cry. *Jesus, Pepper, get it together.* No need to turn to mush because a decent guy was kind to you.

"What?" he murmured.

"Nothing."

He pulled her into his arms. "You look sad."

"No, not at all. In fact, I'm really happy."

Because it happened. This wonderful thing happened.

"We probably should talk."

Here it comes, Bast's final benediction.

The thaw is upon us and so is the end of our little sojourn here. It's been great. You've been great. And I hope you can leave this place, knowing you're not an utter failure at sex and that I've also forgiven your sins against me. Go in peace to wreak havoc on the world.

He opened his mouth ...

... just as someone opened the door.

They looked up. Reid stood at the bedroom's entrance, his brow creased in confusion.

"Bast ..." He switched his dark gaze from his brother to her, then back. Before he could say another word, a big bundle of fur and energy rushed by and jumped on the bed.

"Hey, Bucky!" Sitting up, Bast threw his arms around the black and white mutt. He shot a wry glance at his brother who was still frozen in the doorway.

Bast broke the stony silence. "How about we get dressed and I meet you out in the kitchen?"

"Sure," Reid said. "Come on, Buck."

The dog returned to his owner and Reid closed the door behind them.

Pepper clutched defensively at the comforter. "He didn't look very happy."

"That's standard Reid." Bast threw back the covers and grabbed his sweats.

"No, seriously, he looked pissed. He's going to wonder why you did this."

Bast looked confused. He waved between them. "This? Is it that much of a mystery?" Before she could answer, he added, "Don't sweat it. Come on out when you're ready."

Once he was gone, she slipped on a hoodie and her jeans. Her civilian clothes, a step back to reality. Chunky wool socks were the finishing touch.

In the kitchen, she found Kennedy making coffee while Reid and Bast eyed each other like they were figuring out how to create a ten-paces-at-dawn situation in the room's cozy confines.

Bast turned and his expression changed when he saw her. Softened. Then he closed the gap between them, cupped her jaw, and kissed her.

She was far too self-conscious to kiss him back, but she did whimper a little. Pulling away, she caught Kennedy's knowing smirk.

"What are you doing?" Pepper muttered in her lowest voice to Bast.

"What does it look like?"

She peered up at him, trying to figure it out. It seemed like a blatant middle finger to his brother, who was obviously still annoyed. Was this some power play? Bast had already admitted that there was tension between them.

Reid was likely pissed at her because she'd set Bast's recovery back.

Or maybe he loved his brother so much he couldn't bear to see him hurt by a troublemaker like Pepper. She understood that instinct to protect. She'd lived it with Kent as she tried to cover up his bad behavior, the kind that was hurting him.

"Pepper!" Kennedy elbowed Bast out of the way and hugged her like they were old friends. "Sorry to barge in on you like this. Would you believe Reid made us leave Chicago at 4:30 this morning? He was worried when Bast only responded with one-word texts." She shot a *you-should've-known-this-would-happen* look at Bast.

"So he thought we'd better come up and check on him. Not that you're anything to worry about, right? Of course not." She answered her own question, but the undertone lingered like a bad smell. *You're not going to hurt my brother-in-law any more than you already have, are you?*

"I don't think so. But I'm probably biased."

Kennedy smiled serenely. "So how are you finding the place?"

"It's beautiful. A perfect escape."

"Yeah, that's what we love about it, too." She touched her husband's arm, a soothing motion. "But tough in winter. Reid sort of panicked when he saw you guys were snowed in, so he talked to Mr. Gunderson next door and borrowed the snowblower. Sorry if we woke you."

"No, it's fine. I was probably going to start investigating that option today, so it's nice Reid did the work."

"Yeah, thanks, bro," Bast said, with a bit of a smirk.

Kennedy laughed, but she didn't add any more explanation. "Okay, how about we get breakfast together and discuss whether you're truly the troublemaker everyone says you are?"

THANKFULLY KENNEDY and Reid had brought croissants, blueberry jam and—yes!—Krispy Kreme donuts, so those did a lot of the heavy lifting. Bast made coffee while Pepper threw together scrambled eggs and bacon.

She took a seat. Bast sat beside her on one side, Kennedy on the other, which left her facing Reid. Great. His expression was only missing the two-fingered prong of "I'm watching you."

"So, uh, how was the trip up?" Pepper asked after everyone had helped themselves. "Are the roads clear?"

"For the most part," Kennedy said. "Even the back roads into and out of Belhaven Harbor, except when we got to the driveway down to this place. Reid had called our neighbor on the way up to ask about the snowblower, and he was already clearing the drive. Such a sweetheart, and then we were able to creep up on you both." She addressed Bast. "Of course, if you'd responded to any of our texts with more than one-word answers, we would have left you alone."

Bast sipped his coffee. "I wanted a little time to myself. That's all."

Reid muttered, "But you're not by yourself."

"No, I'm not," Bast said coolly.

"So how's the wrist?" Kennedy asked because somehow *that* had become the safest topic of conversation.

"Not too bad."

"Guess it doesn't hurt to have a distraction," Reid said.

"Bro ..." Another warning from Bast.

"I just don't understand what's happening here. You can't play and the reason is—"

Bast held up a hand. "I forgave you instantly. Believe me, it didn't happen so quickly with Pepper, so back off."

Reid narrowed his eyes. "Forgiving is one thing. But setting up house is another."

Okay, enough. "We're not setting up house. Your brother was kind enough to get me out of the city when I needed it because the press were being pretty awful. That's all."

"Actually, Pepper drove me. To protect my wrist."

That wasn't good enough for Reid. "But now you're ... together."

"Reid, drop it," Bast said.

"We're not together." Pepper didn't want to be the reason another friendship, especially one between brothers, was strained or destroyed. "We're just hanging out until the roads are clear."

Which they now were.

The snow globe had smashed, the world outside was at the gates. It was time to set this dream time aside.

28

BAST SHOULDN'T HAVE BEEN SURPRISED that his brother was being a jerk. This was standard Reid, who had been a dick for as long as Bast could remember, but for reasons of self-preservation Bast preferred not to dwell on.

However, he'd been thinking about it more over the last few days. How much he adored Reid as a kid and didn't get any of that back. The shoves, the punches, the bullying—all because Reid was in pain. And now Reid wanted to play the role of the "good" big brother and police his relationships.

Only ... it wasn't a relationship. Pepper had just said so.

We're not together. We're just hanging out until the roads are clear.

Which was a fine thing to say. The perfect response to Reid's jibes, so why was Bast annoyed by it?

The rest of breakfast passed with Pepper and Kennedy's chatter keeping things loose. Afterward, as it was clear Bast and Reid needed to talk, Ken and Pep volunteered to do the dishes. The brothers headed out to the patio looking toward the dock.

"This is a lovely place," Bast said, anxious to ease the tension between them. "A real haven."

"It is. Reminds me a little of Grenville. I'm going to build a rink in the neighbor's barn."

"I loved that rink." Just like the one they had as kids. "Those days seemed simpler."

Reid shook his head slightly. "You always thought so. That selective memory of yours."

"So I haven't forgotten what a dick you were. Now you seem to be going to the other end of the spectrum, overcompensating with the big brother protective schtick. I'm sorry about not texting you long manuscripts about my progress."

Reid narrowed his eyes. "I can't help worrying."

"Yeah, but you don't need to."

His brother's gaze flickered toward the kitchen. "Don't I?"

"If you're going to blame Pepper for this, then you have to accept your part in it as well."

"I'm not blaming her for the accident. I understand that. I just don't understand *this*. Why is she here, Bast? Why are you two ... a thing? She's bad news. Look what happened with Gallagher."

"So everyone keeps saying, but you don't know her like I do."

"You met her once a few months ago and now, after four days of banging, you know her?"

"Tell me you didn't know you and Kennedy had something from the first time you met her."

"We didn't. She would serve me Americanos at the coffee shop and insist on talking to me. It was very annoying!" He sounded so peeved at the memory, that Bast couldn't help laughing.

"And when she moved in and you spent more time with

her and realized that the thought of her leaving broke something in you—"

"Which took several weeks."

"But you knew, bro."

Reid gave him a long hard look. "From the first minute.
But that was different. I ... I needed someone to take a
chance on me. To open me up."

"I wasn't enough."

He gave Bast a sharp look. "What does that mean?"

"I tried to get you to open up. To come out with my
friends in Chicago. To do things together." To repair what
was broken between them.

Reid considered this. "I wasn't ready to be your friend
yet, not after everything with Henri. Not after how I'd
treated you. That didn't mean we couldn't be friends, but I
needed to break first. Hit a low point. Our relationship was
too complicated for me to turn around and admit all my
faults."

"I was there, waiting for you to reach out, Reid."

Reid took a moment before he spoke. "It wasn't about
you. I was completely to blame, I know that. Kennedy made
me realize that I couldn't do this one-man show forever. But
I'm grateful for all the times you bought me ice cream to
tempt me to lose my diet and invited me to your place for
poker with the enemy." He placed a hand on Bast's shoulder.
"I failed you, but I can make up for it. And part of that is
giving you advice."

Shrugging away, Bast leaned against the patio railing.
"Even if I don't want it."

"Especially if you don't want it. If you're comparing this
with me knowing Kennedy for a short time, are you saying
you're ... in love with Pepper?"

No.

Maybe?

He had no idea. But he did know that he wanted more. He craved more.

"I like her. A lot. And I'm not saying anything beyond this is going to happen. But Pepper's had a raw deal. You don't know what really went down with Gallagher. I do. Pepper is not the villain here."

Reid shook his head. "Bast, you make friends easily. Women throw themselves at your skates. Let's face it, you're kind of a pushover." Obviously, their childhood pattern was too ingrained for Reid to see his younger brother clearly here. "You're easy with everyone, never a bad word, even when you should have stood up for yourself more."

"Like with you?"

He nodded, a little sad. "I was cruel, and it damaged our relationship for the longest time. I have a shit-ton of regrets about that, but now I want to be here for you. To give you all the advice I should have dispensed long ago. This girl is using you, like that Marina woman you used to date before you got injured. I don't know what Pepper's told you, but whatever it is plays on your generosity and kindness. These aren't bad traits to have, but when someone takes advantage, I can't stand by."

Anger was building in Bast's veins, rushing to the surface. He hauled back the harsh words he wanted to say, the things that proved he wasn't always generous or kind. "You heard her. We're not together, just hanging."

"Yeah." Reid ran a hand through his hair, then petted Bucky. "I just don't want to see you hurt. You've suffered enough. You have a gift, and I've no doubt it's frustrating not to be able to use it for so long. You're the kind of guy who gets bored. It can be easy to see gaps and want to fill them with things ... or people. You're in a vulnerable position right now."

"Ready to be fleeced?" He hated the idea that he might be considered gullible. But he knew Pepper was a good person, and he shouldn't have to justify that to anyone.

"What I see is a girl latching onto another famous athlete, causing havoc, and leaving him in some sort of emotional rubble. I just hope you used condoms. Though it'd be weird that you brought some here of all places."

When Bast didn't respond, Reid shook his head. "Are you nuts? You didn't use protection? Whose idea was that?"

"That's none of your business."

"She is gaming you."

Bast shook his head, annoyed as fuck. "You've got it all wrong. Gallagher's no saint."

"Sure, he's a jerk and has pretty poor passing skills, but he was doing okay before he met Pepper. Was coming back from injury—just like you are—and then boom, she arrived."

"Reid—"

"I just can't let you get involved with this kind of mess. I was in Denver when it all went down. Gallagher was crushed when they split up. It's not that he was a good friend or anything—kind of a dick, to be honest—but it really fucked with his head. He wasn't the same man after she dumped him, and I can't watch this happen to you."

He knew Reid was being protective, that his guilt was framing some of what he was saying, that he wanted to be there for Bast the way Bast had been there for him those first days in Chicago.

"If I tell you that you have nothing to worry about, will you believe me?"

Reid inhaled deeply. "No. Because I saw how you looked

at her, how you kissed her, how you've jumped in at every turn to protect her. You're too far gone, and I can't let this go on."

"Fuck you, Reid."

His brother raised an eyebrow. "Okay."

"Seriously, I can't fucking deal with your passive-aggressive bullshit right now. I get it, your life is perfect. Your career is flying high, and you've got the dog and the wife and the gold medal. Good for you."

"Bast—"

He couldn't stop, though he really should. "Well, there's a chance I might not get back to where I once was. That this …" He held up his wrist. "Is never going to be as strong as it needs to be. I've got to live with that. Maybe *you've* got to live with that. So excuse me if I'm taking comfort where I find it."

Reid looked grim. "I see."

"Do you? Glad to hear it."

With that final jab, Bast headed back inside.

WHILE BAST AND Reid talked out on the patio, Kennedy and Pepper worked on the dishes, though it was clear the feisty blonde wanted to speak more openly.

"The tension is killing me," Pepper had said. "Are you going to say what you need to say?"

"Oh, good, you're not completely insensitive to my speaking sighs." She grinned and leaned against the countertop. "Don't worry, I will be talking to Reid on the way back and letting him know this is none of his business."

"Thanks. But that's not really what's on your mind, is it?"

"No? Okay, then. What I want to say is that I don't know a thing about what went down with your ex, but I do know that you were treated abominably. He had an entire organization behind him, and I'm guessing you had zilch. No one is all one thing or all another. I don't need you to tell me you're a good person, I just need you to be good to Bast."

Not expecting that. "Be good to him?"

"Yeah. So you and he joined forces to get away from the press, but whatever's happened between you has changed him. I don't know you well enough to decide if it's changed *you*. But he—" She looked toward the patio with a soft look, then back again. "He's one of the nicest guys I know, but I've always worried that he's too nice. That he keeps up this good-guy front and pushes his emotions down deep. Too deep. But not when it comes to you."

She chuckled. "I don't think I've ever seen him as *into* anything as I've seen with you. Sure, hockey. But that's something that's a natural extension of his personality. He doesn't usually push back with Reid. Their dynamic is very much one where Bast is the easygoing one, but not today. Today he's protective of you, and it's nice to see. He needs a purpose, something other than hockey."

Pepper shook her head. "That's not me. I'm not ... I'm not anyone's reason to do anything." And she most certainly didn't want to be. That pressure to be right for someone was something she could never live up to again. "We're here because we both needed an escape, and he rescued me." She added more quietly, "When he shouldn't have."

"When he shouldn't have," Kennedy repeated. "That might be a reaction to a particular event, but he's carrying it a bit far, don't you think? The minute we came in, he made sure we knew that you were under his wing. Under his protection, with that kiss."

That kiss. She could still feel it on her lips, the weight of his care. But that was reading far too much into it, surely. She could explain it to Kennedy like she was one of her preschoolers, and in doing so, she might convince herself.

"I think that was more of a way to tell Reid to back off. I don't know their dynamic, but like all younger siblings, he probably doesn't like being told who he can and can't see or be with. Believe me, younger sibling here."

"So nothing more than a little fraternal power play?"

"What do you want me to say, Kennedy?" That Pepper adored when he gave his brother a dark scowl and kissed her like she was the only person in the room? That being under Bast's wide wing left her feeling safer than she had in years? "This is just a proximity thing. It started as friction, and it's a small place. You really should have a guest room!"

"There's a comfy sofa."

"Not that comfy," Pepper muttered, rather ungraciously. Although it was plenty comfy for when she lost her virginity.

She would not be sharing *that* with Kennedy.

"Thanks for letting me stay, even though you had no idea I was here."

"Oh, I wouldn't say I had *no* idea. I saw the footage of Bast bundling you into that car, and Elle mentioned that you had to leave town for a while when I was dropping off groceries at the Kershaws yesterday. I can't say I was completely surprised to see you here. Or that I was disappointed." She added a wink.

"Please don't read into this more than you should."

Kennedy smiled in sympathy. "Well, we all resist the big changes. No one knows that more than me."

Good for her. But Pepper was done with big changes. Done with being the butt of the joke. She was just looking for a quiet life, and playing house with Bast Durand was not that.

"Listen, thanks for being so ... kind. You didn't have to be."

Kennedy hugged her. "That's your problem right there. You don't expect people to be nice to you, and when they are, you're suspicious of it. Might be time to let that go.

Enjoy the moment." Abruptly turning pale, she held up a hand. "Just a sec," and quickly left the kitchen.

A couple of minutes later she came back in.

"Are you okay?"

"Yeah, fine. Just ..." She pointed to her stomach.

Pepper gasped. "A baby? Oh, wow." Of course she had to hug her. "That's so amazing. Does Bast know?"

"Not yet." She wrinkled her nose. "Reid's over the moon, but he's worried about rubbing it in, given Bast's run of bad luck."

"I think he'll be thrilled."

Kennedy grinned. "We're mostly worried about the effect on Bucky. He's had all the attention for the last year."

"Aw, he's going to make a great big brother."

Reid walked into the kitchen, his frown activating—or staying in place, depending on your viewpoint—on seeing his wife hugging Pepper. Feeling awkward, Pepper stood back.

"We need to head back, Ken."

Over breakfast, they had mentioned that the Rebels were playing at home tonight. Reid and Kennedy had spent less time at the cottage than it took them to get here. Pepper was filled with a sense of longing for the kind of love Reid's journey here demonstrated. From the way Bast had spoken of him, she suspected old-school Reid wouldn't have done something like that before he met Kennedy.

She smiled at Pepper. "Okay, duty calls. Let me know when you're back in town, and we'll meet up for a drink."

Ten minutes later, Reid and Kennedy were on their way, and Bast and Pepper were alone again.

"How come you barely spoke to Reid when he left?" She couldn't help noticing that they were rather terse with each other.

"Said all we had to say."

So their conversation on the patio hadn't really resolved anything. "He's just trying to protect you."

"You're taking his side?"

She smiled. "I can see his point of view. Obviously his guilt about why you were injured in the first place is still weighing on him. He thought you were back in the game, that he could finally put that guilt behind him and enjoy his time on the ice with you, and bam, here you are. Because of me, which I know was accidental, but it doesn't change the facts. And it brings up all those shitty feelings he thought were buried. No one wants to be reminded of the crap they thought was buried."

Bast threaded his arms over his strong chest. "He was such an ass about it. Like he doesn't trust me to know my own mind."

"He's your big brother. That's what they do." She knew this from experience. They weren't always right, but the good intention was there. "Maybe cut him some slack."

"We had a fight."

"About me?"

"Sort of, but more about my injury. How I might not make it back, and how we've all got to live with that."

"Ah." She put her arms around his waist and held him tight.

He wrapped her up close and kissed the top of her head. "I didn't mean to blame him. I guess I haven't been completely honest with him about how much the injury messed with my head."

"Okay, so this is a good start. You should talk it out properly. Tell him what's going on."

He drew back. "And what is going on?"

"That you've been keeping some of this resentment

inside. That you can't help how you feel. Bottling it up can only get you so far."

She knew from personal experience. Kent had screwed her over, and worse, she had let him. All because she thought it was the "cool girl" thing to do. That she was being the classy one. But it had festered inside her. So she knew exactly how Bast was feeling, even if he couldn't voice those emotions.

"That's a pretty smart thing to say."

"I'm a pretty smart girl." His sweet kiss to her forehead was a little bit too perfect, so tempering was needed. "Or he could be completely right. I'm bad news."

"Believing your own hype, are you?"

"Hmm."

He raised an eyebrow. "Don't hmm me. Reid doesn't have all the information. And I'm not going to betray your confidence."

"I appreciate it. But that doesn't mean you should leave things unsaid with him. You need to clear the air. In fact, we both do, back in the real world."

He pushed her onto the table. "The real world. Sounds awful."

She smiled. "It does. But I need to get my life together. Back to the job hunt. Talk to my dad and Connor. Stop running away. And you need to figure out your next steps and talk to Reid."

He didn't look too happy about it, almost like he didn't want this to end. But that was likely wishful thinking.

"I kind of want to tell everyone to go fuck themselves. Is that an option?"

She peered up at him, at his lovely face, one she'd love to see over and over. "You kind of already did in that presser."

That made them both laugh.

After a moment, he said, "What can I do to help, Pepper?"

The sweetness of that made her eyes sting and it took her a moment to find the words. "You've already done enough. More than I could ever have wished for."

For some journeys, it was necessary to continue the path alone.

30

"THERE'S MY LITTLE GUY!"

Pepper hunkered and stretched out her arms for Hatch, who waddled over as fast as his toddler legs could carry him. He smelled warm and safe, and a little bit sweet, which was probably because of the gummy he was chewing on.

"He missed you," Elle said. "Kept asking 'Peppa?'"

"Aw, I missed him, too. Again, I'm so sorry for bailing on you."

Elle waved it off. "Are you kidding? I don't blame you for wanting to get away. The press can be such assholes. So how are things with your dad?"

Pepper smiled at Elle, who was unsubtly hinting that Coach Calhoun might be in the wrong here.

"We haven't had a chance to talk yet." Bast had dropped her off late last night, and her father was still sleeping when she left this morning. "I'm disappointed that he didn't stand up for me at the presser, but I also understand it. The team's his baby."

Elle's nostrils flared. "You're his actual baby. No one's

saying he can't be pissed, but everyone recognizes it was an accident."

The door to the living room opened and in walked Theo. Bounded, more like. The man was more puppy than human.

"Look who's home," Pepper said to Hatch.

"Dada!" Hatch stretched out his hand towards his father, who scooped him up and hugged him. It wasn't long before Hatch was squirming.

"Too tight, buddy?" Theo kissed his son on the cheek. "But I love hugging you until your eyes pop out and roll away and get eaten by the cat. That's my favorite thing."

Hatch giggled, clearly not understanding a word of it.

Theo winked at Pepper. "Welcome back, Rowdy. Enjoy your vacation?"

"I liked getting away from the city if that's what you mean."

"That is *not* what I meant, and you know it. Word's out you've been holed up with Mini-Durand. I heard you even broke out the hot tub—or maybe broke it in?"

"Theo," Elle said, a warning in her tone. "That's Pepper's business." She turned to Pepper. "I didn't say a word."

"But someone did."

"Kennedy mentioned to Sadie that you and Bast were helping each other out—"

Theo smirked.

Elle rolled her eyes and went on. "In a rescuing each other kind of way. Anyway, there was mention of a hot tub, I suppose, so everyone sort of assumed? Now Gunnar's not usually one to gossip, but he made the mistake of commenting to Tate Kazminski, who *is* one to gossip. Once Kaz is in the mix, it's gossip game over."

Theo chuckled. "The only reason Elle-oh-Elle here didn't say a word to you already is because she wanted to pretend we hadn't discussed it at breakfast this morning before I headed in for practice. I tried to get Durand Senior to spill. He's keeping his cards close, but then that's Duracell for ya."

Elle considered her. "So you two are what now? Dating?"

"Peppa!" Hatch reached for her, needing the attention re-focused on him.

Theo laughed. "Get in line, buddy, because Bast wants her, too."

"We're just friends," Pepper said as Hatch clambered into her arms again.

"Sure, sure." Theo took a seat and stretched out his legs. "Guessing you don't want to get involved with a dickhead like Durand, anyway. The guy's the worst."

Elle looked at her husband suspiciously. "What are you talking about? Bast is one of the nicest guys on the planet."

"All an act," Theo said blithely. "I know nice. I'm the epitome of nice. But Durand has won a Stanley Cup, the Hart Memorial twice, and can get any chick he wants. No one can be that talented, a magnet for the ladies, and not be a little bit arrogant."

"You're talented, a magnet for the ladies, and not in the least bit arrogant," Elle said with a smirk at Pepper.

"I'm a special case. Got it all: looks, sense of humor, stellar hair, hot wife, great kid and another one on the way."

Pepper covered her mouth. "You're pregnant?"

"Sorry, babe," Theo said to his glaring wife, not sounding sorry at all. Sounding so proud it made Pepper's heart speed up. There must be something in the water at Rebels HQ. "Have you talked to Pepper about what we discussed?"

"Not yet, doofus. I was hoping to ease into it. She's had a very traumatic week."

Theo took another look at Pepper, this time in a pitying way. "You know all this bullsh—"

"Babe," Elle cut in with a chin-nod to Hatch.

"BS, then, with the press and social media. It'll pass."

"Maybe, and the easiest way to do that is to keep a low profile." And not have anything to do with Bast. Only now they were linked forever—and not just because of the on-ice crash.

The journey from Michigan back to Chicago had been quiet, neither of them willing to address what the last few days might have meant. It just seemed easier not to over-complicate things. Both of them had work to do, and it was probably best they put Belhaven Harbor in their rear view.

They'd reached her dad's house at about midnight and sat in the car for a few moments in the cooling dark.

"Are you sure you're okay to drive?" she'd asked. They'd switched about an hour ago, and he was back in the driver's seat. Pepper felt like a passenger again, unable to control the way forward.

"If I said I needed you to drive me home, would you?"

She turned to him. The faint light from the street fell perfectly on his cheekbones.

"Do you need me to do that?"

Because she would. She'd do anything for him. And if she drove the extra ten minutes to his place, she would offer to help him with his duffle because his wrist was still sore. Once inside, maybe Bast would just say, "Stay. Never leave. Be mine forever."

And if he didn't? Oh, she wasn't sure she could survive that.

"I don't know that I need you for that. I've already abused your good nature for far too long."

He looked straight ahead out to the streets, now devoid

of snow but still a touch icy. Maybe she should drive him all the way. Keep him safe to the end just as he had done for her.

"Bast, I don't know what to say except that no one has ever been as kind to me as you were these last few days. No one has treated me with such respect and compassion." She leaned in and cupped his jaw. "I'll never forget it."

"Don't sell yourself short ever again," he said gruffly. "You're amazing, and if Connor or your dad or any other fucking idiot can't see that, then send them to me."

She sniffed. "Okay, hero."

His answer was a kiss, the most perfect meeting of lips. The man was determined to ruin her for all others, which she deserved, she supposed. It was only right that she should come out of this experience irreparably changed.

Reluctantly, she pulled away, marveling at how he chased the air between them for a split second.

"You'll be okay?" she asked, meaning the drive but also a mini pep talk for herself.

"I'll survive."

"Let me know how it goes with Reid."

He nodded, and she found just enough strength to get out of the car.

He'd waited until she was inside her father's house, then waited a few moments more. She almost ran out and begged him to take her back to his place, for this not to be the end. But he drove away, taking her bravery with him.

She tuned back into the present. Theo was still talking.

"Low profiles are kind of overrated. You're just letting someone else control the narrative."

"What am I supposed to do? Take out a full-page ad telling everyone they've got it all wrong, and I really can't be held responsible for my ex-fiancé's deterioration in play? Or that what happened to Bast was a terrible accident for which I am incredibly sorry?"

Theo shrugged. "Maybe? Okay, not exactly that, but you might want to think about using social media to your advantage. You wouldn't believe the number of sponsorships I've received because of my Insta thirst traps. Sure, I do less of that now because the trap worked ..." He thumbed at Elle who was rolling her eyes affectionately. "But it's paid for Hatch's college, and I'll have enough put away for the next of my spawn. Hoping for twins this time."

"Uh, congratulations, you two! We've kind of gotten off the topic." Pepper was only too glad to change the subject. "I'm so happy for you. Guess that groin injury didn't cramp your style. The boys are flowing!"

Elle grinned. "Thanks. We're thrilled, but it's still hush hush for now." Quick look at her husband, who grinned. "Now, about what I was going to ask you before Big Mouth here crashed the stage. Would you think about becoming a nanny full-time for us? Hatch adores you, and now that he's walking and talking, he needs the kind of care that someone as qualified as you can give."

She hated to disappoint them, but she needed to think about her future here. "I'm actually thinking of finishing my degree, maybe transferring my credits to DePaul or another Chicago area college."

"Oh, that's great!" Elle was sweet enough to not let her disappointment show. "But maybe you can help out part-time. Depending on your schedule. At least, keep us in mind."

"Of course. You've both been so kind, especially after all the negativity in the press."

Theo took her by the shoulders and gave her a little shake. "You need to stop thinking you're a problem,

Calhoun! Listen, I don't know why you broke up with Gallagher, and I don't care. But I'll tell you this: I never liked that guy. He was such a prick to me during the All Stars game four years ago. Called me Pretty Boy! Didn't surprise me that he got sent down to the AHL. Not a great player, and I'm thinking, not a great person." He knocked gently on her forehead. "You need to get out of your head and start thinking with your heart."

At one time she'd thought that was what got her into trouble, that she was too soft-hearted. But now she realized that it was a strength—one she'd leaned into while she spent those days with Bast.

She had no idea what lay ahead, but she was determined that whatever happened, her heart would lead the way.

31

WALKING into the Rebels front office for a meeting with Fitz, Bast ran into Hudson Grey, who was coming out of Dr. Huang's office, his eyes a little red.

"Hey, Bast, you're back. How was Michigan?"

No secrets around here. "Snowy. How are things with you?"

"All good."

"Really? You look kind of upset."

Hudson waved it off. "No, not at all. Or not now. I'm always like this after a chat with the doc. It's really cathartic."

Dr. Huang was a sports psychologist, and while Bast had seen his fair share of them over the years, he'd never emerged from the office of one in tears.

"So, that's going well for you, then?"

Hudson laughed because Bast sounded rather suspicious there. "Yeah, it is. I have some anxiety issues, so it helps to talk to someone impartial about that."

Bast's surprise that Hudson would just admit that so readily must have shown on his face.

"You think I'd want to keep that to myself, huh?"

"I guess. Or maybe not. People are a lot more understanding of anything related to mental health these days."

Hudson smiled. "Yeah, it took me a while to get there. I used to do breathing exercises, meditation, a lot of DIY coping strategies. But after I had a panic attack on the ice last season and some other stuff happened with my guy, I figured it was time to seek professional help. I actually have a different therapist, but every now and then, when I need a friendly ear, I come see the doc here." He gestured to Dr. Huang's door. "That's what she's there for."

"It's good to have the option, I suppose."

Hudson gave Bast a wry smile. "It's not for everyone."

"Yeah, I know, but sometimes taking that first step is the hardest. I've been thinking that maybe I should talk to someone."

Hudson nodded enthusiastically. "Yeah, or you could try Tara. She passes for a first-step therapist around here. Very discreet."

Bast would not be spilling his guts to his hair stylist. The only woman he wanted to talk to about any of this was Pepper, but it wasn't fair of him to unload his issues on her. She had enough going on.

"I should let you go, Hud. Good talking to you."

"Yeah, you, too. Gosh, I forgot to ask. How's the wrist?"

He had just come from a session with Kelly, one of the team's PTs, where he'd squeezed a rubber ball and was told to stop trying to grind it into dust.

"It's hard to say. I've been telling everyone I'll get there and not to worry, but sometimes that can get ... tiring."

"Putting on the perfect front can be draining as hell."

True. Bast had been faking his cheer for so long now that he wasn't sure what his real personality was anymore.

"I want to play. I'm just not sure when or if it's going to happen." Not what anyone wanted to hear, but the candor felt good.

"Well, if and when you make it back, I can't wait to be on a line with you."

Bast smiled. "Me, too." He watched Hudson head off, marveling at how the younger generation—by all of three years—seemed to have it figured out.

In Fitz's office, he took a seat.

"How's it going?"

"Better in some ways, not so good in others."

"Talk to me."

Bast spent the next thirty minutes letting Fitz in on his concerns about not making it back to full capacity, how he worried about letting his new team and his brother down, and how he might want to talk to someone professional so he wouldn't come crying to Fitz every ten minutes.

"You're always welcome, Bast," Fitz said, sounding like he meant it. "But I'd like you to do this right and talk to Dr. Huang. She can make a call on whether you just need time with her or if something else needs to happen here. But I'm really grateful that you talked to me, and I want you to keep the lines of communication open." He grimaced. "Man, that sounds so fucking corporate. The only thing missing is 'my door is always open'. I hope you know what I mean."

"I do. Thanks, Fitz."

The boss smiled. "Before you go, we need to talk about what happened in the presser last week. I know you weren't in the best frame of mind, and maybe we made a mistake with the timing. I want to apologize for forcing you to do that."

"I probably could have been a bit more understanding, but I don't like to see people piling on."

"About Pepper?"

He nodded. Just hearing her name set his heart racing. He missed her so much, and it had been less than twelve hours!

"I should have been paying attention when I came off. I also talked to Danny, and he said he sent her on without checking the ice was clear, so Pepper bears no responsibility here. I'm wondering if we should put out some sort of statement to that effect."

"Saying that you were ogling some hot blonde in the crowd, so maybe lay off the mascot, guys?"

"Well, yeah."

That made the GM laugh. "Social media has already outed you. Not sure anything we say will make the situation better from a PR point of view."

"I'd still like something to be done. I should have done it myself on Insta or whatever, and I still could, but I'd like the team's input here."

Fitz tapped his fingers on his desk. "Work with Sophie on it. We're happy to support both of you." Fitz held the pause for a long beat, then said, "So about Deacon. I hear you're reluctant to make an apology. I understand that, but it leaves us in a tricky position from a legal standpoint."

Bast remained silent.

"You need to work with us here, Bast. We can get all this —the statement from the org supporting you and Pepper, the apology to Deacon—squared away in one well-worded release. And all you have to do is say sorry and make a charitable donation."

All you have to do … it sounded so easy, but he'd shoved Deacon for a reason. To defend Pepper, and he sure as hell didn't think he should have to negate that with an apology that implied Deacon's behavior was correct. Kit was also adamant he should make amends, but right now Bast was feeling so damn stubborn about it all.

"I'll think about it."

"Okay. So how was Michigan?"

Et tu, Fitz? It was bad enough that his phone was filled with snarky comments and hot tub emojis—or a fire symbol along with a bathtub combo, which Kershaw had informed him was the closest anyone could get.

"Damn, this team is pretty gossip-y."

Fitz shook his head. "You don't know the half of it."

32

———

PEPPER INHALED a deep breath and knocked on the door to her father's office.

"Come in!"

"Hey, Dad, got a sec?"

Her father looked up from his desk. She waited for his expression to turn grim, but it never did.

"Pepper, honey, you're back."

"Yeah, last night. I didn't want to wake you. Thanks for getting my car and luggage back home."

The words were barely out of her mouth when her father rounded the desk and took her in his arms. "I was worried about you."

"You were?"

"Of course. I shouldn't have sent you off with Durand like that. I wasn't thinking straight."

She swallowed. "You were thinking of the team, Dad. I get it."

"Well, that's been my problem, hasn't it?" He sounded different. "Have a seat, honey."

"O-okay." She took a seat and waited for him to speak.

"I've been worried about you over the last few months, Pepper. You've been so unlike yourself, and I didn't want to pry too much. I liked Gallagher, and I'll admit that some of the stuff being said about you in the press got into my head. Your brother didn't help."

That hurt to hear, but she hadn't done herself any favors by keeping it all inside.

"I'm not going to say I was completely blameless, Dad. But I did leave Kent because I didn't see a way forward. Everything the tabloids said, and all the things that happened to him afterward—that can't be placed at my feet. But I do blame myself for not standing up for myself sooner."

Her father nodded his encouragement, so she went on.

"When everything fell apart, it was like this domino effect on my life. The broken engagement, the press getting involved, losing my internship, failing out of school. It was all so overwhelming, and I did not handle it well."

"And I wasn't much help."

She shrugged. "You were going through your own stuff with Mom. Neither of us were in a position to help each other. I get why you'd want to just focus on work, and then when your personal life, meaning me, interferes with your professional life, the team, that had to be tough for you. I'm sorry I made things harder."

He held up a hand. "Pepper, no more apologies. You've prostrated yourself enough, and I'm the one at fault here. I've been an idiot, and I'm sorry. Which I would have said even if Durand didn't show up here this morning raging about how I'd gotten it all wrong."

"Really?"

"Yep. Said I've been an idiot where you were concerned.

And he was right. You know I hate saying that about anyone, Pepper, especially when it contradicts my own thinking."

She chuckled. "I know you do."

"So you want to tell me what's going on there?"

"There?"

His eyebrow scooted north of his hairline.

"With Bast? Nothing whatsoever."

John Calhoun looked at her squarely. "He's just running around telling everyone that you've been wronged by the world, and nothing's going on?"

She couldn't believe he was still taking her part. Again, back in the real world. "We talked while we were stuck in Michigan. He's a good listener, and I think we helped each other."

"Hmm." Her father sighed. "You could do worse than Durand."

"I know, Dad. I was engaged to Kent Gallagher, remember?"

His grin was wry. "He went out of his way to defend you. Durand, that is. A week ago, and now again today. Pretty much told me where to go both times."

Her heart thumped wildly. "He's a good guy."

"Yep."

"Honestly, Dad. Bast and I have each other's backs. That's it. We're friends." After so long without someone in her corner, it felt good to know he still cared enough to maintain his defense of her.

And if she said the word "friend" enough, she might actually believe it was true.

~

ON LEAVING her father's office, Pepper ran into a cloud of perfume and blondness. Tara pulled her into a vise-like grip.

"Rowdy Rebel, Star Destroyer, you're back!"

"Like a bad rash."

"Come into my parlor."

Pepper followed Tara into the room she'd set up as her salon.

"Have a seat and let me trim those split ends. Have you been using the conditioner I recommended?" She rubbed Pepper's dry locks. "Never mind, I can tell you've been a naughty girl. Now, did I see you coming out of Coach's office?"

"Yeah, we had a nice chat. Things are good."

Tara nodded sagely. "That man is so tense. I get barely a word from him when he's sitting in my chair."

Pepper tried to imagine her father responding to Tara's efforts to draw him out. To be a fly on that wall. "He's not the chattiest guy."

"Oh, I get it. Tough with a gooey center."

The door opened and in walked Mia Wallace, munching on a pretzel.

"Oops, sorry, T, didn't realize you—oh, hey, Pepper, just the woman I want to see."

"Really?"

Mia was Vadim Petrov's sister and was also married to right-winger Cal Foreman. While she'd always been friendly to Pepper, she couldn't imagine why she'd want to seek her out.

"Yeah, we're launching the Athenas soon, and we're looking for a new mascot."

The Athenas was the new women's hockey franchise in

Chicago, coached by Isobel Chase, one of the Rebels' co-owners, and spearheaded by Mia.

"We're thinking Athena, goddess of wisdom and warfare, so the costume might be more of a Grecian theme. I think you could totally pull it off. You're so statuesque."

"Or she could dress like a Greek urn? Would that be weird?" Tara said. "Oh my God, we could do amazing things with your hair! Like ringlets or something snakelike."

"Hey, there," Pepper said before Tara got carried away. "If you haven't already noticed, I'm kind of infamous in mascot circles."

"What? Because of the Big Dump?" Mia chuckled. "That's what Cal's calling it, which I heartily co-sign. I know you're probably not ready to laugh about it, but some of the videos people created on TikTok are wild." She turned serious and sent a baleful look Pepper's way. "Sorry, I'm guessing it's still kind of soon."

"No, it's fine." She'd gained enough distance to see the funny side.

"And not your fault," Tara said as she snipped the end of one strand of hair. Kind of shorter than her usual, but maybe she could do with a new look. "Flirty-eyes Durand was looking at that chick's breasts as they Windexed the Plexi. The videos should be focusing on that!"

Pepper smiled. "Thanks, Tara. I appreciate it." To Mia she said, "Sorry, but my mascot days are behind me."

"Damn. I think you would have been awesome at it. You're the only woman I know in the mascot biz. But not to worry! I'll find someone. Just trying to keep it in the ladies' circle." She picked up some hair mousse and sniffed it. "So Pep, I heard you spent a lot of time with Bast Durand in a hot tub in Michigan."

Pepper's cheeks heated. "Does everyone know this?"

"Leave her be," Tara said, then under her breath, "You should be telling *me* everything first. I'm your stylist."

"There's nothing to tell. I drove him to Michigan, and we got stuck there."

"In a hot tub, though?" Tara mused. "Sounds romantic."

It was. "It was good to get away, get some perspective. But now we're back in the real world."

Mia wrinkled her nose. "What happened in the hot tub stays in the hot tub?"

Pretty much. "He's a great guy, though," Pepper said after a beat. "What he did at that presser was really generous."

"Yeah, but it's the least he could do," Tara said. "He had to absorb some of the flak."

"Right. But people so rarely take a stand in public like that. Especially when it's easier to stay quiet and under the radar." She knew that strategy a little too well. She'd been living it for the last year. "And then, when I needed to get away from the press, he was there, too."

"When he made you drive him all the way to Michigan so you could be stranded." Tara again with a sly look at Mia. "What a prince."

"He was helping me out there, too."

"Well, well, well, this is interesting," Mia said, shoving her screen in front of Tara's face.

Tara scanned it and said, "Huh."

"What is it?"

Mia passed off her phone to Pepper. On the screen was the press releases page on the Rebels website.

November 15—Chicago Rebels Press Office

Six days ago, an unfortunate accident occurred on the ice when Rebels player Bastian Durand collided with Rowdy Rebel, the team's mascot. After a full investigation, it's been determined that this collision was a result of a miscommunication between rink-side staff and the mascot, and that the person wearing the Rowdy Rebel costume was not at fault. As the footage surrounding the incident has been parsed almost as much as the Zapruder film, it's possible that online sleuths might come to a different conclusion. We look forward to the multiple podcasts investigating the incident. Rest assured that Bastian Durand will be keeping his eyes forward from now on and will not be distracted by pretty faces in the crowd. We wish him a speedy recovery and can't wait until he avoids a clash with Rowdy Rebel at some future date.

"This is—" Pepper looked up at Mia and Tara. "Some kind of official absolution. Right?"

"Full investigation, it says." Mia took back her phone. "I can't imagine they put that out without Bast's approval."

"Uh huh," Tara said. "It kind of makes him look like a doofus. Which might just be the most heroic thing he could have done in this whole mess."

Pepper's heart was full to bursting.

"Guess all those things you said were right, Pepper," Tara continued. "He really is a good guy—despite his flirty eyes!"

Yet another example of Bast protecting her. He'd already done so much. Maybe it was time she contributed to the rehabilitation of her rep. Recrafted the narrative.

"I have an idea, and I wondered if you guys would be willing to help. But it needs to be a secret, at least for a while."

Mia grinned at Tara, then turned to Pepper. "A secret? You've come to the right place."

33

Hey there! Did you have anything to do with this press release?

What press release?

Bast …

Just saying what needed to be said. Of course Internet opinion might already be set in stone, but I don't mind stirring things a little :)

You didn't have to do that, especially as it involved you admitting to being less than focused at your job. I appreciate it.

Told you I've got your back, Tequila Girl. So how are you?

PEPPER

Good. Better. Talked to my dad. Heard you got there before me!

BAST

Just the usual coach-player check-in. How did it go?

PEPPER

Really good. We've made up.

BAST

Excellent. Any word from Connor?

PEPPER

He's been calling and texting, but I'm letting him stew for a while.

BAST

Love it.

PEPPER

Speaking of difficult siblings, have you talked to Reid?

BAST

Not yet. Next stop on the Apologies and Absolution Tour.

PEPPER

You'll be fine. I think in all this we forget that, while our family doesn't always agree, they love us all the same. Reid will understand because no one loves you more.

BAST

…

BAST

I said once you were good at this, and I meant every word. You're a special person, Pepper, and special people deserve special gifts. Take a look at this.

*"Who says you have to say it with flowers? The
ultimate gift for your ex: Chicago Zoo has
named a cockroach in Kent's honor. Congratulations, Kent!"*

PEPPER

Oh my God, you did not! I am dying here.
Thank you!

BAST

Just a little fun. Later, sweetheart.

34

───────

REID OPENED the door to Bast and nodded. "Hey, come in."

"Sure you want me to?"

"I'm not the one who got pissy at the guy trying to look out for him."

Bast gusted out a sigh. "Let me say hi to your better half first."

He headed inside and found Kennedy in the kitchen, cooking something spicy enough to make his eyes water.

"Hey, Ken."

She gave him a tight hug and on tip toes, kissed him on the cheek. "How are you?"

"Feeling like an idiot."

"Oh, yeah? Meet your Idiot Twin. So dinner's going to be a little while, but Bucky needs a walk." She smiled at the dog who had come bounding in. "Don't ya, fella?" She leaned in to Bast. "Be nice to your brother. He feels awful."

He opened his mouth. Closed it again. Kissed her on the forehead.

Outside, the air was crisp like snow was on the way

again. Bast put his hand in his jacket pocket and walked alongside his brother as they headed to Riverbrook Park across the street.

Reid let Bucky go to chase something, then turned to Bast. "I'm sorry about what happened in Michigan."

"I'm sorry, too."

Reid looked uncomfortable, even for Reid. "What you said about how we've all got to live with it—with your injury—is that what you've been thinking this entire time?"

"I didn't think so. I thought it was all good, that I'd moved past it. But then I realized that maybe I'd glossed over it because of the upside: it brought us closer. Only, now, part of me wishes it didn't have to happen that way. That we could have gotten over that hump and become friends without me sustaining this injury that might be career-ending."

Reid looked crushed. "You forgave me too quickly."

"It's not a matter of forgiveness, Reid. It's the fact that it laid bare some issues I've not dealt with properly. I was depressed after it happened, but I kept that to myself. Marina dumped me, you were headed to the Olympics in my place, and Dad was being his usual dickweed self. I probably should have talked to someone, but I thought I'd do what I always do. Smile the fuck through, which might not have been so healthy. And now, I feel—stuck, I suppose. I know the re-injury just happened, but what if I don't get back full function? What if this is it?" He swiped at a tear. Jesus, this was why he didn't want to talk about this. It brought out this needy part of him, that little kid who wanted his brother to love and protect and tell him it would all be okay.

Reid curled a hand around Bast's neck and pulled him

close. "I can't promise you'll get all the way back, but I'm with you no matter what happens."

Bast gave a watery chuckle. "I wanted us doing this together. Playing as teammates as well as brothers."

"That could still happen. I'm going to work with you to get you back on top, but—"

"I have to accept it might not happen. I'm not saying any of this to make you feel guilty. I've had it up to here with other people's guilt."

"Okay, got it." Reid drew back and gripped his shoulder. "But my love for you and my concern about where you're at doesn't stem from guilt. I failed you when we were kids, but now, I'm here for whatever you need."

"I-I know you are. And you're happy, which is another reason why I've not wanted to rock the boat with rehashes of what happened. You're in a good place."

"And you will be, soon. I don't want you to ever hold back to save my feelings."

Bast sniffed. "Damn, these days, you're so perfect and well-adjusted that it's scary."

Reid chuckled darkly. "I'm far from perfect. But I want to be for Kennedy and ..." He hesitated, then said, "She's pregnant. We're having a baby."

Bast could feel his mouth drop open. "That's—oh my God, that's amazing!"

Reid smiled, a little embarrassed. "I know. I'm thrilled and terrified, and I want so badly for everything between us, you and me, to be okay. I'm going to need you through all this because I'm pretty sure I have no clue what I'm doing."

Bast wrapped his brother in a hug. "You're going to be amazing. You've had all this practice with Bucky, and Kennedy's a force of nature. She's going to be a great mom. And I'm going to be the best uncle."

Reid leaned back. "And I want to be the best brother to you. That's the only reason I pushed so hard about Pepper. You're the nicest fucking guy in the world, the brother I love more than anything, and I don't want to see you hurt again. About this Pepper business, I should have trusted you. I was just worried you were in a dark place, susceptible to a huckster."

That made Bast laugh. "Pepper is about as far from huckster material as Bucky is from being a good guard dog."

Bucky was currently barking at a bush.

Reid gave an indulgent smile. "Saw the Rebels press release today. You have a hand in that?"

"A bit. I just want everyone to lay off her, and I needed it clarified that she wasn't at fault and no one in the org thinks so."

"It was good. So how are things? Are you two ..." He waved the rest.

"We two are ... no two." They'd had a nice text exchange after the press release went viral, and she'd made it clear that she was in a good place. That she was doing just fine without him.

At his brother's frown, he added, "I'm not sure either of us is ready for a relationship. She has some stuff to work out, and while I'd like to be able to fight all the dragons for her, I've got to let her do that for herself."

"But you want her?"

He growled his frustration. "So fucking much, Reid. I thought it was just because I wanted what you have, what every guy I know seems to have. Or that I've been a miserable fuck for a year and need the warm comforts of a woman. But I haven't thought of anyone else since I met her at Jimmy's Tap. And now that I know her, I can't imagine anyone else coming close. But she doesn't want to date a hockey player—"

"Did she say that?"

"Not in so many words. But she's been through hell at the hands of the hockey-industrial complex, and I just want to protect her. The easiest way to do that is to leave her alone."

Reid snorted. "You don't believe that for a second. You're the guy who stepped up and told all those assholes where to go when they poked at her. And I know you said you needed her to drive you to Michigan, but that wasn't why you took her there."

"Oh, yeah, Mr. Know-it-all, why did I take her there, then?"

Tell me because I have no fucking clue why I do anything anymore.

"You were falling in love with her, and you wanted to keep her safe."

"That's not what happened!" Bast stared at Reid who was shaking his head, still with the disgust, but mixed with something else: pity. "I was pissed to all hell with her, and I wanted to punish her for—"

"For what? The Big Dump? Because that's not what you were mad at her for."

Bast scoffed. "So why was I mad at her?"

"Because when you met her, you wanted her and then found out a whole host of reasons why it could never work. Coach, Connor, Gallagher. You were mad at her because she was the woman of your dreams, and it had just turned into a nightmare. But then I lent you my lake house and look where we are. You made it through the wilderness—"

"*Like a Virgin*? Are you paraphrasing *Like a Virgin*?"

Reid smiled. "Somehow you made it through."

Bast shoved him, which made Reid laugh and Bucky bark.

"It's okay, boy." Reid knelt to reattach his lead. "Bast and I are all good." He looked up and smiled, acknowledging the truth of that. "You're crazy about her, bro. Let her know."

"All this wisdom in the head of a complete asshole. How does that happen?"

"I recommend therapy."

~

Two days later ...

AFTER HIS PT APPOINTMENT, Bast headed to the players' lounge where he found Reid making a kale smoothie while Cal Foreman looked on in horror.

"Baby Durand," Foreman said, his lip curling. "Tell me you don't eat this junk like your brother."

"I'm more of a sandwich guy."

"Excellent. I'm making a turkey-gouda special. You in?"

"Hit me." He took a seat at the counter while Reid poured his green goop into a glass. "So, anyone up for giving advice?"

"About your woman in the hot tub?" Gunnar Bond called out from the sofa where he and Levi Hunt were watching *Days of Our Lives*.

"No. About Deacon."

Dex O'Malley pointed from the lounge's well-worn leather lazy boy. "Not denying he has a woman, though. Or the hot tub. We'll stick a pin in that."

Reid sipped his smoothie, and excellent actor that he was, did not retch. "What's the latest on Deacon?"

"I'm being told I need to apologize. Fix this before the lawyers take over."

Foreman looked up from a jar of light mayo. "That guy needed to be put in his place. You were doing the right thing by Pepper."

Bast thought so. It was good to hear someone else agreed.

The mouthy Southie, as Foreman was known, wasn't finished. "O'Malley, you're up."

Bast startled at finding Dex beside him at the counter. "Jesus, you're quiet."

"That I am. So what gives with Pepper?"

"We're just friends." He caught Reid's eye, complete with raised eyebrow, and added a feeble "I like her."

Dex nodded. "And?"

"And nothing."

Foreman shared a glance with Reid. "Is he always this chatty?"

Reid smiled at Bast. "He's giving her space."

"Probably for the best," Foreman offered. "Right now, she doesn't need Baby Durand punching out reporters or issuing public apologies on behalf of the org, not when she's busy turning herself into a TikTok superstar."

"A what?"

"Yeah, she made some videos. Well, they're edited together—"

"Stitched." Erik Jorgenson had just arrived and opened the fridge door. "Funny, too."

"What the hell are you talking about?"

"On TikTok," Erik said, as if Bast was completely clueless. Which he was.

Foreman passed a sandwich over to Bast. "Open up the TikTok app, dude."

"I don't have an account."

Reid had his phone out, and after a few seconds of searching, he handed it over. A video was already playing so Bast started it over.

Tommy Toga, the New York Spartans mascot, was skating around, munching on grapes, which was his schtick. Then boom! He bumped into Kyle Henninger, a forward for New York, who went down with a thud. The mascot took a moment to consider his handiwork before offering Henninger a grape and yelling "Toga this!"

Okay.

Cut to another mascot, this time Vancouver's Sammy the Shark under a cartoon wave filter when he encountered the Gills' Cully Tipton. Not a crash this time, but Cully turned tail while chased by the shark who got him against the boards after five seconds and started gnashing on his shoulder.

What the f?

Next up was Big Cat, the Boston Cougars mascot, who seemed to be stalking the team's goalie, Finn Ferguson, in a jungle ... and on it went with ten second vignettes of the NHL's mascots taking out players all over the country in funny and funnily specific ways.

"This is fucking wild," Bast muttered. "Are the Rebels in here?"

"Last one," Erik said. "The best one."

Sure enough, there was Rowdy Rebel, and Bast's pulse jumped at the sight. The gray rat-fox-duck combo was skating along to a whistling soundtrack, not a care in the world. In the other direction came Theo Fucking Kershaw, also whistling and wearing ... no!

Bast's toque. Gwen's damn crooked zig-zag pattern was unmistakable.

Was Kershaw doing an impression of a certain Canadian hockey player?

This was confirmed when the guy yelled, "Mon Dieu! Magnifique!" and the camera cut to a very made-up Tara Becker, sitting in the front row waving vigorously and fluttering her eyelashes. She leaned her substantial chest against the glass and—wait a second. Was that a tattoo of his name?

Bam! Both Fake Durand and Rowdy Rebel went down with Theo howling like a banshee. What a ham.

"Kershaw going for a Daytime Emmy here," Bast muttered, while the idiot yelled, "My face! My beautiful face!"

He rewound and played it over.

Erik chuckled as he extracted a Tupperware of meatballs from the fridge. "I thought it was a pretty good impression. It only took five takes."

Reid and Bast both said, "You were there?"

"Yeah, they filmed it yesterday after practice. Casey did the editing, and Mia and Kennedy were on hand to direct. It was very professional."

"My Kennedy?" Reid asked.

Erik squinted at him. "Is there more than one? And they captured the essence of what happened perfectly."

Bast shot Erik a look. "I know that. I've already told everyone it was an accident."

"Sure you did," Foreman said soothingly. "And you did a nice caveman impression in that presser and after, making it clear how you feel about her."

"I was just defending her because no one else would."

Dex pointed. "Exactly. But now it looks like Pepper's taking charge of the story in her own way. Good for her."

Bast checked the comments on the TikTok account, which was called Mascot Mania.

Fucking hilarious!

Sammy the Shark munching on Tipton. Classic.

Mascot Powerrrrr!

Yeah, Kershaw nailed bumbling Durand to a T.

He smiled to himself. Pepper had said the mascots had her back; now it looked like they'd banded together to defend one of their own. Was this her idea? Because if it was, he was so damn proud of her. For the last year, she'd let the media dictate how she should run her life. Now she was using it to change the story and get them on her side.

It might work. Judging by the comments, people were getting a kick out of the mascots and the players making fun of themselves. Combined with the official statement, it could only help people see the Bast Durand debacle in a different light.

Neither would it hurt to weigh in on the issue and show his support.

He hearted the bumbling Durand comment, then added one of his own, with a note because it was Reid's account.

Hey Kershaw, stop stealing my jokes! (- Bast D.)

Let's see if that made a difference.

Pepper picked up the phone.

"Hey, dickhead."

"Hey—wait a second. Is this my sister with the potty mouth? The TikTok superstar?"

"Sure is. How can I help?"

"You haven't answered any of my calls."

"I haven't been in the mood."

Connor exhaled. "Saw your video thing. It was funny."

"You think?"

"Yeah, I do think. Can't believe you were able to get all those mascots and players involved. You could've asked me."

She sighed. "Really, Connor? You've been a complete jerk to me since I broke up with Kent. I understand that he's your friend, but I can't believe you took his side."

"That's not—okay, maybe I haven't been as understanding. I don't know what happened."

"It shouldn't matter!" She dug her nails into her palm, seeking calm. "I told you that things didn't work out between us. Sometimes that happens. Sometimes things should remain private, and it's no one's business. But you decided that wasn't enough for you. Because it's just Pepper being Pepper. Well, you know what, Connor? I don't care what you think."

"Aw, Pepperoni ..."

"I hate that nickname." She hung up on him.

She was tired of letting him run roughshod over her. He was supposed to be there for her, not act as though she was an inconvenience. No more.

He texted:

Sorry. Can we try again?

She called him back. "This should be good."

"What do you need me to do?"

She scoffed. "Uh, how about stop being a jerk and be a bit nicer to me?"

"When am I not nice to you?"

"The sharing of memes and gifs with your hockey bros?"

He thought on that a second. "Like Durand? He showed you that?"

"No, but he told me. And look, it doesn't matter. I'd just like you to stop treating me like your idiotic younger sister. Even when I'm acting like your idiotic younger sister."

"Okay. I can be less of a dick."

"Can't wait."

He chuckled. "Don't hold your breath. But before I turn over this new leaf, I need to ask you a few questions. You and Durand in that cabin—"

"Lakeside cottage."

"What happened?"

"It's none of your business, Connor. The last time I let you interfere in my love life, I ended up engaged to Kent."

She could hear her brother's discomfort, and she had to say she was enjoying it.

"You said 'love life'. So that means that you and Durand are a thing?"

"We're not doing this. You're not allowed to have an opinion."

As usual, her brother wasn't listening. "I mean, he's a good dude and he stood up for you at that presser. So I guess I approve."

Bast Durand, her knight in hockey pads. It still gave her a warm feeling, even though it was mixed with regret that they were in this weird space.

Text buddies. Hooray.

"Your approval is neither wanted nor needed. Button it, Connor."

"What? But you're my sister."

"Button. It."

He laughed. "What'll we talk about then?"

"Mom and Dad. Like always."

A couple of minutes later, she hung up. Telling these men in her life how she felt was so empowering. Why had she waited so long to take control?

And what would happen if she took it a step further ... and told the one man she cared about the most what was on her mind.

Could she possibly be brave enough for that?

35

THE EMPTY NET was about as busy as it could get after a Rebels win, which was to say it was heaving. Bast put his head around the door, saw Dex O'Malley standing on a table—of course—then felt the buzz of his phone.

He headed outside again. "Kit? What's up?"

"I've heard from the *Sun-Times'* lawyers. There won't be any lawsuit. I've got that in writing."

Bast's heart lifted. Perhaps it had been weighing on him more than he'd cared to admit. "Any idea what brought about the change of heart?"

"My understanding is that someone in the Rebels org promised exclusive access to an interview for Deacon."

An alarm went off in his brain. "Someone?"

"Seems Deacon was happy to get media access to Pepper Calhoun in exchange for agreeing to drop any charges against you. Have you seen those videos she made with the mascots? Maybe *she* needs representation."

Was he hearing this right? There was no good reason for Pepper to talk to the press, not after all the shit they'd put her through. But if she was worried about Deacon coming after him, maybe she'd put all that aside and give the prick an interview.

To save Bast's ass.

Since the Rebels' press statement and the TikTok mascot campaign, Bast had wondered if she might be ready to hear what he had to say. Now learning that she might have intervened on his behalf to get Deacon off his back sent a burst of joy barreling through his veins. She had his back just like he had hers, and that was about the best news he'd heard all week.

"Thanks for being in my corner," he said to Kit. "I know it can't have been easy for you to agree—"

Kit coughed.

"—or *pretend* to agree with my stance here."

"I love that you have principles even if it shoots you in the foot. You're a good guy, Bast. Talk soon."

"Yeah, take care." He hung up and headed into the bar, ready to celebrate a Rebels win.

The first person he saw was Pepper. She was seated on the opposite side of the bar, wearing a toque.

His toque.

Kennedy was explaining something with her hands. Whatever it was made Pepper laugh, but then she turned slightly, her eyes checking the door like she was expecting someone.

Their gazes met and he knew. Fuck, he knew.

Déjà vu, the best kind, where you realize that something's happened before and it's inevitable. He'd already fallen and now he was having a hard time picking himself up off the dusty-ass floor.

He needed to talk to her, tell her that she was it for him. From the first night in Jimmy's Tap, and he'd been fighting it ever since. But he hoped his actions might have spoken loud enough for him, especially as his words could barely describe the depth of his feeling.

He was in love with this woman.

It might be too soon for her to accept his pursuit of her, but he needed her to know he'd be here. Waiting until she was ready.

Rounding the bar, he was waylaid by a half-cut Dex O'Malley and a familiar woman, who screamed his name.

It came to him quickly. "Kylie!"

Throwing her arms around him, she smashed her tattoo-free chest to his.

She saw him sneaking a peek. "It was temporary. I didn't want to commit to you just yet."

That made him laugh. Dex circled her waist. "Think you might get a tattoo of me, babe?"

She smiled sweetly at him. "Well ..."

He left them to discuss it, but his path was foiled again when his brother stepped into his sightline. For fuck's sake.

"Hey, congrats on the game," Bast said, his eye wandering over Reid's shoulder. "Nice goal in the third."

"Thanks. And thanks for coming out tonight. The boys appreciate it even though you might not feel like it."

"No problem. Could we talk lat—"

Petrov, the Rebels' captain, patted him on the back. "Humpty, you are here at last. We thought you might have fallen over again on your way over."

"Very funny." *That* nickname had better not stick.

Kershaw nudged him. "Still in testing, but I'm liking how it sounds, non?"

"Your French accent is terrible, by the way."

"Yeah, but like all good impressions, it's the *essence* of the character that matters. And the essence of you is that you like the attention from the ladies, and it tripped you up big time. I'm just giving the fans what they want."

That got a few chuckles from the crowd, the one that was standing between him and Pepper. He was fully prepared to ram his way through if that's what it took.

"So what are you doing here?" Theo asked.

Bast speared him with a glare. "I might be injured, but I'm still part of this team."

"No, I mean *here* here." Kershaw thumbed over his shoulder. "Shouldn't you be making nice with Pepsi Cola? Heard she got you off the hook with Deacon."

How was it the world and his wife knew his business before Bast knew it himself?

"I'm trying to get through, but everyone else wants to talk my ear off and give me stupid nicknames and crack jokes about my ability to stay upright."

Petrov raised an eyebrow. "I thought you were the nice one."

"Speaking of nice ..." Theo leaned in. "You'd better not screw over Peppa. My kid loves her, so if I have to choose between a teammate and my nanny, she's gonna win hands down."

Bast felt his lips curve. "Don't worry, she's safe with me."

He just wasn't sure he was safe with her.

"Now, if you don't mind getting the fuck out of my way, I have somewhere to be."

Laughing at the new, not-so-nice Bast Durand, his teammates stepped aside, and he carved a hasty path toward Pepper. Kennedy grinned when he arrived.

"Hey, favorite brother-in-law!"

"Hi there." He gave her a kiss on the cheek. "Bye there."

"Uh, charming." She winked at Pepper. "Careful around this one, Pep." And then she left as instructed.

"Hi," he said. "You okay?"

She blinked at his abruptness. "Yeah, I am. Are *you* okay?"

"I suppose." He felt kind of grumpy. He was glad to see her—thrilled to fucking see her—but he didn't like an audience. He didn't like not knowing how the next few minutes were going to go. "Can we go somewhere private?"

"Sure—"

But he was already pulling her toward the corridor where he knew there was an office from the multiple times he'd drunk here with the team during his rehab.

He opened the Staff Only door and pulled her inside.

"Sorry about that, but I'm kind of sick of everyone butting in and having opinions."

She smiled. "Agreed. But on the whole, people mean well, don't you think? They just want you to be happy."

"Sure, sure." He'd planned to do all the talking, find out about this Deacon business, tell her what was going to happen—they would date and have tons of sex and screw the haters—but now he realized that he'd much rather hear Pepper speak. "How are things? Really?"

"Good! I talked to Connor, aired some grievances. Now we'll see if he follows through on his promise to stop being an ass."

"Wouldn't bet on it." He smiled. "Sounds like you've been taking charge. TikToks, media interviews, your life."

"Oh, you heard about that?"

"The whole world heard about it. I loved that video, by the way. Striking a blow for mascots everywhere!"

"Right? I saw your comment. Nice to see the players not taking themselves too seriously."

"Hmm. Not sure I enjoyed Kershaw's impression of me, though."

She rolled in her lips. "A little too close to the bone?"

"Maybe." But he couldn't keep it up. "Nah, he did good. And so did you. I'm so proud of you, sweetheart. And I don't know what you said to Deacon that got him to back off."

She waved it off. "He reached out after the TikTok video went viral, and I saw an opportunity. Two birds, one puck. He's agreed to let the issue with you drop."

"You didn't have to do that."

She placed a hand on his chest. "Just like you didn't have to support me. But you did. Because you're the kindest, most generous, most decent guy I know. Beautiful, inside and out. You had my back from the beginning, Bast, and if I can do this one small thing for you, I will."

It was no small thing, and she had to know it. Keeping his feelings in was so hard ... which meant that maybe he shouldn't. Maybe he should open his heart. "You're fucking amazing, you know that?"

Her cheeks flushed. "I'm starting to see that maybe I'm not such a disaster after all. Did you talk to Reid?"

"Yeah. It was good to get it out there. You were right. I'd been holding onto the resentment about the injury, how it changed my relationship with Reid. He was hurt, but he got it. I don't want to lie to him anymore. I don't want to lie to anyone." He searched her face. "That includes you, Pepper."

"Oh. I never thought you lied to me."

"I did. When I drove you home a few days ago." He leaned in close. "I said I'd survive."

Her lip wobbled. "And ... that was a lie?"

"Yep. Because I won't, not without you. I'd be a shell, shuffling around, wondering why I didn't tell you that I needed you to drive me home. All the way. That I needed you to stay with me and never leave."

Her breath hitched. "I went inside my dad's house and

waited a couple of minutes, trying to screw up the courage to come back outside and tell you I didn't want it to end. But by the time I'd managed to find a modicum of bravery, you were gone."

He touched his forehead to hers. "I thought you needed the space. That's what I've been doing since I returned. Giving you all the stupid space, trying to be your friend, but talking to Reid, I realized something."

"What's that?"

"I don't want to play it safe. This last year, I've had to because of my injury. And I've spent that time trying to come to terms with the possibilities of a life outside hockey. I'm going to fight like hell to play, but I'm also going to prepare myself for any changes that come my way. Reid and I are going to set up a foundation, raise money for kids who need it."

"Like Cecy? Oh, Bast, that's fantastic. And you and Reid doing that together? I love it."

"Not sure how much time he'll have for a new venture with the baby on the way. Have you heard about that?"

"Kennedy told me. I'm so happy for them."

He nodded. "Me, too. Life's happening so fast for them."

"For you, too."

She was right. After so long with nothing happening, now it was a mad, crazy rush. "Reid told me something I couldn't figure out for myself. Asking you to drive me to Michigan—"

"Asking?"

"Okay, demanding it wasn't so I could punish you. It wasn't even because I needed to protect my wrist."

"No?"

"It was because I was already half in love with you. I needed to keep you close, protect you from the media storm, and figure out this connection between us. Because it was too strong to ignore."

She bit her lip. "I thought I'd imagined it."

"No, it was there from night one at Jimmy's Tap, and then I messed up by not trusting it when I found out who you were. By letting all the shit out there"—he gestured to the bar—"get in the way of something potentially amazing in here." He grasped her hand and placed it over his trip-hammering heart. "And when we met again, I know it was a disaster, but I'll be honest: running into you on that rink was the best thing to ever happen to me. I couldn't see it imme-diately, but I see it now."

She shook her head. "I can't believe you're so accepting of it all."

"The wrist will heal. It might take a while, but it'll get there." It felt like they were talking about more than this tricky joint. "And if I have you in my corner, I know I can do anything. Because you're a special woman, Pepper. You want to take care of the world—your dad, your ex, all the little kids with their spongy brains. But you also need someone to take care of you."

Her eyes were shiny. "We both do. Thanks for taking care of me, Bast. I loved how safe you made me feel—"

"Loved? Past tense?"

Her smile was tentative. "Is present tense on the table? Or future tense? I don't want to assume anything."

"Assume away. Take it as read." He placed his hands on her hips and pulled her close, chest to chest, heart to heart. "Past, present, and future. This is what I want."

Her eyes sparkled, those gorgeous hazel eyes he wanted to wake up to forever.

"I can't believe it. I fell for you back in our snow globe world, and for a while, I sort of hoped it would stay like that.

Inside the glass where I could look at it like a memory. One that might ache for a while but would eventually fade."

He drew back. "You wanted to keep it to the lake house? Not bring what happened back to Chicago?"

"I thought that was for the best." She shook her head. "But there I was, repeating the mistakes of the past, running away from my feelings. How strongly I feel about you. I needed to fix things in my life—Kent, my family, my career—and as soon as I felt on a more secure footing, I might be able to figure out what to do about you."

"And what kind of decision have you come to?"

She leaned in close. "That I can solve my own problems, but it doesn't hurt to have a team of people on my side. And if I was to choose one person to be my co-captain, it would be you, Bast Durand. I want to wear your toque and your jersey. I love you. I know it's fast, but I don't want to miss a second of making a life with you."

Joy danced through his veins. "Can't think of anything I want more."

Before he could seal the deal with a kiss, in walked Tina, the bar's owner. She raised an expressive eyebrow. "Look, I know you lot bring a shit-ton of business to this bar, but you don't own all the private spaces as well."

Bast winced. "Sorry, Tina. Just needed a quiet spot."

"Let me guess, you two are madly in love after your smashing meet-cute on the ice."

"Uh, nailed it," Pepper said.

She gestured a hand toward them. "I should take a commission, given the number of people who profess love for each other in my bar. Off with you. I'll get the most expensive champagne on ice."

"My girl likes tequila," Bast said as he clasped Pepper's hand and led her outside. In the corridor, he backed her against the wall. "I know everyone's going to have something to say, so I need to kiss you now before the world gets involved."

Those whiskey-bright eyes sparkled as her lips kicked up at the corners. "Make it a good one, Superstar."

Which is exactly what he did.

EPILOGUE

June

PEPPER STOOD IN THE WINGS, waiting for her name to be announced. Of course the delay gave her plenty of time to run through all the ways this could go wrong.

They mispronounced her name.

Or forgot it.

Maybe someone screamed at her "You got Peppered!"

Or she took a facer in front of a thousand people.

Buck up, Calhoun! You're better than this.

Seeking her usual source of calm, she checked her messages and re-read a recent text exchange.

BAST

Sweetheart, I hate that I can't be there for you. Probably grounds for a break-up?

PEPPER

Absolutely. How dare you think Game 5 of the conference finals is more important than my graduation?

Just kidding. I get it. I'm so proud of you.

BAST

Thanks. I promise I'll make it up to you. In both NSFW and non-NSFW ways.

PEPPER

I will hold you to that. For now, just focus on winning that game. Best graduation present ever.

Reading those words soothed her to an extent. While she would have loved to see his smiling face in the crowd, she contented herself with the knowledge he had been there for her over the last six months while she finished her coursework and internship. There'd been another storm of media attention after Kent's PED use was made public by a Diamonds' employee who didn't agree with the cover-up. But her family, friends, and surprisingly, the Rebels org, had closed ranks, ensuring she was protected until it blew over. As it inevitably did.

She'd never known such love and support, and having this man in her life made her realize how long she'd spent short-changing her expectations of the people around her.

Another name was called. She shuffled closer to the stage, closer to getting that final approval. After today she would have her bachelor's in early childhood education and would be qualified to teach little ones and fill their spongy little brains with all sorts of information. She already had a job lined up for the Fall at Riverbrook Pre-School.

Now she was close enough to the stage entrance to be able to peek out at the audience. Elle was there with Kennedy (eight months pregnant!), and while Pepper would have loved to see Hatch, his mom didn't think he'd be able to sit still long enough. (*You want disaster, Pepper? Just invite my hyperactive son to your graduation!*) Connor had flown in from Denver—unfortunately the Diamonds missed the cut for playoffs this year—and was sitting beside her dad, who really should be in New York for the Rebels' game but told the org that attendance at his daughter's graduation was a deal-breaker, and he'd fly out after. (Of course no-one in the Rebels' front office would have made a fuss.) Beside her dad was her mom, who was about to embark on the Camino de Santiago with a couple of girlfriends next week. She'd asked Pepper to join her, but the prospect of six weeks walking the Spanish countryside didn't appeal as post-graduation R&R.

Not when there was a Michigan lake house and a hot tub waiting for her ...

Later tonight, they'd all head to her dad's house to watch the Rebels-Spartans game, which was about the best graduation celebration she could think of.

Another name called, another shuffle forward.

She took an extra peek, mostly because her eyes were drawn to a movement in the row where her friends and family were sitting. Was that—no!

He was here!

"No fucking way," she muttered.

She got a few funny looks from her cohort. Definitely not appropriate language from a soon-to-be early childhood education specialist.

Bast had just sat down beside her mom and was leaning

over to say something to Connor. This was crazy! He should be in New York, getting ready for tonight's game.

Instead he was here, watching his girlfriend get a piece of paper?

"Pepper Calhoun."

She was frozen, except for the tears threatening to burst the banks, staring out at this perfect man who had ... lied to her and said he was in New York when it was clear he'd never left the state of Illinois.

"Pepper Calhoun."

Someone nudged her. "That's you."

"Oh, right." She headed out, carefully putting one foot in front of the other, and took the scroll from the Dean.

"Congratulations, Pepper."

"Thanks."

The cheers and hoots were loud, but not enough to drown out her thumping heartbeat. Turning to the audience, she took in the sight of all these people who loved her enough to celebrate this day with her—and while she knew Bast loved her because he told her often enough, she had always been an actions-speak-louder kind of person.

Bast was, too.

He was here, on one of the most important days of her life, on one of the most important days of *his* life. It meant the world to her, just as he did.

"Did you really think I'd miss this, sweetheart?" Bast's grin could not possibly be wider.

"Uh, yes! You have an important game. Tonight. In New York. This is the last place you should be."

The last hour had been absolute torture while she sat

through the rest of the graduates getting their diplomas (we did it!) and what should have been a very inspiring commencement speech by the amazing Judy Greer (DePaul '97), but which Pepper couldn't focus on because her boyfriend was here.

He pulled her close, putting her brain in the usual scramble because he was in her life, loving her to the max. "I got a special dispensation to attend."

"Basically, like my dad, you told them you were doing this and they could take it or leave it."

He shrugged. "Pretty much. What are they going to do? Fine me?"

"They could. I love that you're here, though."

The last seven months had been amazing as Bast fought his way back to full fitness and Pepper finished her degree. They saw each other as much as possible—she practically lived at his condo, which was the perfect place to study while he was on a road trip—and she couldn't wait for the summer.

But first he had a Cup to win.

He nuzzled her nose. "So, what would you say if we just got out of here?"

She peered up at him. "You mean, snuck away? Perhaps to ... New York?"

His jaw dropped. "How did you know? Did Connor blab?"

"No." She would kill her brother for withholding such vital information later. "But you know that I would never in a million years forgive you if my graduation made you miss Game 5 of the conference finals. I'm guessing you've already chartered a plane like some big shot and my dad, Connor, and maybe my mom are invited to fly to the game with you?"

He grinned. "You really do know me. Cecy and Gwen will be there, too, if that's okay."

"Of course it is. I can't wait to see them."

Bast and Reid had started their foundation three months ago—Hockey Cares—and even got Gwen on board to help lead the effort. The support was so great they were branching out to accept all children who need financial support during a medical crisis. Pepper was so proud of her man and all he had achieved.

All he *would* achieve—because she had no doubt he was going to be back on top soon.

He took her hand, clasped it tight. "You ready for the next adventure, Tequila Girl?"

She threw her arms around his neck and kissed him, marveling at how the worst day of their lives had led to forever.

"Let's go win this thing."

ACKNOWLEDGMENTS

Thank you to my editor, Kristi Yanta - I gave you something very rough and your notes were, as always, completely spot on. Thanks also to proofreader Julia Griffis for your amazing attention to detail.

To my cover designer Michele Catalano Creative, thanks for another great Rebels cover.

To my agent, Nicole Resciniti, thanks for another great year.

And finally, to Jimmie — thanks for all your support this last year as we adjusted to life on the road. It's been wild and I'm so grateful you're on this epic journey with me.

ABOUT THE AUTHOR

Originally from Ireland, *USA Today* bestselling author Kate Meader cut her romance reader teeth on Maeve Binchy and Jilly Cooper novels, with some Harlequins thrown in for variety. Give her tales about brooding mill owners, over-sexed equestrians, and men who can rock an apron, a fire hose, or a hockey stick, and she's there. Now based on the road, she writes sexy contemporary featuring strong heroes and amazing women and men who can match their guys quip for quip.

ALSO BY KATE MEADER

Rookie Rebels

GOOD GUY

INSTACRUSH

MAN DOWN

FOREPLAYER

DEAR ROOMIE

REBEL YULE

JOCK WANTED

SUPERSTAR

WILD RIDE

Chicago Rebels

IN SKATES TROUBLE

IRRESISTIBLE YOU

SO OVER YOU

UNDONE BY YOU

HOOKED ON YOU

WRAPPED UP IN YOU

Hot in Chicago Rookies

UP IN SMOKE

DOWN IN FLAMES

HOT TO THE TOUCH

Laws of Attraction

DOWN WITH LOVE

ILLEGALLY YOURS

THEN CAME YOU

Hot in Chicago

REKINDLE THE FLAME

FLIRTING WITH FIRE

MELTING POINT

PLAYING WITH FIRE

SPARKING THE FIRE

FOREVER IN FIRE

COMING IN HOT

Tall, Dark, and Texan

EVEN THE SCORE

TAKING THE SCORE

ONE WEEK TO SCORE

Hot in the Kitchen

FEEL THE HEAT

ALL FIRED UP

HOT AND BOTHERED

For updates, giveaways, and new release information,
sign up for Kate's newsletter at katemeader.com.